Brenda,

Thanks for your support!

Peace + Blessings,

Victoria Wells

a Special SUMMER

A Novel

Victoria Wells

Xpress Yourself Publishing, LLC
P. O. Box 1615
Upper Marlboro, Maryland 20773

This book is a work of fiction. Names, characters, places and incidents are either products of the author's imagination or are used fictitously. Any resemblance to actual persons, living or dead, business establishments, events or locals is entirely coincidental.

All Xpress Yourself Publishing titles are available at special quantity discounts for bulk purchases for sales, promotions, premiums, fund-raising, educational or institutional use.

ISBN-10: 0-9799757-7-8
ISBN-13: 978-0-9799757-7-6

Library of Congress Control Number: 2007939704

Printed in the United States of America

Interior and Exterior Designed by
The Writer's Assistant
www.thewritersassistant.com

Visit Xpress Yourself Publishing World Wide Web at:
www.xpressyourselfpublishing.org

Dedication

My first novel is dedicated to the memories of my beloved maternal grandmother, Bertha Lee Bunn and my beloved brother, Billy Riddick. Missing you, loving you, wishing you were here with me.

Acknowledgments

I want to give thanks to my Savior & Lord, Jesus Christ for loving me just the way I am. I thank Him for His mercies that are new with each morning. I thank Him for blessing me with wonderful parents, Leroy and Mildred Riddick. Mommy and Daddy, I love you so much for always directing me to all that is good. Thank you for always telling and showing me how proud you are of me.

To my family, I love you all with everything that I have. Mardi, I know I don't say it all the time, but I appreciate all that you are to me. Thank you, my love, so much for always supporting me in all of my endeavors over the last twenty-one years. Martia, Leroy, & Melanie, I am so proud of all of you. I am truly blessed each and every time you call me "Mommy."

Although I thank and love all of my siblings for their support, I must follow my heart and give special shot outs. Robin, thank you for believing in me from the very first moment I told you about writing my book. Sandra (Bertie) thanks for spreading the word about my book in Virginia and selling copies for me. I'm looking for you to do the same with the re-release of *A Special Summer*! Omar and Cindy, it meant so much to me that you came down to my release party and went back home selling copies for me! I know y'all got my back and are going to do the same this time around!

To my spiritual parents, Dr. Reverend Wilbert Richardson and Gwendolyn (aunt Dolly) Richardson, you both mean the world to me. Thank you for all of your love and support over the years. Pastor, thank you for being a true Shepard and knowing my heart and not judging me. 'Cause Lord knows I was terrified to tell you I was writing a romance novel. I still remember that day in your office! I can't express the joy I felt when you and Aunt Dolly told me how proud you were of my story.

Victoria Reese and Esther Wells, what would I do without your friendship? Vicky, who would have guessed that meeting as freshmen at Saul H.S. we would still be tight and best friends? And Esther isn't it strange how the deaths of our brothers created an unbreakable bond between us? I thank both of you for loving me and being true friends, even when you tell me my stuff stinks!

I can't forget all my peeps at Jefferson! Thanks to all of my sickle cell patients for showing me much love over the years. Your strength and determination to live with such an agonizing disease keeps me in check more than you'll ever know. I love you! To all the nurses, doctors, clerks, transportation, dietary, registration, Jeff Bookstore, and anyone else I may have forgotten, thank you for supporting me the first time around and asking, "When is your next book coming out?"

To my fairy godmother, Gayle Jackson Slaon, I still don't think you believe how much of a blessing you have been in my life. I could never thank you enough for mentoring me and sharing your experiences with me about the business.

To my publisher, Jessica Tilles, how can I thank you for giving me this opportunity? How can I thank you for giving me a voice? I cannot find the words to express how much I appreciate you for believing enough in my story to want to publish it. Thank you for always being available anytime of the day or night.

If I've forgotten to acknowledge anyone, please charge it to my head and not my heart.

Peace and Blessings,

Victoria

a Special SUMMER

Prologue

Even though it was a brilliant July morning with birds singing their melodies, the sweet smell of honeysuckle drawing bees to their nectar, Summer's eyes stung from the tears threatening to escape as she peered out of her bathroom window.

"Oh, no, this can't be true. It's not true." Summer whispered to herself as her hand shook uncontrollably. Trying to convince herself she was hallucinating, Summer closed her eyes tight then reopened them again focusing on the bathroom vanity. There was no mistaking, the home pregnancy test strip screamed in her face a big, fat, pink, positive sign. It was confirmed. Summer Jackson was pregnant. *A baby. What am I going to do?*

A wave of nausea swept through her so fast she barely had time to jump up off the toilet to lift the lid to empty the contents of her stomach, which she had just consumed twenty minutes earlier. Summer flushed the toilet then staggered to the sink, rinsed her mouth, splashed cool water on her face and patted it dry with a hand towel. Slowly she sat on the floor, pulled her knees to her chest and wrapped her arms around them. Rocking back and forth, she stared at the ceiling as tears spilled down her face. Her right temple pounded as she remembered the last time she'd been with Nicholas 'Nick' Stiles.

Summer believed the evening would end as usual; they would go back to his place for some serious loving. Over the past few months of their relationship, she found herself helplessly falling in love with him. Tonight was the night she would confess her love to him. Nick was her everything, all she wanted in a man. He had been the one she had given her virginity to without hesitation.

Instead of confessing her love, Summer sat stunned in a dark car in front of her townhouse as Nick told her he was leaving in two weeks for several months to set up a new division of a trucking company, one of many business enterprises.

"Summer, it's best if we don't see each other after tonight." Nick's tone had been cold and distant.

Summer sensed that Nick had been distant all evening, but she never expected him to drop a bomb such as ending their relationship. From where she stood, everything was fine. Struggling to control her voice, Summer wanted to know, "Best for who Nick?"

Becoming irritated, Nick responded harshly. "Look, Summer, I told you from the door that my work comes first. That I'm not into long-term relationships, let alone long distance ones. I thought you understood, when it's over, it's over."

Nick's words had been so cold, so blunt, Summer winced with every syllable. She had understood what he'd said, however, his *actions* told her something different. They told her that he'd changed his mind about having a long-term relationship especially since they had exclusively been seeing each other for nearly a year.

Without saying another word, Summer grabbed her purse that had fallen to the floor and exited his vehicle. Once inside her townhouse she leaned against the door and slid to the floor before bursting into tears. One month later, here she was again, on the floor crying. This time because she was carrying a baby belonging to a man that no longer had any use for her, let alone a baby.

Summer knew what she had to do. First thing Monday morning she was calling her gynecologist's office to schedule an abortion.

Chapter 1

Philadelphia, Pennsylvania
Five Months Later

Twisting and turning, placing pillows under her back then taking them out. This went on for two hours. Becoming frustrated, Summer glanced at the red digital numbers on the clock. 1:30 a.m. Grabbing the remote control from the nightstand she turned on the television and pulled herself up in bed. Saying a prayer of thanksgiving because it was a very early Saturday morning, unlike the night before when she had to get up in five more hours to get ready for work.

Flipping through the channels, Summer smiled to herself as she acknowledged the reason for her recent restless nights. Tenderly she placed her palm on her rotund, seven-month belly. It always amazed her how her baby seem to be in tuned to her touch as she felt the life inside of her move, then settle down from her touch.

Every time Summer felt movement in her womb, a flash of guilt stabbed at her. Guilt over the fact she'd almost terminated the life growing inside of her. Summer shuddered whenever she thought about the day she walked into the outpatient procedure office with the goal of ending her pregnancy. Thank God the nurse on duty was a woman she'd went to nursing school with. Ginger immediately sensed how distraught Summer was. She convinced Summer to go home and think about what she was about to do. "I just don't want you to make a decision you'll later regret for the rest of your life."

Giving Summer a tight squeeze as she hugged her, Ginger sent her on her way to think things over.

Summer now referred to Ginger as her angel. At that time, all she could think about was how cold and uncaring Nick had treated her. She couldn't understand how he'd just made love to her one week, then turn around and dump her the next week.

A lump formed in Summer's throat as her mind traveled back to over a year and a half ago when she met him at a benefit to raise money for cancer awareness in the African American community sponsored by the Philadelphia chapter of the NAACP.

The night they met was a beautiful, crisp fall evening. Summer and her friends, Starr Avery and Ava Peretti were so excited about getting tickets to the benefit. Ava's cousin was a disc jockey at the local R&B station WDAS and was able to hook them up with tickets because they were staff nurses on an oncology unit at Thomas Jefferson Hospital. They could not believe the number of dignitaries, politicians and celebrities in attendance. "Tell me that is not Will over there," Summer squealed.

Summer was gorgeous in a bronze, form fitting evening gown, with a V-shape bodice that dipped in the front, flaunting a curvaceous size six figure.

When Summer, Starr and Ava sauntered into the plush ballroom, several male eyes were drawn to the trio of gorgeous women.

As a waiter came by with a tray of sparkling white wine, Summer grabbed a flute, "Mmmm, this is good." She said savoring the taste of the sweet wine.

Giggling, Starr nudged Ava with her elbow. "You better watch her; she's enjoying that bubbly a little too much. You know after two of those she's gonna try to find the nearest corner to climb into to get her sleep on."

Summer wasn't the least offended by Starr making fun of her. It was true; the slightest bit of alcohol rocked her to sleep like a newborn baby. Summer's face broke out into a lively grin as Ava pointed out, "Aw, leave her alone and let her get her drink on, because you know we won't be getting any tickets to this shindig next year."

In unison the trio snapped their fingers and bobbed their heads. "I know that's right! Haaaay!"

Realizing they were somewhat loud and now the center of attention from a small group of distinguished looking men who'd over heard their conversation, the young women eyed each other before breaking out in laughter. One of the men looked at them as if to say, "What are they doing here?"

Putting a manicured finger to her lips, Ava emphasized as she straightened her back, held her head up high and pointed her nose in the air, making fun of the stiffs nearby. "Sssh. Let us conduct ourselves like highfalutin ladies..." a wicked smile replaced the serious expression as she added, "of the night."

The man nearly choked on whatever it was he was drinking.

This sent them into another fit of laughter. Summer nudged Ava, "Crazy, speak for yourself! I ain't a lady of nobody's night!"

"Ditto for me too!" Starr added.

Summer and her friends were having a fabulous time as they chitchat and spotted the movers and shakers of the city. Summer declined every invitation to dance, whereas Ava and Starr got their jam on every chance the offer came their way, which was often. It wasn't that Summer was stuck up or anything, she was just painfully shy when it came to men.

Coming off the dance floor, they returned to the spot where they'd left her standing.

"Girl, you better dance the next time a fine brotha comes over here. What's the matter, your dance card is all full with the invisible man as your partner?" Ava ribbed her.

Summer rolled her eyes. "You know I can't dance, Av."

Throwing a hand on her hip, Ava challenged. "Come on Summer, every black girl has a little bit of rhythm."

Starr added her two cents by putting her thumb and forefinger close enough not to touch as she squinted her right eye. "Just a little bit."

Sucking her teeth as she places an empty flute on a passing tray. "If MC Hammer one and two will excuse me, I have to go to the ladies room."

As Summer turned to leave, a familiar face caught her eye. Looking over her shoulder while walking, she attempted to get Ava's attention. That new cute doctor at the hospital Ava had the hots for was on the other side of the room. However, she was too engrossed in a conversation with a man she'd danced with earlier in the evening to notice Summer was trying to get her attention.

"I'll tell her when I come back." Summer mumbled low to herself.

Turning her head back around in the direction, she was walking, Summer collided with what felt like a brick wall. She was startled not by the solid form in front of her blocking her view and path, but more by the chilled fluid that was now rolling down her cleavage.

It had taken Summer a few seconds before she became aware she'd run dead smack into a man's chest. Embarrassed, she could feel her caramel complexion flushing. Gazing up into an onyx set of eyes, Summer gasped as her legs turned to noodles. If she didn't do something fast she was going to hit the floor. Hard. Not wanting to embarrass herself further, she grasped onto the lapels of the stranger's tuxedo. Her body was doing strange things as she held on for dear life pressing her chest against the man's rock hard chest in an attempt to keep from falling to the floor.

Firmly supporting the small of her back, the stranger pressed her even further into his solid form.

"Whoa, are you okay?" The voice was deep and sexy.

Nodding her head staring at the stranger's broad chest up close and personal, Summer responded softly. "Yes, I'm sorry. I wasn't paying attention to where I was going."

The closeness of the man's strong body felt oddly good to her. As she became intoxicated from the powerful scent of his cologne, Summer inhaled deeply, sensations stirred in her she'd never known existed. Sensations that suddenly frightened her, causing her to retreat from the close contact. Cautiously she stepped back.

"Oh, my goodness, I'm so sorry for grabbing on you like that." She knew not only was her face probably a tint of pink, but her ears most likely were bright red as well. They were burning up with embarrassment.

Slowly Summer lifted her head to meet the stranger's dark gaze with wide expressive eyes as she timidly asked, "Did I get your tux wet?"

A sexy grin curved his full lips. "No, but I see you're all wet." He told her as his eyes pointed to her cleavage. Reaching into the inside pocket of his tuxedo, the sexy stranger removed an embroidered handkerchief with the initials *NS*, and handed it to her. Their hands touched sending a shock of electricity through Summer as she accepted the white cloth. Stepping around the sexy stranger, she scurried off to the restroom without saying another word.

Standing in front of the mirror, Summer frowned as she dabbed at her cleavage with the handkerchief. The scent of his cologne from the fabric drifted beneath her nostrils as she patted her bosom. Summer closed her eyes and inhaled deeply to drag the masculine scent deep into her lungs.

Brotha was fine! Denzel Washington in *Training Day* fine! Summer thought to herself that he had to be at least six feet three inches of chestnut brown, rock hard muscle. The man's chest and shoulders were so wide they'd completely blocked her view. Oh Lawd! Not to mention his set of dark piercing eyes, straight nose, chiseled jaw and thick full lips draped by a perfectly trimmed goatee. Summer shivered just thinking about how gorgeous the man was.

"Earth to Summer, earth to Summer." Startled by Starr's intrusion, Summer jumped putting her hand to her chest. She was so caught up daydreaming about Denzel's clone back in the ballroom she hadn't heard her friend come into the ladies' room.

"Girl, you scared the day lights out of me! Don't sneak up on me like that!"

"Oh my bad. I was coming to check on you girl."

"Did you see me make a fool of myself out there? I can hardly walk let alone dance. I'm so embarrassed." Summer moaned.

"Come on, girl, it was an accident. Shoot, besides the way dude was holding you, I don't think he cared at all you bumped into him spilling his drink. Now come on let's get back out there, he's probably looking for you."

Starr didn't wait for a response. Grabbing Summer's hand pulling her towards the door she was determined to get Summer to talk to the fine brotha. Starr didn't know what Summer's problem was. All night she stood on the sidelines people watching. Summer was one of the most gorgeous women she knew. And what Starr loved about Summer was that she didn't flaunt or use her beauty the way some women did. If anything, she was totally oblivious to her pretty looks. She deserved to have a handsome man pay attention to her, even if it's for only one night.

Summer yanked her hand away, "Wait a minute, Starr, I haven't peed yet." Thrusting the hanky in Starr's hand as she ran into the stall, "Here hold this, and don't remind me of how I made a fool of myself."

Starr automatically inhaled the hanky. *Mmmm smells good.*

"All right, hurry up girl. By the way did you get cutie's name or digits?"

Blowing out of the stall, going over to the sink washing her hands, Summer frowned. "No, girl, I just grabbed his hanky and high tailed it out of there. I told you I was embarrassed. Didn't have time to get no name, let alone digits."

Snatching paper towels from the dispenser, Summer checked her reflection as she dried her hands. Spotting a stain on her gown, she groaned.

"What's wrong?"

Pointing to the stain, "This."

"Summer, it's not that bad. I can hardly see it."

"Are you sure?"

Nodding her head, "Yup, now come on, and let's go so you can get Mr. Hottie's digits."

Feeling in a lighter mood, Summer giggled. "Girl, you are crazy out of your mind. But he is fine, ain't he?"

Now Summer was the one dragging Starr by one hand while snatching the hanky from her with the other hand. Even if she didn't talk to him she could stand in a corner and watch the sexy stranger the rest of the night remembering what he felt and smelt like.

Lifting the hanky to Starr's nose, Summer did a little jig. "Smell this girl, he even smells good too."

Starr's dimples popped out as she grinned at her friend. "I already did and if you don't get the digits then I will!"

Summer laughed. "Don't even make me cut you, girlfriend, okaaay!"

Scanning the large room, Summer spotted the handsome man talking to a woman who was obviously attracted to him. Summer shook her head. *Sistas can be so desperate, just look at her acting all hoochie.* The woman kept inching closer to the sexy stranger sticking her silicone breasts out. Summer bit the inside of her cheek to keep from cracking up. Every time the woman inched closer he'd ease back as if she were emitting a rancid odor.

As Summer made her way over to him, he caught a glimpse of her out of his periphery. Excusing himself, he turned his attention to Summer, strolling across the floor meeting her half way. Summer noticed Miss Desperate was not at all pleased. Mr. Hottie had left her standing alone in the middle of the room. When the woman saw what, rather who, snagged his attention she gave Summer a dirty look before huffing off in the opposite direction.

Summer's steps began to falter as the fine man swaggered towards her. The man simply embodied sex appeal. Goodness gracious he moved with the grace and agility of a large, strong shiny, black leopard.

Summer's heart began to beat rapidly as they approached one another standing within only a few inches of the other. Nervously she licked her bottom lip before biting on the corner of it.

"Umm, I just wanted to give this back to you. Thank you." Handing the handkerchief back to the handsome stranger, she attempted to make a quick getaway. No way was she going to make a fool of herself again in his presence.

Letting out a low sexy chortle, "No, you don't," he wrapped a hand gently around Summer's elbow, slowly turning her to face him.

"I didn't catch your name, Beautiful."

The brilliant white smile he flashed made Summer's knees weak as his dark eyes penetrated her.

Tears slowly slid down Summer's cheeks as she replayed that night in her mind again for the hundredth time. Turning off the television, she laid on her side as she quietly cried in the dark. She wanted to know how in the world she had managed to become a twenty six year old, pregnant, soon to be single mother. *I trusted him,* is what she told herself as she finally drifted off to sleep exhausted from crying.

Chapter 2

"Mr. Stiles, the pilot is preparing for takeoff, please fasten your seatbelt." The flight attendant informed Nick as he read over the annual report of his current business venture in textiles. Returning the reading material to his briefcase, he fastened his seatbelt settling back into the leather chair. Nick closed his eyes as he listened to the plane's engines; this is what he loved about owning his own aircraft… solitude.

Back to Philly, that's where he was headed. Nick missed everything about Philly, from the hustle and bustle of pedestrians on Chestnut and Walnut Streets at lunchtime as they rushed in and out of eateries trying to get a quick bite, to the more leisurely elderly folks walking pint size canines in Fairmount Park. Even more than this, he missed watching the Eagles do their thing on their home turf at the Lincoln Financial Field. Yes, he was ready and welcoming the idea of coming back home.

To Nick's amazement setting up a new division of his trucking company out of the states went more smoothly than expected. With all the major kinks worked out, he was able to return home to start up another project. He had his eye set on a major textile company that was in financial turmoil. He was usually fair in his dealings, however, if need be he could be a ruthless and cunning S.O.B. Nick planned to make the company a fair offer, but if they refused he would just have to get down and dirty.

Staring out the window, Nick ran through a mental checklist of all the things he had to do once the plane landed at Philadelphia International. Summer Jackson crept into his thoughts. Nick let out a curse under his breath. He felt terrible about how he had ended things with her.

He still remembered how her pretty brown eyes moistened from tears ready to spill. How the stunned expression blanket her face as he spewed painful words. The worse was how her petite frame trembled as she made her way to her front door.

Over the past five months he often thought about Summer. Wondered what she was doing, mostly late at night when he was alone. Gazing out of the plane's window into the dark night sky his mind wandered to the first time he laid eyes on her. He'd noticed her the moment she'd entered the ballroom.

❧ ❧ ❧ ❧ ❧

Summer was exquisite in a bronze gown that made her light complexion glow. Nick studied her face that barely had any make-up applied to it. Her eyes were a medium brown framed by naturally arched thick brows. Eyelashes so long they nearly touched her cheeks whenever she blinked. High cheekbones, a small nose, and full perfectly shaped lips complimented her beautiful face. Lips, Nick told himself he could kiss all night.

A woman's hair was always a complete turn on for Nick, most of that night he kept his hands deep in his pockets to keep from running his fingers through her thick black lustrous waist length mane. Usually he was attracted to taller women; he was meticulous, they had to stand at least five feet eight inches. Summer's height was only about five feet five inches tall, accentuated by three-inch heels.

Although she was petite, she had nice breasts, not too small, yet not too large, just the right size to fit in his palms. A tiny waist that flowed into round feminine hips and a nice firm behind that would stop traffic on Broad Street during rush hour.

What intrigued Nick was that Summer was oblivious to how she unintentionally caused male heads turn as she strutted by. The girl had no idea whatsoever she was a real live walking brick house, all natural, and no artificial parts. Nick was even amused that other women in the room were envious of her beauty with the exception of the two women who accompanied her. "Hump, now she knows all that's not her hair." Said one woman, while her friend commented, "Mmmm hmm, that weave must of set her back a few pennies," the two haters hackled.

Ignoring the snide comments, he studied the trio. Nick found each of them beautiful; however, there was something extra about the petite beauty, which drew his attention.

Nick smiled to himself remembering the encounter that gave him the opportunity to meet Summer.

From across the room he had watched as she refused dance after dance from would be suitors. Nick was pleased when she literally ran into him causing him to splash his drink down her cleavage. Temptation told him to wedge his tongue between her breasts to remove every drop. Logic ruled and instead he opted to offer his handkerchief.

He waited for what seemed like an eternity for Summer to come out of the ladies room. While waiting for her he was approached by a woman who decided to mosey on over and strike up a conversation with him. He attempted to be polite as the woman chattered on and on about nonsense. Nick wasn't the least bit interested as his eyes darted from the entrance of the ladies room back to the cosmetically enhanced nuisance sticking out her fake boobs.

Witnessing the collision, boob lady decided she'd better get her butt in gear before the little floozy came back. As she pranced over to Nick her main objective was to distract him. The spark of interest in his eyes was unmistakable as he held Summer close. *I'll have to show him what a real woman is all about. Not some little girl trying to be grown. Tonight, he'll be holding me close…all night.*

Nick knew it was rude to abruptly end the conversation with boob lady who blatantly threw herself at him. However, he couldn't help but be mesmerized by Summer's beauty as she timidly made her way towards him. The graceful sway of a woman's hips had never aroused him as it did that night as he watched her movement. Without a choice, his body on its own volition set itself into motion, meeting her halfway, closing the distance between them.

Being so close to Summer again for the second time that night had him fully captivated. *This one is different.* Nick was an expert when it came to women. She was rare in some sort of way, which meant she'd be a challenge. He was used to women throwing themselves at him, ready to do whatever, wherever, but not this one. She'd actually attempted to flee his presence the moment she returned his handkerchief. If he hadn't been so eager to know who she was, Summer would have made her escape. Nick could still hear the softness of her voice. "My name is Summer Jackson."

❧ ❧ ❧ ❧ ❧

Restlessly, Nick shifted in his seat as he told himself he had to see Summer soon. He felt she at least deserved an apology for hurting her the way he had.

The more he thought about her over the past five months it became clear to him that Summer was in love with him. It was evident in all the special little things she'd do for him.

Things she didn't have to do, things she wasn't obligated to do, like making sure his dry cleaning was sent out and picked up without being asked to do so. Sensing he had a trying day she'd bring him a double scotch, sit in his lap, loosen his tie and delicately place kisses at the base of his throat, relaxing him, and evaporating the stress away. Or simply listening intently as he went on and on about whatever was on his mind at the time.

Damn. I messed up bad, real bad.

Chapter 3

Early November, the Previous Year

Summer, you have a call on line three," Ava yelled.

"Ava, take a message for me please. I'm about to medicate Mr. Smith." Summer yelled back as she stood at the medication drawer filling a syringe with pain medication.

Padding over to Summer Ava reached for the syringe. "Here, give it to me. I'll give Mr. Smith this, you go answer the phone." Ava motioned to Summer with her hand as if she were shooing a fly away.

Briskly, Summer went to the phone snatching up the receiver. It always annoyed her when she was interrupted, especially when she enjoyed spending time with a patient. Mr. Smith was about to tell her about the time he caught the ball at the 1985 World Series. Summer had zero aptitude for sports; however, she loved to see the twinkle in her patient's eyes when they shared their stories with her.

Who in the world is this bothering me? "Hello, this is Summer Jackson. How may I help you?"

"Well, you're one hard lady to catch up with, Miss Jackson."

The sound of the voice was deep and sexy. She knew it could only belong to one man, Nick Stiles. She'd been making every excuse in the book, and then some not to take his calls for the past week. Pressing her lips tight together, *I'm gonna kill Ava.*

"Hi Mr. Stiles, how are you doing today?" Summer could have kicked herself; she sounded like a complete nerd. *Good, maybe he'll leave me alone.*

"It's Nick, and I'm fine now that I'm talking to you."

She shook her head. *Oh, this brotha is a hot mess.*

Cutting to the chase, Summer wanted to know, "Is there a reason for your call, Mr. Stiles? I mean Nick?"

Nick chuckled. "Right to the point, I like that. I was calling to see if you would have lunch with me?"

What! Is he crazy? I can barely talk to this man let alone eat in front of him. "I'm sorry, Nick, but I can't."

Summer rolled her eyes at Starr as she mouthed, "I'll go." Starr didn't even know what or where she was consenting to going to. For all she knew the man could be a serial killer.

"Why?" He asked in a tone that made Summer raise an eyebrow.

"Why?" *Because I said so!*

"Yes. Why can't you have lunch with me?"

This was something Nick wasn't used to. Women always jumped at the chance to be in his presence.

Letting out a deep breath she explained. "Because I can't get away from the unit for more than thirty minutes."

Summer stomped her foot, signaling Ava to shut up as she yelled in the background, "I'll cover your patients for you."

Nick didn't want to push the lunch issue or her excuse for not having lunch with him. He'd heard one of her coworkers offer to cover her patients. Leaning back in his leather chair he said, "I see. What about dinner? You work the day shift right?"

This brotha won't quit! "I…I don't know." Coming up with any lame excuse she added, "I don't stay out late on the nights I have to go to work the next morning. My day starts pretty early."

Nick wasn't dissuaded. "I'll have you home by ten."

"I'm sorry Nick, but I can't."

Nervously, Summer breathed heavy into the phone waiting for his response.

Silence.

When he didn't say anything, she took that as her cue to end the conversation.

"I have to get back to my patients, thanks for calling. Goodbye, Nick."

Nick couldn't believe it. The young, beautiful woman that haunted his dreams every night since meeting her actually turned him down. That never happened before.

Stroking his goatee, *Miss Summer is a shy one*. It's been years since he encountered such a shy woman. Most women he met were the aggressors, with nothing shy about them. This was definitely a change, a refreshing change. His primal instincts immediately kicked in, the chase was on.

Swirling his chair around facing the window he gazed out at the surrounding skyscrapers hovering over William Penn. *This isn't over.* When Nick was determined to have something, he went after it until he got it. And that included Summer Jackson.

Hanging up the phone, Summer hissed at Ava and Starr. "Y'all make me sick, the both of you." Yanking a chart from its holder, "Ava, why didn't you tell me it was *him* calling again? I told you I didn't want to talk to him."

Sucking her teeth, Ava snapped, "Then you shouldn't have given him your work number."

Summer threw her hands up in the air and huffed. "I didn't think he would call. We pretty much said everything we had to say. I told him I was a nurse in a hospice unit. He told me his mother had died from pancreatic cancer three years ago and that he had attended and donated money to the benefit every year since. I told him I had to go. He asked for my number, I gave him this one. I didn't think he would call."

The truth was Summer always had some crazy reason as to why she didn't want to go out on a date. She didn't know how to tell her friends it made her uncomfortable when men ogled her. Not to mention on those rare occasions when she did go on a date by the end of the evening the jerk thought because he brought dinner that gave him the privilege to fondle her. So whenever her friends set her up, she always found a reason to break the date. Once, she even went to the extreme of working a shift in the emergency room on a Saturday night when there had been a shortage of nurses to get out of going on a blind date. The sham wasn't a complete lost though. Summer enjoyed the hustle and bustle of the emergency room so much that occasionally she worked a shift here and there when the ER was short staffed.

Starr eased up next to Summer, putting her arm around her shoulder. "What's the matter Boo? You act as if you don't deserve to go out on a date or something. I know you get tired of hanging with me and Av all the time."

Laying her head on Starr's shoulder, "I don't know. It seems like every time I like a guy he turns out to be a jerk. The only thing they're interested in is the booty and you know I'm telling the truth."

"I hear you girlfriend, but give the brotha a chance. Okay? It seems like he's feeling you girl, and I mean strong. Brotha is definitely sweating you."

Summer thought about it for a second. "I'll see. Let me get into Mr. Smith's room. He was about to tell me a story about the Super Bowl."

Ava who was standing within earshot laughed at Summer. "Crazy girl, it's the World Series, not the Super Bowl. One is football, the other baseball, duh!" Ava knew this because Mr. Smith told her the same story two days ago when she was his nurse.

"Whateva!" Summer threw over her shoulder as she bounced down to Mr. Smith's room.

When she was out of hearing range, Starr questioned Ava. "Do you think she'll go out with him?"

"Hmmm, maybe, I hope so. She's such a pretty girl."

"Brotha ain't too bad to look at either."

Ava nodded her head in agreement. At the same time they blurted out, "They'd make a cute couple."

Nick was determined to break Summer's resolve. After a week of daily phone calls, flowers and Godiva chocolates, she agreed to a date on Friday night.

❧ ❧ ❧ ❧ ❧

Pulling a black long sleeve wrap Donna Karan dress from her closet, Summer was anxious to get the night over with.

"At least I finally get to wear this dress I spent all that money on," she said to Ava and Starr who were sitting on her bed as she hunted through her closet for the perfect pair of shoes.

Starr flipped through a magazine while Ava flicked from one cable station to the next. Looking up from the magazine, Starr agreed with her. "Yeah girl you did spend some bucks on that dress, but it's gonna look cute on you."

"Thanks, Starr." Holding up a different shoe in each hand, "What do you guys think, the pumps or the wedges?"

Ava turned her attention away from the television. "I like the pumps."

"Yeah, me too," Starr said.

"Okay, it's the pumps then."

Spontaneously, Ava and Starr jumped off the bed and start doing the Beyoncé booty bounce while rapping the old MC Hammer hit, Pumps and a Bump .

Summer cracked up. "You two are fools! Y'all know that right?"

"We know!" They'd agreed as they continued to rap and booty bounce.

Shaking her head, Summer threw the wedges in the closet and joined Ava and Starr in acting a fool. They were having too much fun for her not to cut up with them.

After about five minutes of goofing off, Summer asked, "What time is it, Ava?"

"Seven fifteen. What time is he coming?" She inquired as she flopped back on the bed and resumed channel surfing.

"He's coming at eight. I had better hurry up. Y'all got me acting all crazy. I'm about to be late."

Starr never stopped her gyrating as Summer rushed past her into the bathroom.

Summer surprised herself. She was showered and completely dressed in less than forty minutes. It certainly helped she didn't wear a ton of make-up. The only things she applied to her face was a moisturizer, eye shadow in gold and brown and a sheer mocha lip gloss that complemented her light complexion. Adding the final touch, Summer sprayed a few squirts of Vera Wang perfume on her wrists and behind her ears.

Standing in front of a full-length mirror, she was satisfied with her reflection. The wrap dress hugged every curve stopping just below the knees to give a full view of shapely legs in sheer black stockings. The pumps showed off well-toned calf muscles, courtesy of daily heel raises. Starr flat ironed her hair and curled it at the ends, letting the long tresses fall down her back.

Giving one last glance in the mirror, Summer headed down the stairs. When her foot hit the last step, the doorbell rang. Her heart began to thump as she went over to the door slowly opening it.

The man was absolutely fine! Nick was wearing a gray sports jacket, black turtleneck and dress slacks with black Kenneth Cole dress loafers. *Mmmm he always smells sooo good!*

Summer was so taken with how darn good he looked and smelled, she hadn't noticed him holding a bouquet of flowers. Handing her the flowers, flashing a hundred watt smile, "These are for you, Beautiful."

Summer blushed. Accepting the flowers their hands touched, sending a current racing through her slightly knocking her off her square. Stepping to the side, allowing him entry, "Come on in so I can put these in water."

Nick watched as she quickly retreated to the kitchen. With each sway of her slim hips her hair bounced full of body against her slender back. Putting his hands in his pockets, he looked around the living room, then into the small dining room. Appreciating the feminine and genteel décor, he strolled over to an entertainment unit. A smile tugged at the corner of his lips as he looked at photos of Summer at various stages in her life. From the photos, he gathered she'd always been a looker.

A few seconds later, Summer emerged with the flowers in a

crystal vase with Ava and Starr on her heels. They'd come down the stairs earlier to eat the take-out they'd ordered.

Stopping briefly to set the vase on the dining room table the trio stood before Nick with Summer positioned front and center.

Pointing to her friends, "Nick, these are my friends, Starr Avery and Ava Peretti."

Taking Starr's, then Ava's hand in a handshake, Nick flashed a charming smile. "Oh, yes, I remember you ladies from the benefit. How's everything going?"

Sharing a quick glance, they both sang in unison, "Good, everything's good."

He engaged in light conversation with Ava and Starr as Summer went to the hall closet to get her coat. Coming back into the living room with the coat draped over her slender arm, "I'm ready now."

"Here, let me help you with your coat," Nick offered as he smoothly sauntered over to her. Taking the coat from her, he helped Summer put her right arm in the sleeve, then her left arm. He lifted the coat onto slender shoulders covering her petite frame. Before Summer could pull her hair out, he gathered the silky tresses in one large hand gently freeing every strain trapped beneath the coat.

Turning to face Nick, Summer gazed at him momentarily speechless. They hadn't even left the house yet and she was feeling unsure of herself. He was already making her nervous.

"Thank you." Summer whispered.

In a deep, low husky voice Nick replied, "It was my pleasure." He loved the feel of her hair. It felt like what he'd imagined, soft, thick silk.

Summer shivered from the deep vibration his voice sent out. She had to say something, anything to help her regain her balance.

"Where's my purse?" She asked her friends who apparently were in a daze.

Ava and Starr were just as taken as they stood staring wide eyed as the fine brotha made a simple act of helping a woman with her coat appear so sensual. Not to mention the way he was gazing at their girl Summer made goose bumps pop up all over them. They could only imagine what she was feeling.

Starr whispered to Ava, "Brotha got it going on."

"You ain't said nothin' but a word."

"Hellooo. Have you seen my purse?"

Snapping out of the trance, Starr pointed, "Right there on the sofa." Taking quick steps to the sofa picking up the purse she handed it to Summer.

Giving each a quick hug, Summer told them she'll see them later. Meaning, "Don't go anywhere until I get back home."

Both the women nodded their heads in understanding.

❧ ❧ ❧ ❧ ❧

"Are you always so quiet?" Nick wanted to know as he intently examined Summer.

Looking up from the menu, Summer was met by intense dark eyes encased in a serious expression.

"Umm, no, not really," she answered barely above a whisper.

"Then why are you so quiet now?"

Hunching slender shoulders, "I guess I'm just a little nervous."

Nick took a sip from his water glass. "Of what?"

Letting out a slow breath, Summer tried to steady the quivering of her voice. "It's been a long time since I've been on a date."

"And why is that? I know you must get asked out all the time." Nick paused as his expression changed from intense to playful. "I noticed all those dudes asking you to dance. But you turned them down, one after the other. You broke a lot of hearts."

He was right. Men did ask her out all the time. However, she avoided men like the bird flu because they usually only wanted one thing… Sex.

Lowering her head avoiding eye contact, she mumbled, "Because I don't like being treated like an object." *Sex object that is.*

Summer breathed a sigh of relief when the waiter suddenly appeared at their table. After they'd order dinner, the conversation moved to other topics. Nick decided to drop his line of questioning, it was clear she was uncomfortable. So instead, they talked about what they did for a living, their families, politics, anything to keep the evening from becoming strained.

Over dinner, they discovered they both were the only child and were born and raised in Philly. Nick had gone to Central High School, the all boys' school at the time, down on Ogontz and Olney Avenues. And Summer to Girl's High at Broad Street and Olney Avenue, just one city block away. Nick teased her about being in elementary school while he was in high school.

Sadness washed over Summer when Nick told her he and his dad had spoken only twice since his mother's death. He shared with her that they never had a good relationship.

He told her the malice between father and son further festered when he decided not to assume his father's role of becoming a lawyer.

Summer couldn't believe Nick's father was the Honorable Judge Henry Stiles, who presided on the bench as a federal judge. Judge Stiles was known for throwing the book at criminals, especially repeat offenders. At least that's how the media portrayed him.

Summer's background wasn't as illustrious as Nick's. Her father had owned a small business as an electrician and her mother operated an in-home daycare center. Summer was proud; however, to tell him she was very close to her parents, even if her mother did drive her crazy at times being overly opinionated about everything. Summer wasn't a bit ashamed to tell him she was scared her parents had decided to move to North Carolina to build their dream home on a piece of land her dad had inherited. They virtually left her in the city with no close family ties so to speak. Aunts, uncles, and cousins were scattered all over the country. Summer refused to move with them. "I don't want to move down south. I'm just fine, right here in Philly."

When her mother pressed her, Summer simply told her, "Mommy, I'm not going. My friends are here and my job is here. Just let me grow up, please." Although she missed her parents, she knew she made the right choice to be totally independent of them and on her own.

Nick was impressed Summer's parents invested their money in the seventies when most blacks didn't know what CD's, mutual funds and saving bonds were. He chuckled when she boasted she began making investments when she got her first job at sixteen with the hope of retiring by the time she was forty-five or fifty.

"That's pretty young don't you think?" "Not at all, I want to enjoy my life. You wouldn't believe how many people get sick as soon as they hit retirement at sixty-five. Most of the time the poor souls didn't enjoy their lives, hardly took any vacations, or spent time with their families because they worked like a dog."

After paying the bill, Nick helped Summer out of her seat and into her coat. As they made their way out of the restaurant, she was conscious of the way his hand rested on the small of her back as he led her outside.

The cold November air was brisk as they waited for the valet to bring Nick's vehicle. Once inside the two sat in silence. Nick's attention on the road and Summer's on the city's passing scenery.

Nick was the first to speak. "It's still early, want to go for a walk?"

10:20 p.m. was the time on the car's interior clock.

"Sure, I could use a walk. I ate too much." Summer groaned patting her stomach remembering the four-course meal she devoured.

Chuckling, Nick said, "Yeah, you sure did." Scanning her petite body from head to toe, "I was wondering where all that food was going."

Playfully punching him in the arm, "Hey, I hadn't had anything to eat since nine this morning, I was hungry. No, make that starving." She said with emphasis as her voice raised an octave.

"Yeah, I could tell."

Sucking her teeth and cutting an evil eye sideways at him, they both erupted in laughter at her reaction to his teasing.

"I'm glad you're having a good time at my expense, Mr. Stiles." Summer's insides did a somersault as Nick flashed the sexiest smile.

"I am having a great time at your expense, Miss Jackson."

Parking the car on Kelly's Drive near Boathouse Row, Nick got out of the vehicle and proceeded to help Summer out.

"So, which direction do you want to walk, Beautiful?" He asked as he gazed down into Summer's flushed face. He was doing it again, making her nervous.

Summer twisted her mouth to one side as if in deep thought. "Ummm, I guess towards Lincoln Drive."

If they made it that far it would be at least a mile walk, give or take. This would allow her to walk off the huge meal and get a chance to spend a little more time with Nick. To Summer's surprise she was really enjoying his company. Besides being the most sophisticated man she'd ever been out with, he was a true gentleman. Not once had he made any unwanted advances. Once she'd gotten over her shyness, Nick had been very attentive when she talked. It was as if he was interested in what she had to say as he held on to her every word.

"Okay, Beautiful, Lincoln Drive it is."

Good. This would give him more time to get into that pretty head of hers. Nick was impressed, he found her rather mature and well versed for a twenty five year old. Usually his rule was never to date women five years his junior. Summer was that and then some, twelve years to be exact. He had figured she was much younger, however, she carried herself with such elegance and grace the age difference didn't bother him at all. She wasn't some young, hoochie momma, gold digger, but rather an intelligent, articulate, young woman.

Nick's lips twitched in a faint smile remembering Summer's offer to help pay the check while back at the restaurant. When he refused, she pleaded with him to let her at least leave the tip. Again, Nick refused. Summer pouted, not even thinking when she stubbornly insisted, "Next time I'm paying."

Yes, there definitely will be a next time, Miss Jackson.

Again, with Summer, he'd experienced something new. Every woman he'd ever taken out expected to be wined and dined, of course at his expense. Nick didn't mind though; that's what a man was supposed to do when he invited a woman out. Summer, however, wasn't presumptuous; she had not assumed he would foot the bill. Nick wondered about that. Had the men she dated been so cheap she was used to helping foot the bill? Or was it she didn't want him to expect any favors at the end of the night because he'd taken her to a five star restaurant? The last thought made him frown.

Strolling at a comfortable pace, Summer found it hard to put one foot in front of the other. She couldn't believe her first date with Nick was going so well. The man looked good, smelled good, and for goodness sake had manners. Not once had he attempted to touch her inappropriately. Certainly, Summer noticed how his eyes glanced over her when she opened her front door for him earlier, how during dinner he made her so nervous when he gazed directly at her, nearly making her drop her fork, or how he would take her small hand as he helped her in and out of his car.

Nick interrupted her reverie. "A penny for your thoughts, Beautiful."

Oh, mercy he had the sexist, deepest voice she ever heard in a man.

Stopping mid-step, prompting Nick to stop as well, Summer turned facing him tilting her head to get a better view of him in the moonlit sky.

"Why do you keep calling me that?

"Calling you what?" Nick was aware of what she was asking, however, he wanted to draw her out, make her talk more.

Lowering her head, avoiding Nick's penetrating gaze, "You know what."

A lazy grin curved his full lips. "No, Summer, I don't know."

Letting out a breath of frustration because she knew he was messing her. "Beautiful. Why do you keep calling me that?"

Taking a finger, he gently lifted her chin to meet his gaze. "Because, Summer Jackson, you are beautiful."

Summer thought she would die as Nick proceeded to lean down, kissing her ever so lightly on the tip of her nose. A current ran through her body causing her to shiver. Maybe it was the sudden gust of night wind that just blew by and not the kiss. *Naw, it definitely was the kiss.*

"Are you cold?" Concern laced Nick's husky voice.

All Summer could do was nod her head. No way was she about to tell the finest man she'd ever laid eyes on that he had reduced her to shivers.

Before Summer could blink, Nick held her in an embrace so close that she had no choice but to lay her head on his strong muscular chest as his chin gently rested on top of her head. Summer's nipples tingled while the butterflies in her stomach fluttered as her breasts, stomach, pelvis and thighs molded to Nick's solid form.

"Does this feel better?" He whispered holding her close, generating heat from his body.

"Yes." Summer answered in a small voice.

It didn't matter she barely knew this man, but this felt so right. Summer's arms that had been at her side freely found themselves wrapped around Nick's midsection.

Closing her eyes, she inhaled the scent of his cologne. She recognized it as the same scent as the one on his handkerchief the night of the benefit. Holding on to Nick, she told herself, *I have to thank my girls,* as she let herself go and simply enjoy the feel of his strong presence.

Nick's breathing became deep and slow, he was fighting to control his manhood as he held Summer close, pressed so intimately against his body. Things had been going so well the last thing he wanted to do was frighten her off. Nick knew women; the one he held in his arms hadn't had much experience with men, if any. He definitely would have to take things at her pace... slow.

Be that as it may, he couldn't control his sudden impulse. Not wanting to miss the opportunity, because he had wanted to do this from the moment he first laid eyes on her. Threading long strong fingers through her hair, cradling the back of her head he slowly pulled her head away from his chest. *Daaayum, I could play in this hair all night long.* Gazing down into her face he trembled at the vision before him.

Summer's eyes were at half-mast with her lips slightly parted waiting to be kissed. Lowering his face he wanted to take her mouth in a wild passionate kiss, *slow, Nick, slow.* Delicately he traced her bottom lip with his tongue. The mere act gave him the response he wanted. A soft moan escaped Summer's throat traveling pass her parted lips into his mouth. Summer opened her mouth wider in submission allowing Nick's tongue further entry to explore her sweetness. After his exploration, their tongues passionately mated until they were satisfied.

Breaking the embrace they gazed into each other's eyes, no words were exchanged. No words were needed. The kiss sealed their fate. Simultaneously they reached for the other's hand as they continued their leisurely stroll hand in hand as if they'd been lovers for years.

Chapter 4

Present Day
Month of December

Why is everyone standing around me shouting in my face? Where am I anyway? That's right. I'm at work. What happened? Wasn't I getting a bag of IV fluids from the cabinet?

Gently patting Summer on the face trying to arouse her, "Summer, Summer are you all right?"

Blinking her eyes and shaking her head to clear it, "Ava, what are you yelling and smacking me in my face for?" Summer sat up frowning while pushing Ava away.

"Girl, you passed out." Ava told her as she backed up to give her room.

"No, I didn't. I just got a little woozy that's all." She waved her hand and dismissed the fact she'd just fainted.

Ava gave her an incredulous look. "Woozy my foot! I'm calling your doctor." Rushing over to the phone she began dialing Dr. Neil, Summer's obstetrician.

"Ava, get off that phone. I feel better now." Summer demanded, down playing she'd just fainted at work. Standing up she was a little off balance. She felt Starr's arm supporting her weight by holding onto what used to be a slim waist.

"Summer, let Ava talk to your doctor. Didn't you just have an appointment yesterday?" Starr questioned as she helped Summer sit in a chair.

"Yes and everything went well. I probably just moved too fast or something."

The entire time Ava was on the phone with the doctor's office she kept Summer in her line of vision.

"Mmm Hmm, I see. Okay. I'll let you speak with her now."

Handing the phone to Summer, Ava wasn't fazed one bit that she was shooting daggers at her, as she took the phone and placed it to her ear.

Not saying a word, Summer nodded her head as if the person on the other line could see her.

"Okay, thanks Sheila. Bye."

Starr looked at Summer with a curious stare. "What did Sheila say?"

"Calm down already. I'm pregnant not deathly ill." Rolling her eyes and sucking her teeth, she knew Ava and Starr didn't mean any harm, but they were more than overbearing at times. "Sheila said that my hemoglobin is a little lower than it was the last time I had blood drawn. And as you Nancy nurses know, that is why I got all dizzy and everything. Sheila said Dr. Neil wants me to start taking my iron pills three times a day instead of twice a day. Okay. Y'all satisfied now?"

"Well, you know what I think?" Ava ignored Summer as she spoke to Starr.

"What girl?" Starr knew Ava was about to send Summer into a frenzy, that's why she was ignoring her.

"Summer works too hard. What she needs to do is take her pregnant self home and go to bed."

Ava stared Summer down, daring her to say anything that would dispute her.

Summer wasn't intimidated by the stare. Crossing her arms under her breasts she shot daggers at the both of them while pressing her lips in a thin line.

"What? Don't be looking at me like that, Miss Thing. I'm not the one selling you wolf tickets." Starr snorted in Summer's direction.

Rolling her neck and pointing her finger, "First of all I can look at you anyway I want to. Second, I'm not going anywhere. It's almost time to go home, anyway, for your information."

Snatching a patient chart off the desk, Summer flipped it open writing a shift note.

Humming a tune, ignoring her friends as they went on and on about how she should start her maternity leave now instead of in the standard two weeks before the due date. *They must be crazy if they think I'm gonna sit up in the house bored to death all day until this baby is born.*

Starr whispered to Ava, "Look at her, ignoring somebody with her little nasty self. I swear she ain't our sweet little Summer anymore since she's been pregnant."

"Mmm hmmm, chile done went and grown a backbone, it's gotta be those crazy pregnant hormones."

"Humph, must be. I can't wait until she has that baby." Starr threw out loud enough making sure Summer heard every word.

"Tell me about it." Ava agreed.

Standing up walking over to Summer, Starr tugged on her ponytail. "Maybe she'll be nice again."

Summer giggled as she nudged her. "Get away from me. You make me sick." Looking Ava up and down turning her nose up, "You make me sick, too."

Ava threw her head back and laughed. "Yeah, I love you too, Boo."

❧ ❧ ❧ ❧ ❧

The week went by uneventful; Summer hadn't had any more fainting spells. Ava and Starr were still being royal pain in the butts. Summer didn't know why she went to work; they had taken to tag teaming her, doing the bulk of her work before she could even get to it. And if they weren't calling her everyday after work, they were popping up unexpectedly at her front door. Not to mention they would call Summer's parents giving them minute by minute updates on her as if they were channel 6 Action News or something. Their over protective actions led to Summer getting calls almost on a daily basis from her parents.

She didn't mine though; she missed her parents something awful since they'd moved down south.

Summer's parents were upset when she told them she'd decided not to tell Nick about the baby. Her mom called him every dirty name in the book; names Summer didn't even know her mom knew since she was an upstanding Christian woman. Whereas her father lectured her mother the man could not be blamed if he didn't know he was going to be a father.

Every conversation usually ended with one of her parents asking, "Have you seen or talked to Nick yet?" Summer knew her parents were hinting at if she had told him about the pregnancy. Her response was always the same, "No, I haven't."

She never explained why she kept the baby a secret from him. She'd been too ashamed to tell them she had allowed herself to get pregnant by a man who made it clear he had no desire whatsoever to be a father. Summer innocently discovered this when he told her about a situation that occurred years ago with a woman he 'thought' he loved. The woman played Nick, making him believe he was about to become a father. When it was discovered he wasn't the father, he set out to ruin the woman for humiliating and making a fool out of him.

After he shared that bit of information with her, Summer just had to know, "What would you do if a woman told you she was pregnant by you again?"

Summer was only curious; she hardly had any plans on becoming a mother before marriage. She was somewhat taken aback when he stared at her with his jaw clenched and eyes cold as ice. "I'd tell her to flush it."

After an awkward second of silence, he added, "Don't find yourself pregnant… at least not by me." His warning was unmistakable. He didn't want to have anything to do with children.

During the time they'd first started to date, Summer read several business articles about Nick. She wanted to know everything about him. She'd learned he was shrewd and ruthless in his business dealings. Nick was referred to as a sheep in wolves' clothing because of his ability to be charming one second, and cut throat the next. Many of the articles reported such characteristics were the reason why at the age of thirty-seven he was one of the wealthiest, self-made African American men on the east coast.

Summer witnessed his wrath once after he found out a trusted employee embezzled $350,000.00 over a two-year period. Nick told her then that he only gave a person one chance to cross him. So if, and when, they did, they'd better make it good, worth their while.

Nick made sure the federal prosecutor filed every charge allowable by law against the man.

Vigorously, Summer rubbed her arms from the chill that ran through her as she thought about Nick. Without meaning to she'd crossed him. She had gotten pregnant and God help her, decided to keep the baby. With all her heart she believed if she'd told him right away he would have demanded she have an abortion. He had told her as much. Heaven forbid if she told him now, he'd think she was trying to trap him into marrying her or worse yet, giving her a large sum of money to avoid a paternity suit. Summer had known Nick long enough to know how his mind worked. He could think the absolute worst of someone when he wanted to.

As Summer sat thinking, a strong emotion weighed heavy on her…fear. Part of Nick's ruthlessness was attacking a person's most vulnerable spot. Summer loved children. Whenever Starr baby-sat her niece and nephew, she would volunteer to help keep the adorable toddlers entertained.

Even though Summer was not pleased with the whole single mother thing, she would love her baby enough to be both mother and father to it. If by any chance Nick believed she had crossed him he'd strike like a cobra at her weakest spot. As much as she loved him an overwhelming sense of fear chocked her. Nick could never find out about the baby…ever.

Brrrg! Brrrg! Brrrg!

The loud ringing of the phone snapped Summer out of her reverie.

"Hello?"

"Hi baby."

A huge smile broke across Summer's face. "Hi mommy, how are you doing?"

"The question is, 'how are you, Miss Summer?' Ava called me, told me 'bout you passing out at work. Why didn't you call your daddy and me baby?"

Summer groaned. Ava had a big mouth; she couldn't hold water sometimes to save her life.

"Mommy, I'm all right, my hemoglobin was a little lower than normal, that's all. I'm feeling much better now."

Summer was trying her best to sound convincing as not to worry her mother.

"All right baby, but the next time you better call me and your daddy. You hear me?" Her mom's tone was firm but loving

"Yes ma'am, I promise."

With that out of the way she and her mother talked. They caught up on the latest as Summer padded back and forth with the cordless phone from her bedroom to the bathroom. She was getting everything set up to take a nice relaxing bath. Lately her lower back had been bothering her, probably from how the baby was laying. Which she didn't understand since the little munchkin moved all over the place, all the time.

The conversation flowed nice and easy. Summer kept her fingers crossed hoping her mother wouldn't ask about Nick. She hadn't seen nor heard from him in months. Doubt she ever would, at least no time in the near future.

Thank goodness, her mother never asked about Nick. Before hanging up her mother told her Ava might stop over to check on her since Starr was away at a conference.

"Okay, mommy, I'll keep an ear out for Ava. Tell daddy I'm sorry I missed him and I'll call later."

"Bye baby."

"Bye mommy."

Finally adjusting the water temperature, standing in front of the mirror piling her hair on top of her head with hair pins, Summer couldn't wait to soak her sore back. Before she stripped out of her clothes she started to call Ava and tell her not to come over. "I just want to be alone tonight." With any luck she wouldn't see Ava until Sunday morning at church. But just in case, she left the bathroom door slightly ajar to hear the doorbell.

Lighting scented candles, strategically arranging them in the bathroom, Summer turned off the light before easing herself down into the soothing water. She didn't know what smelt better the rose scented candles or the lavender bath salts she added to the water at the last minute. Whichever it was she was totally relaxed. Taking baths always reminded her of Nick.

The first time they made love she was a virgin. Nick had been gentle with her, yet she still was sore and swollen. Wanting to ease her discomfort he drew a bath for her in his Italian marbled Jacuzzi. When he returned to let her know her bath was ready she attempted to walk to the bathroom.

"No, Beautiful, I'll carry you." As he lifted her in his arms, Summer tucked her head in the crook of his neck. She couldn't believe how he was taking such good care of her.

Although her heart ached over losing Nick, memories like the one she just had made her smile. Things with him from the beginning were always good. That's why for the life of her she couldn't comprehend his logic for ending their relationship.

When the baby moved, Summer shifted her attention to her belly. She placed her hand on her stomach and rubbed a soft circular pattern as she closed her eyes and hummed a lullaby. This usually calmed the baby's movements.

She was definitely having a Calgon moment. Moments like these, reminiscing about Nick and his ability to be tender was giving her a glimmer of hope. *Maybe if I call his office he'll speak to me and then I can tell him. He'll understand.*

Summer daydreamed pleasant thoughts of the man she still loved as her eyes closed and she drifted into that state between deep relaxation and sleep.

Summer's eyes popped wide open at the sound of a loud obnoxious doorbell.

"Great timing, Ava."

Chapter 5

Turning off the ignition, Nick had second thoughts now that he was outside of Summer's house. The clock on the interior of the Benz read five minutes after ten. Glancing up at her bedroom window the light was on. She was home. Summer always was a homebody; she was probably reading a book or watching television.

Hesitating for a minute, he swung the car door open stepping out heavy-footed. The day had been trying. Negotiations did not go as expected with the textile company. It was going to take longer to add this one to his collection.

Nick had no business there. He was not in the best frame of mind, but he had put going to see Summer off long enough. He'd been in town for over two weeks now.

Taking long purposeful strides, he made his way to her front door. Extending a long finger, he rang the bell.

Gingerly, Summer rose from her sitting position in the tub. Trying to hurry, reaching for the towel quickly drying herself off, she grumbled, "Ava, why are you bugging me now?"

Snuffing out the candles Summer clumsily quickened her pace. Reaching on the back of the door for her thick pink terrycloth robe she donned it as she searched for her slippers.

Surveying the room, *where are my slippers?* Deciding to forget her search because Ava was ringing the doorbell like a madwoman, she left the bathroom in a hurry.

Holding on to the banister to keep from falling, Summer was really going to *wring Ava's neck!* Didn't she know her big belly got in the way these days?

Nick became increasingly aggravated. What was taking her so long? The thought crossed his mind she had someone in the house with her. He clenched his jaw, bawling his large hands into fists at the thought of another man touching her soft, delicate body the way he'd been privy to.

He spent restless nights tossing and turning in his bed remembering how her petite body felt beneath his. How he had to position himself just so to keep from crushing her with his weight. Imagining her with someone else in such an intimate way made him see red. This time Nick didn't ease up off the doorbell.

When her foot hit the last step, Summer swore, *this girl has lost her ever-loving mind.* Waddling over to the door, snatching it open she began tearing into Ava.

"Girl, are you cra–"

Immediate disbelief, panic, terror, and then fear overtook Summer as her heart began to wildly pump in her chest. Her first instinct was to slam the door shut, lock it, run, hide, and pray he'd go away.

Nick must have sensed what Summer was thinking, her reaction to him was frightening to say the least. He couldn't believe how her facial features transformed from one of annoyance to fear within milliseconds. Quickly, he wedged his foot in the doorway and with one strong arm pushed the door open before she could shut it.

With all her might she tried to close the door. But her body and the little life in her womb betrayed her. Her arms suddenly had no strength as she pushed against the door that wouldn't budge. A sudden sharp kick to the ribs left Summer gasping for air, and releasing her hold on the door sending her awkwardly stumbling backwards.

Stalking forward while simultaneously slamming the door shut with his foot, Nick couldn't believe his eyes. He had to be seeing an illusion, a vision, or a dream. *This can't be.*

Summer jumped and took a step back at the sound of the slamming door. Advancing another step towards her, he wore an incredulous expression as his eyes roamed her from head to toe. He couldn't believe it. Summer was pregnant! Pregnant!

Retreating another step, Summer's mind was racing. *Maybe I can make it to my bedroom if I run fast and lock the door and then he'll leave. Right?*

Nick was terrifying with his bulging eyes, flaring nostrils, and pulsating jugulars that were completely consuming him. Never before had he responded to her with such a crazed temperament.

Summer's mouth suddenly became dry, she wanted to swallow, but could not. Wanted to say something, but no words would form in her brain to leave through her lips. Remembering she didn't have any clothes on under her robe, self-consciously she gathered the front of the robe near her breasts with one hand.

An evil smirk marred his features. *Always the modest one, I guess that changed. Little tramp went and got herself knocked up.*

Again, Nick advanced to close the distance between them. As Summer lifted her right foot to take another step back, he barked, "Don't you dare move another inch, Summer Jackson."

Startled by his outburst, she let her head drop as the tears she fought to keep sealed behind lids fell one by one.

"I see you've been busy, Miss Jackson."

Nick's tone was cold and sarcastic as he closed the distance between them. He didn't care she was crying. He did care however, she'd met someone and gotten pregnant while he could not even look at another woman, let alone bed one.

He continued his insult through clenched teeth. "Didn't take you long to let some punk crawl between your legs."

Summer was appalled at how Nick was speaking to her. Jerking her head up, attempting to give him a disgusted glare, she backed down from the daggers he threw at her more than the harsh words he spewed slapping her in the face.

"Nick, what are you talking about?"

"You know damn well what I mean. I go away for five months and come back to find you pregnant!"

Finding courage she said, "Did it ever occur to you I was pregnant before you left?"

He rubbed his hand across his face and spat out in disbelief, "What are you saying, Summer? Are you trying to tell me it's my baby?"

Tears that, momentarily dried, began to spill again. Summer could not stand to have Nick look at her with such anger in his eyes so she averted her gaze to the other side of the room and focused on a still life that hung over the mantle. "Yes," she whispered.

Frustrated, he grabbed Summer by her upper arms and forced her to make eye contact with him. His grip was so tight she winced at his touch. The space between them so oppressive she felt his hot breath on her face.

Through clenched teeth he hissed, "Speak up, Beautiful, I can't hear you."

Summer's lips trembled as she whispered, "Yes, Nick, it's your baby."

Feeling like he'd been kicked in the midsection, Nick released his hold on Summer as he stumbled back. Only once had he believed he was going to be a father. He was in love, so he thought with Veronica Taylor. Nick begged her to marry him; he wanted to make an honest woman out of her. Give their child his name, but Veronica refused his offer of marriage. It became apparent to Nick why she had refused him when an ex-boyfriend showed up and demanded a paternity test to prove that the baby was his. Test result later confirmed the ex-boyfriend was the child's father.

Veronica's scheme had been to use the baby as a means to Nick's bank account to start a business, which she'd successfully accomplished.

Humiliated and feeling like a complete fool he swore one day he would get revenge.

Five years later, Veronica owned and operated a successful boutique on Fabric Row at 4th and Christian Streets. The very building she had leased to run her boutique out of was the very building he would later, unbeknownst to her, purchase as prime real estate. All Veronica was aware of was there was a new owner of the building.

Nick raised the rent so high, at the end of each month she was scrambling to pay the bills. Months of juggling finances to pay merchants, employees, back rent, late fees, and legal costs forced her to close the doors of her business. In the end, Nick's retaliation financially ruined her.

She had lost everything. Her business, her home and her new modeled Volvo she fell in love with the second she spied it on the showroom floor.

To add insult to injury, Veronica's ex-boyfriend turned out to be a deadbeat dad. The child support he paid, when he paid it, was hardly enough to feed the poor child.

Nick never showed any remorse; it was his money she'd swindled as capital to start up her business. Twisting the knife deeper he leased out the building to the local fashion design school on the Avenue of the Arts for a nominal monthly fee.

Several years later here he is again in the same predicament of being played like a fiddle. He had told Summer about Veronica and her conniving ways. How she had stooped so low as to claim a child was his knowing it was a damaging lie. Nick made it clear to Summer that he never wanted to be in that position again. "I have no intentions of being anyone's father...ever."

Walking to the other side of the room, putting distance between them, he asked, "How far along are you? When is the baby due?"

"I just turned seven months. The baby is due the end of February."

Gathering up her courage again, Summer waddled over to Nick. Touching his arm she pleaded, "Nick, please let me explain."

Snatching away from her, he roared, "Take your hands off me! Explain what? That you're practically ready to deliver a baby that you claim is mine and you didn't tell me."

Summer tried to interrupt. "Nick, I—"

"Shut the hell up! I thought *you* were different, Summer! But you're no different than the rest of those skanks! What were you going to do? Huh? Hit me with a paternity suit!"

She cried, "No! Nick! I wouldn't do something like that! I never asked you for anything!"

Pacing the small living room back and forth like a caged animal, Nick kept his gaze on Summer, who was too afraid to move.

"Summer, I don't know what the hell you would do! And you didn't have to ask me for anything! I pampered you like a spoiled little brat! But that wasn't enough for you, was it? I can't believe you would do something so stupid as to get yourself pregnant!"

Summer stared at him in disbelief and sobbed uncontrollably as Nick ejected his venom. He was being so cruel. Did the raging lunatic think she had conceived a baby on her own?

"Thought you were clever not telling me, didn't you?" He stopped his pacing, towering over her. "Because you knew I would've told you to get rid of it! I told you I *never* wanted children!"

Shaking her head, backing away from Nick's tyranny, Summer placed a protective hand on her belly.

Completely paralyzed by Nick's barbaric behavior she braced herself. The building storm was about to erupt into a full-blown monsoon.

Shoving his hands in his pants pockets to keep from shaking Summer, Nick continued with his line of attack.

"You wanted to start this little game, Summer. Now I'm going to finish it for you. I told you I only give a person one chance, one, Summer to cross me." Nick rubbed both hands over his short-cropped hair in frustration, letting out a deep breath. "Summer, you crossed me."

This is what Summer feared more than anything. He was going in for the kill. She had to make him understand. Begging she said, "Please Nick, I…I never meant to. Let me explain, help you understand."

Banging his fist against the wall, "No, Summer! You need to understand that a paternity test will be taken! For all I know *it* may not even be mine! But if *it* is, trust me, you'll never see your precious baby… ever!"

Nick stormed out the door, slamming it shut.

Summer's heart-wrenching sobs could be heard as Nick made his way to his vehicle.

❧ ❧ ❧ ❧ ❧

Kevin sat at a table in the back and looked at his watch. *This had better be good.* He was already in hot water with Trina. Tonight had been the second time he bailed out on her at the last minute. A wry smile crossed his face as he thought about all the ways he would make it up to her.

Trina was not the type of girl you would take home to mom, but for the present time she would do. Trina was a straight up freak in the bed. Kevin blew out an annoyed breath as he mumbled, "Nick better have a damn good reason for dragging me down here."

He checked his watch again and signaled for the waitress to come to his table. He had just told her ten minutes ago he was waiting for his brother and would wait to order when he arrived. Agitated, Kevin suddenly needed a drink.

"Yes Sir, what can I get for you?" The waitress asked as she showed off a set of deep dimples when she smiled. Kevin was a sucker for dimples.

"How 'bout your number and a shot of Hennessy?" Kevin winked as he flashed his Mack Daddy smile.

Flattered by his come on the waitress blushed. "I'll be right back with your drink, Sir?"

Kevin leaned back in his chair and grinned as he watched the young woman seductively sway her hips as she strutted away. That's when he spied Nick thundering through the door. *What the hell is his problem? He looks like he could kill someone with his bare hands.*

Nick and Kevin Dawson had been boys since their high school days at Central. Since the age of fourteen the pair had been more like brothers than friends. They even referred to each other as brothers in the literal sense. The bond they shared was almost psychic in nature. The mere sight or sound of the other's voice always revealed if trouble was headed their way. Whether it was an affair gone wrong or a business deal gone south, the other always knew when something was out of kilter. Tonight there definitely was a problem with Nick. Kevin knew something was up when he called, telling him to meet him at Warm Daddy's.

When Nick approached the table Kevin stood, the two greeted each other with a handshake and masculine hug.

Kevin was the first to speak as he gestured for Nick to sit. "Brother what gives, you look like you could spit fire?"

Before Nick could respond, the waitress was at the table giving Kevin his drink.

Roaming Nick over, appreciating what she saw. Smiling seductively, her voice dropped a sultry octave, "What can I get for you, Sir?"

"A double scotch." Nick's tone was flat letting her know he wasn't interested.

Embarrassed by his dismissal the waitress quickly fled their table as she muttered, "I'll be right back with your drink, Sir."

"Man, did you have to be so cold?" Kevin asked as he chortled.

"Brother, I am not in the mood for *any* females tonight." Nick responded tersely.

"Whoa. Dude, what gives?"

Nick dropped his head and pinched the bridge of his nose. "Summer's pregnant," he grinded out through clenched teeth.

Kevin was aware Nick was going to see Summer tonight. However, in a million years he would have never guessed that the bomb Nick just dropped would be responsible for his friend's foul mood.

Kevin choked on his drink and waited for the waitress to leave as she sat Nick's drink down in front of him. Kevin cleared his throat and tried not to choke again.

"Is there anything else I can get you gentlemen?

"No thanks," Kevin said.

The second she was out of hearing range, he wanted to know. "Whose kid is it?"

Even he knew Nick didn't want children. *Damn, I thought Summer was one of the good girls."*

"She says it's mine." Nick drummed his knuckles on the table.

"Daaayum. Man, are you sure it's yours?"

"Yeah, man, most likely it is. She says she just turned seven months. If that's the case, it's my kid." Nick grimaced as he let the strong liquor slide down his throat.

"Get the hell out of here, man! Summer's seven months pregnant and you're just finding out about it." *Deep.*

"Yup, my brotha, just found out tonight. That's why I had to see you. I needed to bounce this off of you."

"Well how'd it go?" Kevin raised his hand and signaled for the waitress to bring him another drink and Nick one too. This was going to be a long night.

"Man, you know I lost it."

Kevin nodded his head. When out of control Nick's temper was beyond nasty.

"Bro, there's only one other time I wanted to put my hands on a woman."

Kevin sat erect, stared at his friend bug eyed as he groaned, "Tell me you didn't, Nick."

Offended his closest friend would think such a thing of him, he said through clenched teeth, "I said I wanted to. I would never hurt Summer. Though I wanted to shake the mess out of her."

Easing back into his chair, "So what are you going to do?" Kevin inquired as he took a large gulp of his drink.

Nick never batted an eye when he said, "I'm gonna get custody of my kid."

"Nick, come on man. What are *you* gonna do with a kid, an infant at that?"

Nick became irritated with Kevin. He always defended Summer.

"Summer should have told me she was pregnant. Instead of doing that, she hid it from me. What was her motive?"

Trying to reason with him, "Come on man, even you yourself said Summer was the best thing to ever happen to you. Maybe she had a good reason for not telling you."

"Like what Kev?" Nick challenged. "I've been trying to figure that one out."

Letting out a deep breath, continuing his defense, "Man, I don't know. All I'm saying is that you should talk to the girl again. Summer is a sweetheart and you know it."

"Whatever, man. All I'm saying is that she should've told me. I'm not letting some scheming, lying, whore, raise my child. If *it's* even my kid. She's probably just having *it* to try to get money out of me. All females are just a like, greedy, little tramps."

Shaking his head in disbelief, "Nick, dude, you know you're wrong as hell. That girl is nothing like Veronica or the other women you traipsed around with for that matter."

Kevin didn't often get angry with Nick, but he bordered on it as he locked eyes with him in a primal stare down. "You can't even compare the two. Summer wasn't some gold digging, hoochie with her hands in your pockets every time you turned around, let alone a whore. That girl loved you. Was heart broken when you broke it off with her. I told you how shook up the girl looked when I saw her downtown on Chestnut Street the week after you left for Canada. What you need to do is give her a break and stop threatening to take her baby. Excuse me, *your* baby.

Remember, you're the one who dumped her with that lame excuse of not wanting to be in a long distance relationship. And, you're the one who said you didn't want any kids. You should be glad she didn't tell you. Maybe she didn't want to put you on some guilt trip about your running off to conquer the damn world."

Nick sat seething. If it had been anyone else ripping into him, he would have given them an uppercut. Kevin had given him much food for thought with his brutal honesty. However, that did not change his position on the paternity test. He didn't care what Kevin said, he was getting a paternity test and do what he had to do, even if it meant getting custody of the kid.

So what, he didn't want to be a father. It didn't matter now, did it? Regardless whether he wanted to or not, it didn't change the fact that he was going to be one. And it was all Summer's fault. Whatever her reasoning, Nick didn't care. All he knew was she would pay one way or another.

"Listen, Kev, I know I'm not straight about this situation. You know how I get when someone I've trusted lies to me. I hear everything you're saying, but I gotta do what I gotta do, man. You feel me?"

Kevin nodded his head. He felt Nick all right; he just prayed that he would remember how special Summer had been to him. If he did, maybe he would have some mercy on the poor girl.

Nick stood, threw a large bill on the table, enough to cover their drinks and a healthy tip.

"Where you headed man?"

Glancing at his watch, it was only a little after midnight and Trina would still be up. If not he'd wake her. He could feel his groan tightening as he imagined her coming to her front door with nothing on but a mere thong. That's how she usually greeted him when he called late at night.

Smiling broadly at his buddy, he said, "To make that booty call you interrupted my brotha."

Nick chuckled. "More power to you, man."

Chapter 6

The holidays passed by like a blur, a distant memory. Summer hadn't told anyone about the night Nick came to visit her; she was still in shock by his reaction to her pregnancy. Although she had not seen him since, he stayed true to his word. On Tuesday afternoon, Summer received a letter from Nick's lawyer, Mr. Steinberg. It was official; her back was up against the wall. The baby's paternity would be determined once she gave birth. At least he wasn't crazy enough to demand an amniocentesis for the results.

When Summer received the letter via certified mail, she immediately phoned the lawyer. Never being in such a position before, she had no idea what to expect. She was anxious to know if Nick had begun the legal process to get custody of her unborn child. Mr. Steinberg assured her custody arrangements could not be initiated until the paternity of the baby was established. He also informed her that a family court judge would have to review the case in order to grant custody to either parent or both parents in the case of joint custody. For the moment, Summer breathed a sigh of relief.

Mr. Steinberg's assurances hadn't meant much to her. Summer found herself crying over the whole mess every time she thought about Nick's threat. Mostly because she knew what the test results would reveal, which meant there was a strong possibility he would immediately file for custody.

Summer had given some thought to hiring an attorney and fighting Nick for custody. The thought of it only gave her a headache and depressed her even more. Nick had enough money to afford the best legal counsel; she would never be able to compete with his caliber of attorneys.

Besides, she had to spend her money sparingly since she had taken an earlier maternity leave than expected. With the stress of her now hectic life, she began to have sporadic episodes of premature contractions.

Brrrg. Brrrg. Brrrg.

Rising up off the sofa, waddling to the phone on the kitchen wall, Summer answered, "Hello?"

"Did you sign the consent form yet?"

This man is making my life a living hell. "Yes." Summer lied. She was too afraid to tell him she hadn't signed that dreadful piece of paper. She had put off signing the document hoping Nick would change his mind. Fat chance. *I'll sign the darn thing after I get of this stupid phone with Ivan the Terrible.*

"Good. Bring the document to my office so I can FedEx it to my attorney."

Nick was determined not to make any of this easy for Summer, he very well could have sent a messenger service to her house to retrieve the document.

Stunned, Summer's mouth dropped open. Didn't this fool know there was supposed to be a blizzard later in the afternoon? Although it had not yet started to snow, she didn't want to take public transportation into Center City. And no way was she going to drive with the threat of a blizzard. The last time she drove in heavy snow her life flashed before her as she slid through a stop sign and nearly collided with a SUV.

"Summer, did you hear me?" Nick snapped, irritated by her silence.

Too afraid to voice her concerns about the impending weather, she didn't want to fuel his anger by refusing to come to his office.

"Yes, I heard you. I'll bring it now." Summer mumbled in defeat.

It's a good thing she kept an outfit ready to wear at all times. She glanced at the kitchen wall clock and noticed it was eleven forty-five. The weatherman predicted the snow wouldn't start for another few hours. If she hurried, she could make it back home before it starts to come down.

Making her way up the stairs, Summer put on a pair of stylish black denim maternity pants foregoing tights and a gray cable knit maternity sweater. She did not want to put too many clothes on since she had taken to having annoying hot flashes at the most awkward times. Summer could just hear her mother admonishing her. "Girl you're gonna catch a cold in your hind-parts going out half naked."

After she got dressed and fixed her hair, Summer grabbed money from the dresser for carfare as she hurried down stairs to put on her boots, coat, hat and gloves. As she proceeded to head out the door, she picked up the dreaded document and shoved it into a large leather hobo bag she slung across her shoulder. Concerned with getting back home before the blizzard hit it totally slipped her mind she had not signed the consent.

Coming up out of the subway at Walnut-Locust, wanting to turn back around and go home because the snow was coming down in large flakes covering the ground, Summer was fighting the tears that were threatening to fall. "I knew this was going to happen. Those weather people don't know what they're talking about. Later this afternoon, early evening my foot. It has to be at least three to four inches out here already." Summer fussed aloud not caring if the passing pedestrians thought she was loco.

Maneuvering in the wind and snow was difficult; the brutal wind was biting at her face and fingertips. Summer wanted to put her gloved hands in her pockets to keep warm, but couldn't, she needed her arms held slightly away from her body to keep her balance. *Why can't I get a stinkin' hot flash right about now? I… am… freezing!*

Summer's face stung from the cold as she glanced up at the tall building at Eighteenth and Walnut. She signed the visitor's log and took the elevator up to the twentieth floor. As the doors opened, her heart pounded as she stepped off into the main lobby of Stiles Enterprise. *I just want this to be over with.*

As Summer approached the receptionist desk, a middle-aged woman greeted her.

"Good afternoon, how may I help?"

"Umm, I'm here to see, Mr. Stiles."

"What is your name and what company are you with?"

"Umm, my name is Summer Jackson and I'm not with a company."

"Oh, yes, Mr. Stiles is expecting you. If you like you may have a seat while I intercom him."

As Summer took a seat, she nervously rubbed her fingers up and down the thick leather strap of her handbag. She watched as the receptionist informed Nick she had arrived. As she waited, it suddenly occurred to her that this was the first time she'd ever been to Nick's office.

Whenever she'd suggested meeting him at work he'd tell her, "I keep work and my personal life separate." Now all of a sudden he didn't care that *his* and *her* personal lives were on display for all to see. Summer could tell the receptionist was wondering who she was since she wasn't affiliated with a company.

"Miss Jackson, you can go back to Mr. Stiles' office. Do you know where it is?"

"No ma'am."

"Straight back to the end of the corridor."

"Thanks."

Waddling down the long corridor, Summer had to stop to remove her hat, gloves and coat. Of all times she was starting to have one of those annoying hot flashes. She was sweating and perspiring all over the place. *Well isn't this a blip, I'm sweating like a freakin' pig.* Before she knocked on the door, she wiped her brow with the heel of her right hand and then wiped her sweaty palms on the leg of her pants. *That's better, now at least I won't look all sweaty.*

Summer knocked on the solid oak door with the gold plaque that read: *Nicholas Stiles, President and CEO.*

"Come in," came the command from the other side.

Summer's breath caught as she walked in the office. Why? Why did he have to be so darn handsome? Nick was the epitome of fine. She couldn't help but to be drawn to the powerful figure talking on the phone as he motioned for her to take a seat in the chair in front of his desk.

She placed her hat, gloves, coat and bag on the chair to her left as she eased herself down into the chair. Fretfully she placed her hands in her lap and studied her nails as she waited for Nick to end his call. Summer was aware of how his eyes traveled over her; she became uncomfortable as his dark eyes focused on her large belly.

As Nick continued his phone conversation, Summer tried not to pay attention to how his tailored navy suit fit his muscular frame. She couldn't see his shoes but knew they were just as fly as the suit. Her gaze traveled to his mouth as he talked. He had the most sensual lips she'd ever seen on a man.

All of a sudden out of nowhere, she had to pee as the fetus shifted and tap-danced on her bladder. Gripping the sides of the chair, pushing herself up to her feet, Summer left the office with the restroom being her destination. When she had to go, she had to go; she didn't have time for an explanation as Nick curiously watched her leave the office. Summer's sudden urge to pee gave her a brief reprieve from his penetrating gaze.

Ending the call, he was wondering where in the heck she ran off to. He leaned back in his chair as he waited for her to return from wherever it was she had gone.

Summer's appearance surprised him. He noticed how radiant her complexion was and how pregnancy hadn't distorted her facial features like it did some women. As a matter of fact, she was even more beautiful to him. Even her hair appeared more luxurious.

Summer had always been a distraction to Nick. As he talked with a potential investor, his attention shifted to her as she placed her right hand on the side of her belly. He wondered if the baby moved as she patted the area where her hand was and softly mumbled as she smiled. As he studied Summer, he could tell her belly had grown since he last saw her. He wanted to touch it, to communicate with his baby the way she had just done. Before Nick would even let his thoughts take him any further a tiny voice popped into his head. *Don't get your hopes up like the last time.*

Summer lightly tapped on the door. She jumped as Nick barked for her to come in.

She avoided his eyes as she timidly sat down in the chair. She prayed for this ordeal to be finished as quick as possible.

Summer's body language spoke volumes to Nick as her shoulders slumped and she held her head down. She was afraid of him. He knew her fear stemmed from the night he showed up at her house unannounced. After he met with Kevin, he realized Summer's surprise condition had been the straw that broke the camel's back. Yes, he was pissed with her, but he wondered if he hadn't had a lousy day if it would have made a difference. Would he have come down on her so hard? As he looked at her, he was reminded of how she cried and tried desperately to give him an explanation.

Clearing his throat, "Did you bring the document?"

Too afraid to say anything, Summer nodded her head.

He watched as she nervously reached into a large black leather hobo bag as her hands trembled.

Summer was so shook up she dropped the heavy bag on the floor. Leaning down she quickly snatched the bag up off the floor and continued to rummage through it in search of the document. That's when it hit her. *Oh, no I forgot to sign it. What am I going to do?*

Summer bit her bottom lip and nervously told him in a small voice as she pulled out the crumpled paper, "I didn't sign it yet."

"I thought you said you signed it?" His tone was low and tight as he gazed at her.

Lowering her eyes to avoid his hard gaze, her voice was barely a whisper, "I meant to sign it before I left home." Digging into her bag again, continuing her search she mumbled, "Where is my pen?"

"What was that?"

"I... umm...I can't find my pen."

He picked up a pen from his desk and handed it to her.

Scooting her bottom to the edge of the chair, placing the document on the desk while reaching for the pen their fingertips touched. She jerked her hand away from his touch as if it burned her skin. Memories from the night a few weeks ago flooded her mind when she tried to touch him and he not so kindly demanded she take her hands off of him. Tears stung her eyes as she relived the stab of his hurtful words. She remembered a time when her touch was what he'd craved. She pushed ancient thoughts aside as she signed what might be the fate of her baby away. She wanted, so badly, to beg him not to make her do this. But, was stopped by the stony mask he wore.

Handing the document and pen back to Nick, Summer bit down on her bottom lip to keep the tears from falling. Determined not to cry in front of him again, after he'd taken the document and pen from her hands she stood and began to put her things on.

Pointing to the window at the blizzard fiercely coming down, "I better get going now; it's getting worse out there."

Nick turned his attention to the window; he sensed Summer's uneasiness the longer she stayed in his presence. It hadn't slipped past him she nearly jumped out of her skin when their hands touched, or how she fought hard to hold tears back as she anxiously made haste to leave his office.

Bringing his attention back to her, "You can't go home by yourself in that storm."

Summer stared at Nick like he had two heads. "I have to get home *now*." *I wouldn't be out here in this mess if it weren't for you,* she wanted to scream at him, but knew better not to.

"Not by yourself, you're not. Sit back down and give me a few seconds. I'll take you home."

It was more of a command than a request. Although she couldn't stand to be in that office another millisecond, obediently Summer sat back down. It was becoming too much of a chore being around Nick, his attitude and behavior towards her was becoming more unpredictable.

Placing his briefcase on the desk, he put files along with that awful document inside before closing it. Nick doubt a courier service would make any last minute runs. The document was too sensitive not to be in his possession until he could have it delivered to Mr. Steinberg.

Standing up behind his desk, walking over to the coat rack grabbing his coat and scarf, donning them, and then snatching the briefcase he said, "Let's go."

Standing at the curb on Eighteenth and Walnut, Summer's teeth chattered as she waited for Nick to bring his vehicle to the front of the office building. She could have waited inside the lobby of the building, but decided not to. She was in a hurry to get home and away from Nick. The sooner she could hop in the car, the sooner and closer to home she would be. Wrapping her arms as far as they could go around her body, vigorously rubbing herself trying to generate heat, Summer was praying Nick would hurry. The black Benz rounding the corner and easing to a slow stop with flashing hazard lights was the best sight she'd seen all day. Well, with the exception of Nick's handsome face. Despite their present circumstances, she still thought he was the finest man she'd ever laid eyes on.

Effortlessly, Nick swung the door open taking long strides to the curb where Summer was. Quickly his arm went snuggly around what used to be a tiny waist as he pulled her close to him. The last thing he wanted was for her to slip and fall on the icy covered ground and hurt herself or the baby.

Summer tensely flinched and nearly lost her balance. She hadn't expected him to touch her like that. Take her by the hand maybe, but not wrap his arm around her. It had been so long since she'd been anywhere near having his arms around her.

Tightening his hold on her, keeping her from falling, he said, "Whoa, careful now, you don't want to fall." A grim expression covered his face when she flinched. It had been the second time in less than an hour she had recoiled at his touch; a touch that at one time ignited her passion. *Does she think I'm going to hurt? She knows I would never do that to her. Doesn't she?*

Gingerly, Nick guided Summer to the vehicle and helped her in her seat without any further mishaps. His mind was elsewhere when she softly thanked him. He was still tripping over how she was responding to him and hadn't heard Summer thank him for helping her in the car.

Summer's heart sank when Nick never acknowledge her thanks. She couldn't win, it seemed that at every turn she did or said something that irritated him. The grim expression that overcast his handsome features when she flinched at his touch said it all. What was wrong with him? He acts as if the last time he saw her they were in each other's arms. *Humph, he was the one who told me 'take your hands off of me.'* So why was he looking all perplexed?

Traffic was gridlock. Nick turned to KYW to get the latest traffic report. With the storm blowing into the city earlier than previously forecast all bridges leading into and out of the city were closing, public transportation was being cancelled and all government offices were closing. The reporter advised the public to stay indoors because the roads had become increasingly dangerous as the snowfall steadily accumulated at a rapid pace.

Summer felt like a noose was being tied around her neck. Gripping the side of the leather armrest, the knuckles on her left hand turned white as her right hand slowly inched to press the button, automatically rolling down the window a bit. She felt as if she couldn't breathe. As soon as the cool air rushed into the window, Summer took a deep breath to get the welcomed oxygen into her lungs. She did this a few more times until she felt she was able to breathe comfortably again. *This can't be happening, not now.* If she had taken the subway, she would have been to Fern Rock by now. From there the walk wouldn't have been too bad. On a good day, she had done the walk in fifteen minutes. So what if it would have taken her a little longer. Besides, she had the option of taking a cab home from the train station.

Glancing sideways at Nick and taking in his strong profile wondering, *why is it every time I do as you tell me I find myself getting into a big mess?* Regret immediately swept through her as she rubbed her belly. She had just referred to her baby as a 'big mess.'

As Nick switched the radio back to the jazz station, the rush of cold air drew his attention to the partially opened window, then to Summer. Her dainty nostrils were slightly flared as she took in deep breaths. Further inspection revealed tiny beads of sweat on her brow she hadn't bothered to wipe away and a petite hand that grasped the armrest so tight he was sure fingernail prints would be left in the soft leather.

"If you're hot I can turn the heat down or off."

"I'm fine now."

Studying her stiff body, "You sure?"

Summer nodded her head. "Yes."

Nick knew she was far from being *fine.* She would probably be fine with swimming in the middle of the ocean with sharks than to be in such tight quarters with him.

Nick shrugged his shoulders and tapped the steering wheel with his fingers to the tune of the song that played on the radio. He was never going to get Summer from Center City to Oak Lane with the magnitude of the blizzard. Now was just as good as anytime to tell her since they hadn't moved two blocks in the last ten minutes.

"You know you're not going to make it home."

"I know," Summer whispered. As she peered out the passenger side window, a single tear slid down her cheek. Quickly she wiped it away before Nick could see it. She hadn't been quick enough though. He saw the tear before it even fell.

Chapter 7

A fifteen-minute drive to Nick's waterfront penthouse had taken over an hour because of all the bumper-to-bumper congestion. Everyone on the roadways was trying to make it home in what was becoming the worst storm of the season.

All of the bumper-to-bumper traffic irritated Nick to no end. Silently the pair rode the elevator to the top floor, twenty-four stories. As they stepped off the elevator into a contemporary living room, Summer was glued to the spot where she stood.

At one time, Nick's penthouse had been like a second home to her. She had been familiar with every square foot of the spacious luxury dwelling. However, this did nothing for the level of uneasiness she was presently experiencing. Summer felt out of place, she wanted nothing more than to be at home curled up on the sofa drinking hot chocolate as she watched old movies.

It was written all over her face, she'd rather walk on hot coals barefoot than be secluded with Nick in his tower.

As he shrugged off his coat, he instructed Summer to do the same. Trudging in the snow and then waiting in it had completely saturated her pants from the ankles up to her mid-calves. She was not surprised when he said, "Your pants are wet. You need to take them off."

Summer looked down to inspect her pants, which was useless; her protruding belly obscured her view. She had been so preoccupied with thoughts of home she hadn't noticed the wet cold fabric that clung to her legs. As she sneezed covering her mouth, "Aaachewww!" her mother's words admonished her again.

Nick said, "Bless you," as he gestured for Summer to hand him her coat.

"Thank you."

"Come with me." Turning and going to the hall closet, hanging up their coats he made his way to his bedroom with Summer lagging behind. Dreading every step, her legs became heavy upon entering the master bedroom suite. The instant she stepped across the threshold memories of being with Nick evaded and crowded every corner of her mind. If she could turn back the hands of time, she would have never made the fatal mistake of treading onto forbidden territory.

After months of dating, Nick remained a perfect gentleman. Summer, however knew it was just a matter of time before they'd become intimate. Every kiss, hug, and caress wore down her resistance. In the beginning the tiny voice in her head warned, *don't do it.* After months of kisses, hugs, and caresses, the tiny voice became a faint whisper, hardly audible. When she decided to take the plunge, share his bed, the voice was buried so deep she never heard its pleas.

Nick was a drug to Summer. She was a clean vessel that tasted of an illicit substance. And like many addicts the first time was a bit awkward, but nevertheless enticing enough, exhilarating enough, to keep going back for more. The addiction so strong she let fundamentals she'd been raised with like going to church fall by the way side. Whenever she asked, "Why don't you go to church with me on Sunday?" The answer was always, "I'm not ready for that yet," which was always followed up with a suggestion to go to a jazz brunch, an afternoon game to see the Sixers or to play a couple sets of racquetball. Initially she tried to resist but the jones for her drug was too strong, too overpowering.

"Summer?"

The baritone sound of her name snapped her back to the present.

"Huh?"

Handing her a tee shirt, "Here, put this on."

Summer's hands fumbled nearly dropping the tee shirt as Nick brushed past her into the walk-in closet to grab a pair of jeans before he left the room.

❧ ❧ ❧ ❧ ❧

Nick snatched the cordless phone out its base on the kitchen wall.

The pickup came on the second ring.

"What's up man?"

"What up with you? You're the one who called me." Kevin chortled.

Letting out a deep breath deciding to jump straight into it, "Summer's here." Nick paced the floor and waited for Kevin's response. He always had something to say.

"Where?"

"Here… with me."

"Get the hell out of here!"

"Wish I could but I can't." Ending the pacing, he leaned against the sink.

"What is she doing at your place, man?"

"She came down to my office to bring the paternity consent."

Deep. Summer actually signed it, poor girl. What is up with my man? Kevin talked to him until he had a migraine and was blue in the face. He'd told Nick to wait until he simmered down a bit before he presented Summer with the document. But as usual, when Nick had his mind set on something, he had the tenacity of a bulldog.

"Man… you made that girl come downtown… eight months pregnant… on public transportation… to bring you a piece of paper?"

Nick cringed at his best friend's accusing tone. "I know man, I know, I was wrong." A hint of regret laced his voice.

"Wrong for what, Nick, making her come downtown in a freakin' blizzard? Or making her sign that damn paper?"

Nick's tone was tight as he clipped out every word. "For making her come downtown, you know how I feel about the paternity thing man. So don't even go there."

He's a lost cause. Changing the subject, Kevin wanted to know, "So how is Summer? Can I talk to her?"

Dragging his hand down his face, Kevin was pushing it as usual. "Man, she's driving me crazy. And no, you can't talk to her."

"Driving you crazy?" There was an air of amusement in his voice. Nick was a trip. He was the one who insisted the poor girl come to his office with the threat of a snowstorm. Serves him right, Kevin thought.

"Man, I'm so confused. She looks so pitiful, I want to take her in my arms one minute and tell her everything's going to be okay. But then I look at her big belly and get pissed off all over again. I don't know if I can take having her here… so close."

"Well you should have thought about that before you made her come out knowing a damn storm was coming. If you had, Summer would be home and you'd be alone."

"Yeah, I hear you man. To make matters worse every time I say something to her she jumps like a spooked cat."

Grunting into the phone, Kevin warned, "Stop acting like a beast and maybe the poor girl will relax some. You need to chill and lightening up a bit."

As much as he wanted to cuss Kevin out, he refrained himself. He knew he meant well. But Kevin would never understand how much this thing with Summer was affecting him. At lease not until something like it happened to him. The way Kevin chased skirts he'd have a heart attack if one of those skirts told him he was about to get caught up in some baby momma drama.

"Listen, Kevin, man I need to go."

"A'ight man, I'll check you later.

"Later."

Chapter 8

Slowly Summer stripped out of her clothes. She took her time to remove every piece. The longer she took, the longer she delayed seeing *him.* She pulled on the oversized tee shirt then padded over to the huge walk-in closet. *Lawd, I know I look a hot mess.* Opening the door to the closet, staring at her reflection in the full-length mirror that hung on the back of the door, she groaned, "I am so fat." Her protruding belly making the tee shirt rise higher then normal made her suddenly uncomfortable with her expanding body. Shrugging her shoulders, "Oh well." Stepping back, gently closing the door, she picked up her wet clothes and headed to find Nick.

He had changed into a white tee shirt that amplified his broad chest and a pair of jeans that clung to muscular thighs. Standing at the island in the center of the kitchen he was preparing dinner as Summer came waddling into the kitchen, entering as quietly as possible.

Sensing her presence, Nick stopped dicing or chopping, whatever it was he was doing to look at her. Heaven help him, she was absolutely gorgeous. The tee shirt stopping mid-thigh revealing shapely legs and bare feet, more skin than he'd seen on her in awhile.

Summer flushed, turning crimson from Nick's gaze. Holding out the wet clothes, she asked in a small voice, "Can I wash these, please?"

"You know where everything is." His tone was indifferent as he returned to his task.

Moving past him to the laundry room she proceeded to set the washer on the proper setting of water, added detergent, and then her clothes. Putting everything back in its place, Summer went back into the kitchen. Nick was still at the task of preparing dinner.

Wanting to feel useful she offered, "Is there anything I can help with?"

Never making eye contact or breaking his focus, blowing her off, he said, "No, I'm good. Go watch television or something."

Nick was not having it. No way was he going to allow Summer to get close to him. Refusing her help had hurt her feelings; he saw it all in facial expression. If he allowed her to get close, it would only confuse him even further. She would become a distraction stealing him from his thoughts. He had to maintain his priorities. The first being finding out why she had played him.

Feeling dismissed, Summer plopped down at the foot of the king size bed. She grabbed the remote from the nightstand and flicked on the large screen plasma television. Clicking through the channels, she peeped at the digital clock on the dresser. It read three twenty-eight. *Good, Martin is about to come on.*

Summer felt like she needed a good laugh to ease the stress that had been building all day. If she wasn't careful, she possibly could start having premature contractions again. Dr. Neil constantly reminded her she needed to remain as stress free as possible. *Yeah right.* So far, everything was cool; as far as the contractions went, she hadn't felt a thing except normal active fetal movement.

Summer was cracking up; the episode of *Martin* she was watching was the one where Gina had killed his momma's bird. Seeing Mother Pane act a fool made Summer remember she had not called her parents or her friends.

Looking out the window at the swirling large white flakes, "Oh my goodness, I know they're having a fit."

Moving over to the nightstand, the red light wasn't flashing which meant Nick wasn't using the phone. Settling on the bed, picking up the cordless phone, she dialed the rowdy one first. Disconnecting the call, "I better get comfortable for this."

Between her parents, Ava or Starr, one of them was bound to give her a tongue-lashing. Calling Ava first would make calling the others a piece of cake. Ava was the most outspoken, didn't care what she said, even if it hurt your feelings.

Scooting up on the bed resting against the headboard, Summer tucked her feet underneath her and began redialing Ava's number.

She picked up on the first ring. *Oh here we go. The chile is sitting by the phone.*

"Hey, Ava."

"Don't 'hey Ava' me. Girl why aren't you home in all this mess?

"How do you know I'm not home?" Summer ask weakly.

Sucking her teeth, Ava huffed, "Caller ID, duh!"

Busted! Summer should have called Starr first. She's nowhere near as high strung as Ava.

"So you know I'm at Nick's." It was more of a statement than question.

"You are where?!" Ava yelled loud enough to wake the dead.

Oh shoot! "Didn't his number come up?"

"No! The ID says 'Private Number'! What the hell are you doing there! Did he force you to go there! Huh! Tell me!"

Ava was hot! She hardly ever cursed no matter how mild the word. But she couldn't stand Nick's guts! *How could she go anywhere with him the way he'd treated her. He had to have forced her. Unless he did something insane like pledge his love to her. Not!* As far as Ava was concerned, Nick was a wealthy, selfish, self-centered man. He didn't deserve Summer or her baby.

Yanking the phone from her ear to keep Ava from rupturing her eardrum, Summer frowned at the phone. "Hey girl, pump your brakes," she hissed. "If you give me half a chance, I'll tell you what's up. But if you yell at me one more time, Ava, I'm hanging this phone up. Are we clear?" Summer knew she had to be as vague as possible with her explanation as to why she was at Nick's.

"Yeah." Ava mumbled with an attitude.

Just as she was about to explain things to her Nick appeared in the doorway. As Summer assured Ava she was okay and would be home as soon as the weather permitted, he leaned against the doorframe and crossed his arms over his broad chest. His presence was overwhelming, making her nervous as he stood hovering like a hawk. Mentally coaxing herself to bring the conversation to an end, Summer cut Ava off mid-sentence.

"Listen, I have to go now. Please do me a favor and call my parents."

"Are you alright?" Ava skeptically questioned because suddenly Summer's voice became really quiet.

"Yes."

"Is *he* there?"

"Yes." Summer's gaze momentarily shifted to Nick then back to the television as if she was watching it.

"Has he hurt you?" Ava gritted out between her teeth. *I can't stand that man!*

"No, I'm fine. I... I really have to go." Summer's voice pleaded.

"Summer, if he hurt's you..." *I'll hunt him down like the dirty rat bastard he is.*

"I'll be okay. Don't worry." Summer again pleaded.

"All right girl, I love you. Call me if you need me."

"I will. I love you too. And please don't forget to call my parents."

Summer partially lied to Ava. She really did love her with all her heart. But call her? Lawd a mercy, no way! If Summer sent out a distress signal, Ava would hike in the blizzard to Nick's penthouse. The Caucasian blood running through her veins would help her brave the elements. The African American blood would give her the endurance to make it. And once there all hell, along with world war III would breakout. Ava likes to cut people… for real. Summer could just see her wielding a butcher knife at Nick like one of those chicks in Kill Bill. Ava was straight up crazy and wouldn't care that Nick was several inches taller not to mention pounds heavier than she was.

"All right Boo, I'll call the folks."

Ending the conversation, she placed the phone back in its base. Thank goodness Ava agreed to call her parents. The last thing she needed was to explain things to them. She was pretty sure they would have the same reaction as Ava, if not worse, especially her mother. The only one who would possibly understand would be Starr. But she would have to wait to call her because Nick hadn't budged. Besides, she was sure Ava had called her once they'd hung up.

Strolling down the hall Nick heard Summer talking. Sure enough, she was on the phone. He wondered whom she was talking to, her voice had suddenly become low and she was giving one-word answers when he appeared in the doorway. Nick assumed she was talking to a man because of the way she was acting. Nick's jaw clenched as he listened to the one sided conversation.

His eyes narrowed as he pushed away from the doorframe, turned and left the room. Summer shuddered from the look Nick threw at her as she slowly stretched her legs out and stood up. His reaction left her wondering what she'd done wrong this time. It had to be something, but what? People just didn't go around giving the evil eye for nothing. Was he mad because she had used his phone without asking? That was totally absurd; he knew she had to call her family. With every unsteady step she dreaded having to sit across a table from him, but what was she to do? She hadn't had anything to eat since that morning, she was famished. Besides, she was at his mercy for the next few days to be clothed, fed and sheltered from the raging elements. What choice did she have? She had to get through this ordeal the best way she could.

But how? Summer wondered as she chewed her bottom lip and lowered herself into a chair.

Chapter 9

Dinner was delicious. Nick prepared a toss salad, grilled salmon, steamed broccoli, and wild rice. Summer hadn't realized how hungry she was. It had been hours since she ate, which was unusual for her. As of lately she ate several times a day. With the events of the day the last thing on her mind was food. Her main concern was how she was going to make it through the next few days without getting into a confrontation with Nick. It was definitely inevitable; the heaviness of it was in the air. Shrugging slim shoulders, deciding not to worry about it, she concentrated on filling her empty grumbling stomach.

The pair ate in silence; there was no dinner conversation whatsoever, which was fine with Summer. Nick was still in a foul mood for whatever reason. She tried not to make too much out his behavior. It was no secret he had taken to being a complete jerk lately.

Summer inhaled everything on her plate. There wasn't a morsel left. She didn't know what to do with herself after she'd finished her meal, so she squirmed in her seat as her gaze surveyed the vast dining area.

She admired a piece of artwork that complimented the room. *That must be new; it wasn't there the last time I was here.* Further inspection displayed a lush green Ficus tree in a corner. *I didn't know Nick had a green thumb. Maybe his new girlfriend brought it.* Nope. Summer was not about to even go there. A hundred times or more the thought charged through her mind he had broken things off so abruptly with her to be with another woman.

She would torture and beat herself up as she pointed out every imperfection. "I'm too short, my legs aren't long enough, my breasts are too small." There had to be something about her that drove him into the arms of another woman.

Summer shook the painful thoughts from her head and sad expression from her face as she went on to survey the room until her eyes collided with Nick's. His gaze was relentless, tearing into her while lifting a wineglass to his lips.

She hadn't been aware he was gawking at her like prey. His eyes were unreadable. Was it disappointment, mistrust, hate… what? Summer didn't know what insane thoughts were running amuck in his head. One thing she did know, Nick was no longer the man she had known or loved. He'd changed so much, she no longer recognized him. On the outside, he appeared as the Nick she knew and loved. However, on the inside he showed her an entirely different part of himself, a part that possessed a black heart. In a million years she would have never believed he would be so downright callous towards her. At first she couldn't put her finger on it, until now. He hated her because she was pregnant. Was being a father so repulsive he would actually hate her? A lump formed in her throat, not so much from the idea of him hating her, but what were his feelings regarding the baby? Not once had he inquired about the welfare of their baby. The only thing he was interested in was getting custody, taking her baby. Suddenly the thought angered her. What was he going to do with a baby? *Her baby?* Have a nanny raise it? Nick definitely was not the diaper changing type.

It's a good thing nothing on his plate was alive as he stabbed his fork into the food. The idea Summer may have been talking to another man on the phone earlier was still messing with him, had him tripping. The way he was grinding his teeth as he ate was sure to have him in the dentist chair before his next six-month visit.

Kevin didn't know what he was talking about. What if she did have a man? After reflecting on what he said, Nick was regretting having Summer agree to, no, rather forcing her to have paternity testing done. That thought, along with Kevin's words went flying out the window after hearing her on the phone. Nick was glad he had gone with his instincts. There may be a strong possibility the baby wasn't his just like the last time. *Damn it, this can't be happening again.*

Bringing the glass to his lips again, holding her gaze he was wondering what she'd been thinking. Didn't she have sense enough not to get herself pregnant? Nick had warned her not to do something so foolish. She hadn't listened. Numerous times he told her he would never marry, let alone become anyone's father. Like most women she probably figured once he learned of her pregnancy he would whisk her off to the nearest church. *Don't bet your life on it.*

Nick was not about to be manipulated by another woman no matter how beautiful she was. If by chance this was his child he would do as planned, file for custody. Not so much because he wanted to be a father, but to make her pay.

Summer more than anyone knew his relationship with his father was another catalysts for his refusal to be a father. Growing up as a child his father was more concerned about his ambitions of becoming a judge, leaving virtually no time for Nick. Nick did not want to subject a child to that. Clenching his jaw becoming angry, what in the hell was he going to do with a baby? Chances were he didn't have to worry about that. Any judge would rule that there was no valid reason to find Summer unfit as a mother. Women her age and younger were raising children on their own all over the world. Even without him her job as a nurse afforded her the ability to raise a child independent of him. He knew filing for custody was futile; however, he would do it just to make her life miserable.

Standing up, Nick muttering a curse under his breath, everything he just mulled over in his mind was useless, a waste of brainpower, if the child wasn't his. Snatching dishes off the table he snapped, "What?" He could tell Summer was about to say something.

Summer's voice trembled in nervousness. "I just wanted to know if you wanted or needed any help." Her small hands worried the cloth napkin, twisting it as she waited for his reply.

Nick pinched the bridge of his nose then gritted out between clenched teeth. "Knock yourself out, Summer."

The dishes rattled as he sat them back down on the table with a thud as he stormed out the room. It was a wonder every dish hadn't shattered.

Relieved to be alone, Summer took extra precautions not to break anything as she loaded the dishwasher. Nick had unnerved her with his foul mood and hard glare. She was literally trembling from head to toe. She could not shake the feeling that he was about to detonate at any moment. The storm was slowly brewing within him. He carried it in his silent demeanor, the way he stabbed at his food, and the hard gazes he threw her way. Summer's thin shoulders slouched at the thought of a confrontation with Nick.

❧ ❧ ❧ ❧ ❧

After she loaded the dishwasher and wiped down the table, she moseyed into the den. Flopping down on the end of the sofa, she picked up an edition of *Black Enterprise*. This was not her idea of leisure reading, but it would do. Page after page were boring articles on how to start this business, how to start that business, first year projected revenue. *Blah, Blah, Blah.* Summer would give anything to have her latest edition of *Essence,* even a nursing journal would do right about now. At least it would be a topic she could relate to.

Covering a yawn she stretched then reached for the remote on the end table and turned the television on. She had not heard Nick enter the room.

"Summer we need to talk." His voice was tight, eyes narrowed into slits.

Jumping, placing a hand over her pounding heart, "Nick, you scared me. I didn't hear you come in."

Removing the remote from Summer's hand, he turned off the television and sat on the coffee table facing her.

Summer was glued to the sofa from the penetrating stare he used to pin her down.

After storming into his office a magnitude of questions came rushing through his brain. When did she get pregnant? When did she find out? Why didn't she tell me as soon as she found out? Was she ever going to tell me about the baby? The most nauseating question he needed answered was, Does she have a man and is he planning on raising the baby? Clenching his jaw at the notion, he started firing into Summer with his inquiry.

"When did you become pregnant?"

Huh? "May… I think." Of course she knew when she'd become pregnant; her body functioned like clockwork, right on time. In fact when she missed her period she knew the exact night it happened.

Irritated by her answer he ran his hand over his face in frustration. "Woman what do you mean, 'you think'? Either it was May or it wasn't," he hissed.

This is it; his dark side was coming out again, the one that showed up weeks ago at her house. Her mind and heart raced as she prayed for the right words to say to keep him from exploding. Fidgeting with her hands in her lap her voice quivered, "It was May I'm sure."

"You go from thinking to being sure. How is that?" His tone reeked annoyance.

Breathing deeply, trying to steady her voice, "Because I had my last period the beginning of May.

This was too much pressure being in his domain with nowhere to go for cover. *I should have stayed home and just suffered the consequences.*

Last May they were an item, which meant the baby was his. That is if she wasn't sleeping with anyone else. Filing the information in the back of his mind, he decided not to hold a full inquisition. Nick muttered a curse as he watched Summer's eyes begin to fill with tears. He leaned his elbows on his knees, which brought him so close she could smell the wine he had earlier for dinner.

"Are you involved with anyone?"

Summer shot up off the sofa as if she'd been struck by lightning, her voice came out in a high-pitched squeal. "No! Nick!" Involved with whom? Didn't he know she'd been crying her eyes out over him for the last eight months? She never even thought about another man. Didn't he know he was the only man she wanted? The man she loved with all her heart and still loved despite the fact that he treated her like crap.

Nick didn't know what came over him as he charged to his feet and challenged Summer's stance. Summer gasped in disbelief, "Niiick!" as she felt herself being lifted off the floor staring directly into dark cold eyes.

Nick ignored her answer. Through clenched teeth, he gritted out, "Are you seeing anyone and are you planning on having him raise my baby?" He hadn't meant to say *my baby*. Or did he?

"No."

"No what!" He barked at her.

In spite of being suspended in air by Nick's firm hold, Summer struggled to pull back from his grip as she told him between sobs, "No, I'm not seeing anyone. You were the last one."

She's lying. "Then who were you talking to earlier on the phone?" Nick knew he had no right, no business to ask her such a question, after all they weren't together.

"Ava. I…I wanted to let her know I was okay." Summer said still trying to get loose from his grip.

It wasn't that he was hurting her; she just wanted to put some distance between them before things escalated any further. Summer could not count the times she worked in the emergency room and women came in battered because an argument had gotten out of control. Nick had never been violent in the past with her.

She didn't think he would hurt her, but he was rapidly becoming out of control. She'd seen warning signs all night long, that's why she attempted to stay clear of him. What if he did hurt her, or worse the baby? Panic set in.

Staring at him through red swollen puffy eyes, Summer pleaded, her voice barely a trembling whisper as tears stained her face. "Nick, you're scaring me, please put me down."

Damn, what the hell am I doing? Nick snapped back to reality as Summer made an effort to free herself by pleading with him. Her facial expression was contorted in a fusion of shock, hurt, and fear.

As he placed her down, Summer's legs quaked as her feet touched the hardwood floor. Nick stepped back and closed his eyes vigorously rubbing his face with the palms of his hands. He prayed that when he opened them all of this would have been a bad dream. *Damn!* Summer wasn't a dream. She was still visibly shaken, apparently traumatized. Nick reached out and took a small step forward, "Summer, I'm…"

His attempt to apologize was halted when she yanked away from his outstretched hand. For once that night Nick used the good sense God gave him and backed off.

As she watched his retreat she wondered, *Why is he treating me like this?*

Summer stumbled a few steps to the sofa, laid down and curled up into a fetal position. Protectively she hugged her belly as tears effortlessly seeped out as she fought to calm down frayed nerves. Where was all this coming from? Why was he questioning the timing of her conception? Hadn't he remembered that last week of May they spent together at his cabin in upstate New York? Did he forget that was the only time he asked her to trust him?

And what was this nonsense about her seeing someone? He should have known better. Summer had too much integrity to date one man while carrying another's seed. Truth be told, Nick was the first man she'd really dated. Sure she went on dates in high school and in college. Those dates usually ended before anything could jump off when the guy discovered she was not about to drop her drawers after a couple of dates. Even with Nick, she had waited months to consummate their relationship.

Laying in the dark, the aching in Summer's heart was overwhelming. All she wanted to do was run off to some faraway place, have her baby and never see Nick again. Just when she believed nothing else he said or did could hurt her, he managed to prove her wrong. He actually entertained the idea she had slept with another man who he thought might possibly be the father of her baby. Summer was devastated. How could he think she would do such a thing to him? To them?

Summer groaned as she felt a faint twinge in her lower abdomen. *No not now.* What had been a horrible night was tumbling into a nightmare. The discomfort in her lower abdomen was a premature contraction raging its ugly head. No doubt from the stressful day ending with the altercation with Nick.

Slowly rising up, going into the kitchen finding the largest glass, filling it with water, she began drinking. Hydration and lying on her left side with her feet elevated should hopefully abort the threatening premature contractions.

After she forced three large glasses of water down, Summer dragged herself back to the den. Resuming her fetal position on the sofa, lying on her left side, the second her head hit the sofa tears began sliding out rolling over the bridge of her nose, down her left cheek, and into her ear. Protectively she cradled her belly. *Why is this happening to me? What did I ever do but love him?*

Summer yawned as her eyelids became heavy as lead as she wrestled to keep them open. Too exhausted, both physically and mentally she succumbed to a state of slumber, praying when she opened her eyes that she'd be home.

Chapter 10

The hallway wall supported Nick's two hundred twenty pounds as he leaned against it in the dark. Listening to Summer's sobbing was stripping him bare, exposing feelings he never knew existed. The sight of her red swollen eyes and tear streaked face sickened him. How had he let himself sink to such a level to treat her the way he had? Despite everything she didn't deserve to be made to feel unsafe, especially with him. Nick had never admitted to loving Summer, however, he'd always made her feel safe in his presence when they were a couple.

Heavy legs carried Nick back to his office as he replayed the scene over again in his head. It's no wonder she was frightened of him. He had literally lifted her off her feet like she was a rag doll. Regret coursed through him at how he handled things, handled her.

I need to check on Summer, make sure she's alright.

Nick took long strides as he hurried to the den. Not wanting to wake her, his steps became feather light. Gingerly he sat on the opposite end of the sofa.

Closing his eyes, leaning his head back on the sofa he thought about what Summer said. *"I had my last period the beginning of May."*

May. What happened in May? Where was I in May?

Nick slowly rotated his head and allowed his gaze to fall on Summer's fetal positioned form. *How could I forget?* He had asked her to trust him and she did. *Summer's carrying my baby.*

Deep within his soul there was a stirring he could not quite explain. It was true. He was going to be a father. But would he be up to the task? Was all of his anger a mask to cover up perceived inadequacies he held about himself?

ờ ờ ờ ờ ờ

Summer was thrilled when Nick requested she spend a week with him at his cabin in upstate New York. After he finalized the Canada deal, he wanted to get away with Summer and decompress. Working fourteen, sometimes sixteen-hour days was starting to take its toll on their relationship. She never made a fuss about all their cancelled dates. Nor did she complain when he promised to show up at her place at eight-thirty and would not arrive until close to midnight because some crisis came up at the last minute demanding his attention.

Always taking everything in stride she'd simply tell him, "I understand." And understand she did. Summer's father worked long hours to make his small business a success. There were many swim meets, school plays and softball games her father missed because an emergency had come up at work. Summer learned at an early age to hide her disappointment if someone she cared about did not come through on what they'd promised.

Nick offered no apologies. Summer was aware his work came first and everything else second, including her. Nick knew she would be disappointed by the slight change in her voice she tried, yet failed to conceal when their plans were altered. He appreciated that Summer was not the whiney, clingy, type that threw tantrums when he had to cancel on her at the last minute.

Whenever he showed up at her house late at night she would always have a surprise for him. Everything from sexy lingerie to wearing one of his dress shirts partially button exposing just enough skin making him want her the second he laid eyes on her. Once, she was so brazen she answered the door wearing nothing but three-inch pumps and one of his silk ties tied in a bow around her neck as if she were a gift. That night they never made it to the bedroom.

So inviting her to the country for a week of solitude, giving her his undivided attention was something he felt Summer was deserving of. Never before had he felt the need to do anything remotely like this for any woman. However, for some inexplicable reason he had a need to do this one special thing for her.

The cabin was small and cozy with a living room, dining room, kitchen and powder room on the first floor. A loft bedroom and full bathroom equipped with a Jacuzzi was on the second floor. "Mmm, you sure like Jacuzzis, I see." Summer teased.

After unpacking, Summer fixed dinner, which they ate on the floor in front of a crackling fireplace. It was an unseasonably cool evening for May. They were so relaxed, neither wanted to budge to load the dishwasher. Summer flipped a coin, which decided it was Nick's fate to load the dishwasher.

Returning from the kitchen, he sat on the floor behind Summer and pulled her to his chest in a bear hug. He whispered as he nibbled on her lobe, "Whatcha' thinking, Beautiful?"

"Nothing."

With one fluid motion, he had her underneath him as he gazed into sparkling brown eyes.

"Now that I have you at a disadvantage, are you going to tell me what's going through that pretty little head of yours?"

The prettiest smile he'd ever seen illuminated her face right before she spoke.

"You make me feel special, Nicholas Stiles." She wanted to tell him more. To tell him that he made her feel loved and that she loved him. But she didn't, because she wasn't sure if he was capable of hearing it just yet. For now she would keep her feelings for him to herself. *Later, I'll tell him later.*

"That's because you are special..." Nick hesitated, "to me." It had been years since he revealed what he felt for a woman. He kept them and his feelings at a distance. However, somehow, some way, Summer had woven her way close to his heart. He would never admit it to himself or anyone else that she had gotten under his skin. Saying she was special would have to be enough.

Nick promised himself he would never fall in love with another woman. Not even one as loving and caring as Summer Jackson.

He covered her mouth with his as he lightly traced the inside of her warm, moist mouth with his tongue. The kiss started off tender. As he deepened the kiss and their tongues mated the kiss took on a passion of its own fueling the deepest longing. He trailed kisses from her throat to her cleavage as he slid his hand under her blouse. Summer released a small sigh as Nick rubbed her nipple through her bra with the pad of his thumb.

Fingering the hem of her blouse. "Let me get you out of this." Nick pushed himself up slightly enough to stare down into her face. Her expression revealed she wanted him.

A mischievous smirk played at his lips, "You do want me to take this off, don't you?"

Summer nodded her head, "Yes."

Lifting the blouse up over her head revealed a black lace demi bra. Summer's breasts were rising and falling with each breath. Nick's already aroused manhood strained against the zipper of his jeans. Summer's stomach fluttered with butterflies as he wedged his tongue between her cleavage then glided it over the swell of her soft mounds. Summer drew in a sharp breath as her back arched to the response of Nick's sensuous caresses.

Nick eased back and slowly unbuttoned her jeans. As he dragged them down silky creamy thighs, a black lacey thong was exposed.

He rose with the agility of a large feline and took a step back to enjoy the view before him. Summer was one of the most beautiful women he'd ever laid eyes on. Nick thought he would explode when she gazed up at him through brown doe eyes as she tugged her bottom lip between her teeth. It took every ounce of restraint not to take her at that very moment. *Pace yourself man before it's all over.*

The rising and falling of her breasts were mesmerizing, begging him to caress and suckle them. Nick took in a ragged breath as his dark eyes smoldering with desire roamed over her flat belly and lazily traveled to her dainty feet. Nick grunted when he spied Summer's freshly French pedicure.

After Nick removed his clothes he towered over her in black silk boxers. As he lowered himself on top of Summer he supported his weight on his elbows. Wrapping a small hand around the base of his head bringing his mouth centimeters from hers she began outlining his full thick lips with the tip of her tongue. Each stroke was slow and deliberate; Nick released a slow tortured groan. Summer was sure this would get her what she was yearning for.

Nick tenderly kissed a trail from her moist lips to the soft mounds of her breasts. Tugging on her right nipple with his teeth through the delicate fabric caused Summer to let out a soft moan.

"Take it off," Summer begged. She needed to feel his hot breath on her skin, the moistness of his mouth.

Removing the bra, he suckled one nipple, then the other. Summer began eliciting soft cries of passions. Instinctively she rotated her pelvis against his hard body as moisture pooled between her legs.

Nick licked a path to her silky triangle as he inhaled her essence. Stroking her inner thighs and spreading her legs, he began worshipping her. Summer's eyes crossed as she lifted her bottom off the floor to meet him. Every nerve ending in her body tingled as he caressed her in the most intimate way. Digging her nails into his shoulders, Summer's moans became louder and louder as wave after wave over took her. As her completion came, she screamed his name. "Niiick!"

With one fluid move he was on his feet removing his boxers, releasing a huge throbbing erection. Placing a hand on either side of her head, positioning himself to sink deep within her walls, Nick hissed a curse under his breath. He was so caught up that he never put on a condom. Flesh touching flesh felt so incredible. It had been years since he had gone au natural. Nick wanted to bury himself deep inside of her without the barrier of latex. He wanted hot, slick, wet, skin-to-skin contact. *Just this once.*

Gazing into Summer's beautiful face made him want her without protection even more. Softly kissing her lips, he hoarsely whispered, "Baby, do you trust me?"

A lazy smile curved her lips. "Of course I trust you, honey."

"Will you let me make love to you without a condom?"

Summer had been so immersed in Nick's foreplay she had not noticed he hadn't protected them. Biting her lower lip, her voice quivered when she spoke. "Nick, I…I don't know? What if…"

"Baby, I want to feel you just this once?"

Summer had never witnessed such intense passion and desire in Nick's eyes. She wanted to love him with everything in her, so she pushed away every nagging thought in her mind about an unwanted pregnancy. Just this once wouldn't hurt.

With reckless abandonment she surrendered. "Just this once."

As Nick slowly entered her, Summer's lids automatically closed.

"Open your eyes baby."

Obedient to his command, brown eyes locked with black ones as Nick went deeper and deeper, inch by delicious inch. Every muscle in his body trembled as she sheathed him. She was so hot, wet, and tight as her walls contracted and squeezed him. "Oh daayum, baby, you feel so tight, so good."

Summer let out a long breathy sigh when he lifted her right leg and rested it against his torso as she wrapped the left one around his waist. Fingernails dug deep into muscular shoulders as he deliberately shifted his hips hitting her spot, over… and over…and over…again.

Summer's body ignited in passion. She never knew skin-to-skin contact could feel so incredible.

Nick and Summer moved to their own sensual rhythm as they slipped into an abyss of sensuality. Sensuality that had them soaring higher and higher into the atmosphere. Summer was the first to come crashing into waves of release. Nick immediately followed with a release so intense he collapsed on top of Summer as the last shudder left his large frame. Quickly rolling on his back, he pulled her petite body on top of his.

"Whew, I thought you were going to smother me." Summer told him as she snuggled and nestled her face in the crook of his neck.

Nick chuckled. "Baby, I would never do that, especially after you've been so generous with the poonanie."

Sucking her teeth in feign annoyance, "You are so nasty."

"Naw, baby, this is nasty."

Summer gasped when she felt his large hand cradle her womanhood, heating things up all over again.

That night they made love again... without a condom.

Chapter 11

"May," Nick whispered. Summer conceived that night in the cabin. That was the only night they had been intentionally careless. He roughly rubbed his face with the palms of his hands. *Damn.* He spilt enough seed that night to make a hundred babies let alone one.

Summer had been hesitant and tried to voice her concerns. However, he silenced her with his need to have her the way he wanted her. In hindsight, he knew her decision was made because she wanted to please him.

Rising to his feet, he went over to Summer's slumbering form. She looked so peaceful. If it weren't for the dried tears that streaked her face, it would have been hard to tell she'd been uncontrollably sobbing just a few hours ago.

Gently Nick lifted her and carried her to his bedroom where he laid her on the bed. Careful not to wake her he pulled the sheet and comforter up to her waist, stopping at her very pregnant belly.

What he did next, he had no control over. Gingerly he sat on the bed beside her. Being so close to her made him want to touch her. It had been so long since he felt her satiny soft skin. Lightly he threaded his fingers through her thick, silky tresses. They were soft just like he remembered. With the pad of his thumb, he traced her lips remembering how they trembled.

As he leaned over and kissed her ever so lightly on the lips he noticed out the corner of his eye movement. Excitement overcame him as he realized the tiny life in her womb was a part of him. Slowly he placed a large hand on Summer's belly as if she were a precious porcelain doll that might break if mishandled.

The moment he made contact with her belly the fetus moved again under his touch. *Amazing,* was the word that came to his mind.

Summer was always in tune with the baby's movement. Even in her sleep, especially when the baby was extra active like now. However, there was another sensation she never experienced before, some sort of external pressure.

Twisting and stretching her limbs, sleepily opening her eyes to investigate the new heavy sensation. She was not prepared for what met her. A set of dark, penetrating, onyx eyes. Immediate panic set in as she remembered how angry he'd been with her. He'd actually lifted her off her feet. Fear seized her as tears formed in her eyes. She wanted to scream, but couldn't because her throat suddenly froze up.

Summer shoved his hand off her belly as she struggled to get away from him. She curled up in a ball in an attempt to shield herself and her unborn child; the dam broke, releasing a flood. When Nick reached out to her, she recoiled at his touch. He was greeted by the same response with his second attempt. In total disbelief, he reached for her again. This time her resistance was verbal. In a broken sob she pleaded, "Pleeease Nick, pleeease don't hurt me. I'm…I'm sorry."

Nick's heart felt like it was being ripped from his chest. *She actually believes I would physically hurt her.* Wanting and needing to console her he inched closer to her.

"Nooooooo," she cried as she scrambled to get away, but had no place to go; she was blocked between Nick's massive body and the headboard.

Nick's voice was soothing as he coaxed, "Summer, baby, I'm not going to hurt you." Inching closer he added, "I just want to hold you that's all. I promise I won't hurt you." His large hand slightly shook as he offered it to her.

She refused his hand until he gave her some reassurances. "Or the baby?" She questioned in a whisper as she wiped her face with the back of her hand.

She was so innocent, so child like. Gently, he grasped Summer's tiny hand and pulled her on his lap. Next he wrapped his arms around her in an embrace as he kissed her forehead. "No, Summer, I won't hurt the baby."

Tears flowed as her rigid body sat stiffly in his lap. Nick wiped away tears as they fell with the pad of his thumb. Repeatedly he assured her he would never harm her or the baby. The more he did this; her body relaxed as her heart rate returned to normal.

From pure mental exhaustion, Summer's body slumped against his chest, allowing herself to be comforted by his words.

Sensing she'd calmed down, Nick let out a breath he'd been holding.

With the rhythmic movement of Nick's solid chest Summer turned to putty in his arms. Closing her eyes, she remembered the last time he held her in his arms all night long. The pleasant memory caused her to unwind further, mindlessly shifting her hips in a position allowing her to snuggle closer.

The tight muscles in his shoulders unknotted as Summer's anxieties faded away. He knew he could be a ruthless, even an intimidating force when he wanted to. However, he never intended to release his wrath on Summer the way he had. Now because his temper had gotten the

best of him, of their delicate situation, she was absolutely terrified. Even though he was pissed, he never wanted this. He never wanted to see the pure look of fear and terror on her face. *I need to fix this.* She had to know that no matter what he would never raise a hand to hurt her or their unborn child.

Again she shifted and nestled her face against the base of his throat. The masculine scent of him was like a drug she couldn't get enough of as her nose brushed against his Adam's apple.

The closeness was so sweet; this was his chance to set things on a right course. Finally all of her defenses were completely down. The slow rhythmic breathing of her chest and steady even heartbeat were all signs that she felt safe again.

"Summer?"

"Hmm."

"You sleep?"

"No, I'm just resting my eyes." She whispered in a drowsy voice.

Nick softly chuckled; she always said that when fighting sleep.

"Summer, I'm sorry for hurting you."

"Hurting me?"

"When I grabbed you and picked you up earlier." Nick's voice was strained from the disgust he felt for himself. He still could not believe he'd done such a stupid thing.

Sitting up in his lap, she leaned back to get a better look at him through heavy eyes, "You didn't hurt me, you just scared me. You were so angry. I thought you were going to …" Her words trailed off as she laid her head back down on his chest. She could not bring herself to tell him she was afraid that things might have gotten violent, that he might have hit her.

Self-loathing overcame his entire being at Summer's unspoken admission. Nick gently squeezed her tighter into his embrace. At that moment he would give all he had to take away the pain he caused her.

"Summer?"

"Yes, Nick."'

Fumbling over the words, "You thought I was going to hit you?"

Silence.

"Summer?" Why wasn't she answering? Did she still believe he would hurt her?

"Yes, I was afraid you were going to hit me."

Pain clearly etched his handsome features. "Why? Why would you think that? I've never hurt you before." Nick's voice was barely a whisper.

No, not physical, but you've hurt me. "I know. But you've been so mad at me lately. I didn't know what to expect."

Nick could not argue with her assessment. "You're right," was all he could say. The moment was too fragile for him to convince her otherwise. No, he would not spoil the tenderness of the moment. Summer was right where he wanted her. In his arms, believing and knowing she was in the safest place in the world.

As he stood up with her in his arms, she wanted to know, "What are you doing?"

"Laying you down so you can go back to sleep, you look tired

Before he could take a step away from the bed, Summer's small hand grasped his hand.

"Don't leave, stay with me. I don't want to be alone." In his arms he had given her a glimpse of what they once shared.

"Nick?" *Please stay, don't go.*

Rubbing his hand over his goatee, "Are you sure?" He was not sure if *he* should stay the night with her. The question was more so for his benefit and not hers.

Gently tugging on his hand, "Yes, I'm sure."

"All right, I'll stay."

Needing to be in his arms again, she scooted her body next to Nick's until her back was firmly pressing against his solid chest. Summer reached behind until she felt a lean muscular arm. Heat surged through Nick as her soft palm caressed down cords of sinewy muscles until their fingers interlocked. Slowly she lifted his hand, bringing it around her body to rest on her swollen belly. Disengaging her fingers from the lock she began making tiny circles on the back of his hand.

Nick wanted to tell her to stop touching him. That was the problem with Summer, she could turn him on with a simple touch.

The last thing he wanted was for her to think he wanted to take advantage of her. Just as he was about to ease his hand and body away, Summer's caressing came to a halt.

Gliding his hand over her belly to an area of activity she whispered, "You feel that?"

"I feel it."

"That's your baby, Nick."

He wrapped his arms fully around her, melting into her. "I know, baby, I know."

Chapter 12

Three days passed before Summer was able to make it back to her home. After that turbulent first night at Nick's, things mellowed considerably between them. There were so many things they needed to say to one another. She had a need to explain fully why she'd kept her pregnancy a secret. He needed to know why she found it necessary to keep him in the dark. Each time one of them began to broach the subject they would falter sensing the timing was all wrong. Besides, Summer didn't want to ruin the short time she had with Nick.

The night they'd shared the same bed for the first time in many months had been special to her. Nick made her feel safe and wanted, almost loved, as she lay in his arms. As he held her he apologized to her endlessly. Turning her to face him, he tenderly kissed her forehead, eyelids and the tip of her nose with each heartfelt word.

The next morning she woke to him lightly stroking her belly with his fingertips. She had never seen such an overtly affectionate side of Nick until that morning. After stroking her belly he proceeded to place tiny kisses over every large round portion of it as he whispered words she was unable to decipher. Summer lay still as long as possible, never wanting the tenderness he was showering on her and their baby to end.

He'd done a great job at convincing her he would never harm her physically. No longer did she fear him in that sense. Her greatest fear was he would hurt her beyond the physical, shattering her emotional and psychological wellbeing. Yes, he'd been so sweet to her for those three days. That meant nothing, whatsoever, if he hadn't changed his position.

On numerous occasions Summer envisioned her baby being literally ripped from her arms. Other times she'd envisioned herself living her life as a fugitive on the run with her baby.

Shaking the nightmares she'd tell herself, "I have to somehow make him understand."

❧ ❧ ❧ ❧ ❧

"Mr. Stiles, everyone is present in the conference room." Nick's receptionist announced over the intercom.

"Thanks Gladys. Tell everyone I'll be there in about ten minutes."

The meeting would have to wait; he was preoccupied with thoughts of Summer, the baby, and the time they'd recently spent together. Murmuring a curse, he was still disgusted with how badly he treated her. He remembered how fragile she was as he held her in his lap. With words and touch he profusely sought to calm and soothe her. A weight lifted when Summer's demeanor became somewhat relaxed. Her stance was still guarded; however, she no longer was a bundle of nerves when interacting with him.

Nick was astounded, yet pleased when she requested that he not leave her alone that first night. Stunned when she nestled herself against him and encouraged him to feel the evidence of life in her womb, she quietly whispered, "*It's your baby*." The softness and gentleness of her touch stirred a profound desire in him. He refused to ruin the tenderness of the moment. Instead he focused his energies on soothing her fears away. Nick sincerely meant every caress, stroke and tender kiss he planted on her beautiful face.

What he felt for Summer as she lay in his arms, he refused to acknowledge. No. He wasn't in love with her. Sure he still cared for her, wanted to do the right thing by her and their baby. But when and how did he go about doing what was right? How did he know for certain she wasn't playing him for a fool? Being a fool once for a beautiful woman was more than enough for him. Never, ever again would he give his heart to another woman.

Confusion consumed Nick. So many emotions warred inside of him as he contemplated what to do about his relationship with Summer, if it could be called a relationship. He wanted to pick up where things had left off with them. After the way he treated her was it possible? Would she be able to love him the way she had before he abandoned her months ago? True, he had held her all night as she slept like a newborn in his arms; however that didn't mean a thing. He would do anything to regain that special relationship with her. Kevin had been on the money. Summer was the best thing that ever happened to him.

Rubbing his hand across his jaw, Nick truly was at a loss of what to do for the first time in his life. If it meant apologizing, he'd do it on his hands and knees if need be. Heck, he would buy her anything she wanted. A bigger house, new car, furs, jewelry, anything as long as things could go back to the way they were before he left the states. Yet another part of him didn't trust her. She tried to manipulate him, or so he believed. Bile rose in his throat every time he relived the night of going to her and finding her pregnant. Deep in his soul he knew if he had never listened to that small voice in his head telling him to go see Summer he would have never known she was having a baby. *His* baby. The possibility of having a child somewhere out in the world and not knowing it infuriated him. Any decent man would want to know if he had a child.

Standing and straightening his tie, he headed to the door. Taking long purposeful strides down the corridor to the conference room, Nick's mind shifted gears. Shedding off thoughts of Summer and the baby, he eased into predatory mode as he entered the conference room and announced, "Gentlemen, we're about to engage in a hostile takeover."

A pin drop could be heard as everyone witnessed the ominous expression Nick wore on his handsome face. The group of professionals quickly grasps the understanding that he was gearing up for battle with every intention of being the conqueror.

Chapter 13

Rushing in the front door to get out of the cold, Summer dropped her things on the floor and plopped down on the sofa. "Five and a half more weeks to go," she said to herself as she patted her belly. Right away, her thoughts went to Nick when she touched her belly. It had been five days since she heard from him. She wasn't at all bothered by it, because she understood they both needed the distance.

Life went on as usual with the exception of Ava and Starr doing round the clock vigils after she spent those three days with Nick. "We just don't want to see him hurt you anymore than he already has."

Both Ava and Starr felt guilty over the situation with Nick. After all they were the ones who convinced her to go out with him. Summer tried telling them things were "okay" between her and Nick. But they knew she was holding back and wasn't telling them everything.

To Summer's surprise her parents were not at all freaked out about Nick's surprise return in her life. Thanks to her dad, Summer was sure of. The only advice her mom gave was, "Watch yourself baby, men can be so complicated, even downright unpredictable."

She understood exactly what her mom was talking about. After spending all night in Nick's arms the next day he became quiet, a little distant. He hadn't treated her rude, hadn't lost his temper or anything, just kindly kept to himself, mostly working in his office. Summer was disappointed when he slept in his room while she slept in the guest room. No way would she have objected to lying in his arms, all night, every night that they were together under the same roof.

Rested after sitting for ten minutes, she pushed herself off the sofa and padded to the freezer. Peeking in, not finding what she was craving, she sucked her teeth. "I don't even believe this." Summer wanted to throw herself in the floor and have a tantrum like a four year old as she discovered her craving was not about to be satisfied. She had eaten the last of it two nights ago. "Shoot, I should've asked Starr to take me to the store."

Brrrrg. Brrrrg.

"Hello?" Summer snapped.

"Have we had a bad day?"

Summer's heart skipped a beat. She was as giddy as a teenager. *He called.*

"Not really." She wanted to tell him she was better now that he called.

"Then what's wrong?" *Tell me baby and I'll fix it for you.*

"I ate all the ice cream. I don't have any more left."

Grinning into the phone, he could tell she was pouting. She looked so darn cute when she pouted. "Sounds like a state of emergency."

"Ha, ha, you're so smart." She sneered. What did he know? He's never been pregnant before with a maddening craving. Shoot! It was a state of emergency.

"Are we getting an attitude, Miss Summer?"

"No, Mr. Nick." Still pouting, "I just want some ice cream that's all."

Chuckling, Nick pictured Summer with her arms crossed and lips poked out.

"Would you like me to bring you some?"

"Would you?" *Please say yes.*

"I wouldn't have asked if I wouldn't, now would I."

"No." She softly replied.

"Raspberry truffle."

"You remembered?"

"Why would I forget?"

Summer was silent. From her point of view he had forgotten everything about her.

He didn't wait for a response. "I'll see you in thirty minutes."

Keeping busy for the next thirty minutes, Summer went on line to Baby Gap on her laptop. There were so many cute outfits for baby boys and girls that she wanted to buy. At her last ultrasound appointment, the technician offered to tell her the sex of the baby. She declined. When asked "why" by family and friends she simply stated, "Because I don't want to know." Which was surprising, because at times Summer had to know everything. Since she didn't know the sex of her baby she selected several neutral items and put them on her wish list. Starr let it slip that she and Ava were throwing her a 'surprise' baby shower. Summer softly laughed. Starr sometimes couldn't hold water. Just as she was about to go to the Children's Place website the doorbell chimed.

Going to the door, looking through the peephole she quickly open the door. Nick was on the other side holding a bag in his hand from her favorite gourmet ice cream store. This time he was smiling instead of glaring hateful at her. Holding the bag in the air playfully, "This is what you want?"

"Yup." Taking the bag standing to the side, Summer let him in.

"Have a seat."

Shrugging off his coat, throwing it over an armchair, Nick took a seat on the sofa. The display on the laptop top caught his attention. *Baby Gap, huh?* He had no idea where to buy baby apparel from, now he had a clue.

Within a few seconds, Summer was back with ice cream and spoon in hand, standing in front of Nick. "Hold this for me." After she handed him the ice cream and spoon she settled on the sofa next to Nick folding her legs Indian style. Comfortable she reached for her treat, utensil, and smiled at Nick. "Thanks."

Nick observed Summer as she dug into the creamy treat and scooped up a healthy portion then put it in her mouth.

"Mmmmm, this is so good." She was engrossed with having her craving satisfied.

"Is it that good?" Nick asked with a raised eyebrow.

"Huh? What?" Embarrassed, Summer's face became flushed as she looked at Nick.

"I said is it that good?" He asked amused by her embarrassment.

"Yes, would you like some?" She shyly offered.

Shrugging broad shoulders, "Sure, why not."

Scooping up a spoonful of the treat, she went still as Nick placed a finger along her jaw turning her face towards his. Slowly, leaning in close, licking a drop of ice cream from the corner of her mouth he whispered, "Mmm, tastes like I remembered."

Summer shivered from the intimate contact. She wondered if he was referring to her lips or the ice cream.

"Do you want some more?" *Oh Lawd! Why did I ask this man that?!*

Summer did not flinch when Nick held her face between his large hands placing a soft kiss on her mouth.

"Sure, I'd love some more…ice cream."

"Okay." Summer whispered as she proceeded to feed Nick.

After she feed him, he removed the spoon and ice cream from her hands. "Here let me feed you now." This went on back and forth, the two of them feeding each other until Summer had enough of the decadent treat. The last thing she wanted was a stomachache at two in the morning.

When she left the room to take the container and spoon into the kitchen, Nick wondered what in hell's fire had come over him. He had lost his mind. The sole purpose of his visit was to invite her to dinner so they could talk, resolve some issues. Instead, he ended up bringing her ice cream and damn near seducing her. He had to get a grip. He was losing focus. He had to get out of there and away from Summer. She was too potent for her own good, or his for that matter.

Disappointment washed over Summer as she came back into the living room. Nick was standing in the middle of the room with his coat on.

"You're leaving?" She wanted him to stay just a little while longer she was enjoying his company.

"Yeah, I have an early day tomorrow." He lied. A little white lie he convinced himself.

"Oh."

Nick noted the sadness in her voice. He pulled her to his chest in a hug as he rested his chin on top of her head.

Summer's arms wrapped around his waist as she laid her head on his chest and inhaled his masculine scent.

"Oh, baby, don't sound so sad."

Summer remained silent; she didn't want him to leave.

"How about having dinner with me on Friday night?"

"Okay." *Dinner, I can do that.*

"There some things we need to discuss." There he said it. He accomplished his purpose for calling and coming by her place.

Summer felt like she was doused with a bucket of cold water.

"Like what?" She asked as she pulled away from his embrace.

Tightening the embrace not letting her go, he told her, "Now is not the time to get into it. I'll call you later in the week. Okay."

"Okay, but Nick…"

"Summer." She knew the tone he used meant 'don't push me' and she didn't.

"All right, Nick."

Kissing her on the top of her head and patting her on the backside, "Good, come on lock the door behind me."

"Hey, boy!"

He winked at her. "Sorry, just couldn't help myself."

Pulling him by the hand toward the door, she shot back, "Yeah right. You know you meant to do it."

Nick loosened his hand from Summer's grip and led her in front so he could get a better view of her backside.

"Looks like it's gotten fuller, rounder, wi–"

"Nick!" Summer yelled as she frowned at him. Dang! She knew she was huge but he didn't have to rub it in her face.

"Oh, come on girl, don't get all offended." Nick teased

"Whatever, Nick." Summer flagged him, but really wanted to give him the finger as she waddled to the door.

Coming up behind her, he pointed to the floor. "Why is your stuff on the floor?" He hadn't noticed the purse and pillow when he came in. There was a subtle change in his demeanor, no longer was he lighthearted.

"I had my childbirth class tonight. I just sort of dropped all my stuff there."

Childbirth class? Doesn't the father go to those classes? Who the hell went with her?

"Who went with you?" The tightness in his voice was evident, but why? Was it jealousy?

"Starr went with me, she's my labor coach."

Nick wanted to tell her if he'd any idea he was going to be a father he would've been her coach. Hell, he at least deserved that much. Instead he said good night and told her to be sure to lock the door behind him.

Ookay, bi-polar man.

Chapter 14

Sitting home alone all day was beginning to drive Summer insane. Several times a day she called Ava and Starr at work. She just had to know the latest gossip at work. Being put on hold numerous times was frustrating. She understood it was necessary; after all they were at work. Tired of their conversations being interrupted, Summer asked them to come over after work to sit with her for a minute. Happily, her friends agreed even though they'd just visit her three days ago. They knew she was bored out of her mind at home all day with nothing to do. She could watch only so many episodes of Maury and Jerry Springer after her soaps went off.

At six thirty on the dot, Ava and Starr let themselves into Summer's house. After she began experiencing premature contractions, they insisted on having a key. "What if something happens to you and you can't get to the phone or the door?" was their explanation.

"Summer, get your free Willy butt down these stairs! Girl, you know you are a hot mess!" Starr yelled out as she walked to the bottom of the stairs.

"What?" Summer played innocent as she padded down the stairs.

Putting her hands on her hips, "Girl, we were just here like three days ago. Wasn't it you who told us we were coming over *too* often when we tried to visit your fat butt twice last week? You nearly cussed us out."

"Mmm hmm, Summer, you know she's telling the truth." Ava said.

Summer rolled her eyes with attitude. "I am not fat, Starr. In case you haven't noticed I'm with child, and Ava stop taking her side all the time. Y'all supposed to be my peeps."

Times like these were when she missed her parents the most. She knew they were only kidding with her; however, she didn't want to be a burden to them. After all they did have their own lives to live. If her parents still lived in Philly she most likely would be at their house. Summer had seriously thought about going to North Carolina to have her baby so she could be close to her parents. Having them close by meant she wouldn't have to rely upon Ava and Starr as much. However, she came to her senses when Starr reminded her, "Girl, stop tripping. You know you and your momma would be going at it." Starr laughed, adding, "She'd be telling you how to be pregnant."

Summer dropped the attitude and mumbled, "I miss seeing y'all everyday."

Both Ava and Starr stretched their arms out and gathered her in a group hug. "We miss you too, Boo."

Summer knew she could always count on her girls. The ringing of the doorbell broke up the huddle.

"Must be the pizza," Summer chimed excitedly. Food had become a close companion after she'd gotten over the morning sickness hurdle.

"Good. I'm starving," Ava said as she grabbed money from her purse to pay the deliveryman.

As they ate, the trio talked about Summer's plans to return to work. Summer expressed she did not want to return to work the standard six weeks after giving birth. She hadn't begun to look for a babysitter or daycare center for the baby. She was seriously considering staying out of work longer.

Talking about childcare arrangements was making her uncomfortable. She hoped Ava and Starr hadn't noticed her uneasiness with the subject. She hadn't the faintest idea where things stood with Nick and his threat of filing for custody. He'd made it clear that they needed to "discuss some things" Friday night. Does it have to do with the custody of the baby? *Of course it does,* a small voice confirmed.

Summer wanted to get off of the subject of childcare issues; her head started to hurt. She decided to tell them about Nick's visit the other night.

Wiping the pizza grease from her mouth with a napkin, Summer came clean with her friends...well somewhat clean. "I have something to tell you guys, but I don't want y'all to get all crazy on me."

Glancing at each other, reading the other's thought, *Nick.* Starr was the one to speak. "Go head Boo, we won't trip."

"Promise."

"Promise." They agreed in unison.

Summer twisted the napkin in her hands she'd just wiped her mouth with. *Why am I so nervous? Shoot, I'm a grown woman.* In spite of her little pep talk to herself she bit her bottom lip and prayed things didn't get too ugly. She knew if Ava and Starr had their way Nick would have been tarred and feathered the night he showed up at her door.

"Nick came over the other night." She braced herself and waited for the explosion from Ava to come.

"He did what! What did *he* want! To kidnap you again!" Starr shrieked.

Lawd a mercy, the sane one is going crazy. "Calm down Starr, you're acting like Ava now!"

"Hey, what's that supposed to mean?" Ava hissed in her defense.

Ignoring Ava, Summer continued. "He was actually very nice to me. He brought me ice cream." Summer smiled remembering how they had fed each other.

Starr was annoyed by the silly smile on Summer's face. She swore if Summer weren't pregnant, she'd slap the yella off her.

"Who gives a rat's behind about ice cream? Why did *he* come over here?" Starr demanded. *This simple child has lost her mind.*

"Yeah, why he come over? I knew he was up to something every since he held you hostage for three days." Ava interjected not making things any better.

Glaring at Ava through squinted eyes, Summer clipped out in an irritable tone, "I was snowed in, not held hostage Av."

Summer was pissed. Why were they tripping so hard? He was the father of her baby after all. Was it so unusual for him to stop by?

Sucking her teeth with attitude, "Whatever, Summer."

The nastiness rising between Summer and Ava quickly simmered Starr. Standing up she got between them, things were about to get ugly.

"Yeah, whatever, Av." Summer stood up putting her hands on her hips, glaring at Ava.

Moving closer to Summer, Starr urged, "Come on sweetie calm down. Don't get yourself all worked up. You don't want to start having contractions again." Gently she eased Summer back to her chair. "We're sorry for tripping on you. Right Av?"

"Yes." Ava dropped the attitude, she felt awful. She had forgotten all about Summer's delicate condition. The last thing she wanted was for her friend to go into labor.

"Tell us why Nick stopped by." Ava's voice was more gentle as an attempt to diffuse the tension in the air.

Tears welled up in Summer's eyes as she stared at Starr, then Ava. No one understood what she was going through, not even her two best friends. Fighting back tears, "Never mind, forget I even said anything." As she stood to walk away, Summer stopped when she felt Starr's hand gently squeeze her wrist.

"Summer, I'm sorry. Please come on sit back down and tell us what's on your heart."

Sliding back into the chair she wasn't sure what to do. She needed to vent about what she was feeling. Who better than her friends? However, the absolute last thing she wanted was to hear them bad mouth Nick. No one was more aware of what he'd done to her than she was. And what was so pathetic was she still loved him in spite of everything. Hadn't they ever been in love before? Why couldn't they understand? At least they could be sympathetic to the fact she was carrying his baby.

Unconsciously Summer rubbed her swollen belly. The gesture did not go unobserved by Starr or Ava. Instantly they felt remorse. They both knew how hard it had been for Summer not having Nick around for the majority of her pregnancy.

This time Ava spoke. "Summer, please tell us what's going on." Pausing to squeeze her hand affectionately she begged, "Don't shut us out."

"He said he wanted to talk to me about some things."

"Like what?" Ava asked as she took another slice of pizza.

Shrugging her slim shoulders, "I don't know, most likely the baby."

Starr touched Summer's hands that were in her lap when she asked, "How did Nick react when he found out about the baby?"

As close as the three friends were, they could not believe that Summer had not told them about Nick's reaction until now.

"He was so mad I hadn't told him about the baby." Summer purposely left out his threat to file for custody.

Holding up her hand signaling she wanted to talk. "Mad? What was he mad about? Wasn't he the one who ended things?" Ava fought hard to keep the anger she felt towards Nick out of her voice.

Sighing, "Yup, Ava, he was." Summer quickly added, "But that doesn't mean he didn't want to know. Besides, it was my decision not to tell him about the baby."

Ava's fuse blew despite her trying to control it. Summer and Starr both jumped when she slammed her palm on the table, rattling drinking glasses.

"No you don't, Summer, don't you dare go blaming yourself. You did what you thought was best at the time."

Starr cut Ava off before she could explode any further. "She's right, Summer. You yourself said he didn't want children and you didn't want him to feel like you were trying to trap him with a baby."

Summer nodded her head. "You guys are right. It's just that everything is changing."

"Everything like what?" Ava asked, as she calmed down a tad bit.

"Well, he doesn't seem so repulsed by the idea of me being pregnant and becoming a father anymore. And he does want to sit down and talk like I told you."

"I'm glad to at least hear that," Starr said.

"Yeah, so am I. I hope you guys work everything out for the sake of the baby." Ava added with sincerity.

"So do I Av. After all it's about the baby."

Removing pizza boxes from the table, attempting to lighten the mood, Ava said, "I better get going, some folks have to work for a living."

Summer sucked her teeth. "Ha, ha, you're real funny Miss Ava."

Standing up, Starr told her she was going home as well. "Like Ava said, us girls have to work. We can't sit home all day eating ice cream and watching that ridiculous daytime television."

"Heifa shut your mouth you're supposed to be on my side! Remember, I do know how you two sneak into patient rooms watching the same ridiculous daytime television, acting like y'all working." Summer chanted and pumped her fist in the air, "Jerry, Jerry, Jerry." She playfully pointed at Ava wagging her finger. "Didn't I walk past a room one day and see you doing that while your patient was at a test? Weren't you supposed to be making the bed?"

Ava and Starr cracked up. The sight of Summer with her big belly imitating those fools on television was hysterical.

"Come on crazy pregnant woman and walk us to the door." Ava teased. "And no, that wasn't me, it was my twin. You know they say everybody has one."

"Okay Av, whatever you say." Summer said as she walked them to the door.

Starr hugged and kissed Summer on the cheek. "Bye honey, I'll call you tomorrow."

Following behind her, Ava hugged Summer and squeezed her tight. "You know I love you, right?"

Summer nodded.

"I just don't want to see you get hurt again, you've been through so much. So when I get excited and start tripping please, please understand it's because I care about and love you, and you." Ava said rubbing Summer's belly.

Summer smiled at her friend. "I know, Av. And we love you too."

Chapter 15

Brrrg. Brrrg. Brrrg.

The offending sound of the ringing phone seemed to be in a faraway distance. Summer thought she was dreaming, except the ringing never stopped. Opening one eye, she looked at the digital clock on the nightstand.

11:45. Who in the world was calling her so late?

"Hello?" Summer answered in a voice raspy with sleep.

"I woke you up?"

Rolling over on her back holding the phone between her ear and shoulder, "It's okay."

"I won't keep you, I just wanted to make sure you're still okay with us getting together to talk?"

"Yup. Friday is fine. Are you coming over here?" She hesitantly questioned. No way was she going back on his turf anytime soon.

"No. I was thinking we could go to the cabin." He said as he sat in his home office tapping a pen on the desk waiting for her response.

All traces of sleepiness evaporated. She was fully awakened by his suggestion of going to the cabin.

What! That's where all the drama started! Nope, no way! Finally, finding her voice, "The cabin?"

"Yes." He said as if it was the most reasonable request.

"Summer?"

"Huh?"

"What's the matter, baby?

Coming up with an excuse that was believable was what Summer was in search of. How could she out right refuse to go miles away with him to a deserted cabin, in the middle of freakin' nowhere? Yeah things for now were cool between them, but what if he went off on her again? A tiny voice in her head reminded her he'd promised not to do that again. *Yeah, whatever,* she told the voice. As far as she was concerned, no way was she crossing state line with him. She didn't care how fine he was, how nice he'd been, or how much ice cream he'd brought her. No, no, no! She wasn't doing it.

"I don't know, Nick. That's kind of far." She stated weakly after talking smack in her head.

"It's only a few hours." Nick reasoned with her.

"I know but—"

"But what? Don't you trust me?"

Silence.

Summer sat on the other end of the phone not knowing what to say. How did she tell him the only time she could trust him is when he was in a good mood?

The silence was becoming deafening. Nick rolled his shoulders trying to ease the building tension. He knew convincing her was going to be difficult, maybe impossible.

"Summer, I told you I would never hurt you."

You already have. "I know you did. It's just that…" Summer's voice was soft as it trailed off.

Counting to ten, keeping his voice even, "What Summer?"

Summer cursed her wayward hormones, as her voice quivered; she quickly wiped a tear from her cheek. "It's just that I make you so angry, Nick." *Here I go again blaming myself.*

The quivering of her voice unsettled him, he could tell she was tearful. Choosing his words carefully he said, "Summer, I just want to talk somewhere where there are no distractions."

Pausing, again searching for the right words. "There are so many questions I have and only you have the answers to them."

Summer understood exactly where he was coming from, really she did. She too wanted to clear the air, explain her side of things. But goodness gracious, being all alone in the woods with Nick was a bit too much. That for sure was something she was in no way, no how, ready or even prepared to deal with.

"Can't we talk here, at my house?" Heck at this point she was willing to go to his place. At least if he wigged out on her she could take a cab back to the safety of her home. And if worse came to worse she could call Starr and Ava to the rescue.

"No, I'd rather we didn't Summer. I promise you I'll keep my temper in check." *As long as you're honest with me.* Immediate guilt consumed him. *See, that's why she doesn't trust you. She knows you better than you think.*

"You promise?" Summer asked in an unsure voice.

Nick wanted nothing more than to hold her in his arms until every ounce of doubt was cast away.

"Yes, Beautiful, I promise to be on my best behavior."

Stillness hung thickly in the air. He had called her beautiful and meant it. There had never been another woman who'd affected him the way Summer had. Her external beauty surpassed that of many; however, it was her inner beauty that swept him away. It was for this very reason he found it incomprehensible she would ultimately deceive him. Nick prayed with everything in him that when all was said and done she would have an excusable explanation that would make sense to him.

Summer's head became foggy as if she were in a haze. He'd called her by her pet name. His tone was gentle, sincere, unlike that night when he resorted to sarcasm.

"Nick?"

"Yeah?"

"You still think I'm beautiful?"

"Always."

"Even fat and all?"

"You're not fat, Summer."

"If I'm not fat, then what am I? I've gained nearly thirty pounds you know?"

"You're still beautiful *and* carrying my baby." Nick wouldn't comment on the weight issue that definitely was a no, no.

Summer was glad he could not see her blushing. "You think you're so slick."

Teasingly he asked, "Woman, what are you talking about?"

"You're trying to butter me up so I won't back out of going away with you. Come on, admit it."

This was the Summer Nick was crazy about he thought to himself as he softly laughed.

"You got me, I give up."

"Yeah, I thought so."

Nick and Summer continued a playful banter for another twenty minutes. Eventually they got around to making plans to have him pick her up Friday morning around eleven.

"Alright, Beautiful, I'm gonna let you get back to sleep." He drawled out as he imagined her curled up nestled against him with her protruding belly.

Covering her mouth stifling a yawn, "Okay, good night, Nick."

"Sweet dreams, Beautiful."

"You too, Nick."

❧ ❧ ❧ ❧ ❧

Stepping out the shower, he grabbed a thick, fluffy white towel and wrapped it around his waist as he hurried to the phone on the nightstand. The first notion to pop in his head was that it was Summer calling to renege. Who else could it be calling so late?

To say Nick was a workaholic was an understatement. He'd remain in his home office working for another hour after he hung up with Summer. It was nearly two in the morning, his eyes were burning with exhaustion. All he wanted to do was get a couple hours of winks in before the new day started in less than four hours. Only she would think of calling so late, taking a chance that he'd still be awake.

Picking up the phone he said in a weary, bone-tired voice, "Yeah, Summer?"

"You wish!"

"Kev, what the hell are you calling me so late for?" Nick demanded, annoyed at his friend.

"Chill man, I was just wondering what happened with Summer? Is she going or what?"

Nick informed Kevin about his plans of taking her to the cabin for the weekend. Kevin had been a little uneasy with the idea. As far as he was concerned, Nick was still being a little hard on her. True, he was not spitting venom any longer when Kevin brought up her name, but hell, nobody knew Nick the way he did. One minute he'd be Mr. Nice Guy and the next, a complete jerk. Kevin wanted to, and would be supportive of his best friend, his brother. However, he thought Nick was pushing the issue of having this "serious" talk with Summer. For goodness sake, they were having a baby. It wasn't like they didn't have the rest of their lives to figure the mess out.

Nick had mad love for Kevin, but at times like now, he had no concept of time. Just because he was a night owl didn't mean the rest of the world was. He should have known if Nick was up this late it meant he was most likely finishing some work and would be heading to bed. Sleep was important to Nick, even if it meant only a few hours. Nick figured he'd better answer his question so he could get at least two minutes of sleep.

"Yeah man she's going."

"Word?"

"Word." Nick said with a hint of smugness. Wasn't nothing slow about him, he knew Kevin doubted Summer would go to the cabin with him.

"That's what's up brotha, do your thing."

"Plan on it my man. Listen, don't mean to be rude, but I got to get some shut eye."

"Oh my bad, it is a little late isn't it?"

Nick shook his head. If he didn't love Kevin like a brother he'd cussed him out like nobody's business.

"Yeah dude it's two in the morning."

Kevin chucked, "A'ight, brother I'll check you later."

"Later, Kev."

"Nick?"

Here we go. "Yeah man?"

"Be cool." No further explanation was needed. Nick understood he was referring to his reckless temper.

"I'm already ahead of you man."

Chapter 16

Friday morning Summer padded between her bedroom and the bathroom as she packed last minute necessities and toiletries for her weekend with Nick. Hopefully the trip would be uneventful. She had finally convinced herself that spending time alone with Nick wouldn't be too bad just as long as he didn't act like a fool. Hopefully, once they'd cleared the air they could get down to what was most important… the baby.

Summer was anxious to know how they would go about raising the baby while living in separate households.

What would they name the baby? Would the baby be a Jackson or Stiles?

Humming her favorite song, *At Last* by Etta James, Summer moved over to the bed and peered inside her suitcase to make sure she had everything. "I have my gowns, panties, bras, socks, slippers…..am I forgetting anything?"

"Whoa!"

A sudden sharp pain in her lower abdomen stilled Summer. Easing down on the bed, she touched her swollen belly, which was now rigid from a contraction. *It'll pass,* she persuaded herself.

Sitting motionless on the bed until it was safe, Summer gingerly stood and proceeded to close the small suitcase as if doing so rapidly would bring on another contraction. Deciding to play it safe, she left the small suitcase on the bed. "Nick can bring it down for me when he gets here."

By the time her foot hit the last step it happened again.

"Ooooh, let me sit my butt down."

Glancing at her watch and easing down on the step, seventeen minutes had past since the last contraction. This was not happening now! Not when she had worked up the nerve to deal with Nick and the twenty million questions he had for her. Finally warming up to the idea of facing him head on, she had to go and start having contractions again. If Summer were a cussing woman, she would've invented a few choice words of her own. "Maybe this'll be the last one."

Willing the contractions to cease, she glanced at her watch again. *Good, thirty minutes since the last one.*

Summer was starved, but was too afraid to move. Her intentions had been to fix breakfast and snacks for the long ride for herself and Nick. The ringing of the doorbell interrupted her thoughts deciding whether she should attempt to do the tasks.

On wobbly feet, she stood taking baby steps to the front door. Hand on doorknob, Summer masked her worried expression with a pasted on smile before she opened the door.

"Hey Nick, come on in." She said waving her hand with an air of excitement.

He frowned at Summer's retreating as she turned and headed towards the stairs. She talked nonstop as her words came out rushed and hurried. "I'm all ready to go I just need you to get my suitcase I thought I was gonna have breakfast ready for us but..."

Confusion marred Nick's features as he listened to her mouth move a hundred miles an hour. *What the hell is her problem?* "Summer, slow down, you're talking too fast."

She spun around to face him. "Huh? ...Aaaawh, this one really hurts." Summer moaned as she sank to her knees and doubled over from the pain. If this is what hours of labor was going to be like she definitely was not up for the challenge.

With a few long strides Nick was crouched down by her side. "What's wrong?"

"I've been having contractions this morning."

With one fluid move, Nick carried Summer over to the sofa and gently laid her down.

Kneeling down on the floor next to her, he had not a clue what to do. *Is she about to have the baby now? And if so, isn't it too early?* Nick felt helpless at the thought of his child struggling to survive because he or she was born too early. It was that last thought that made him ask, "Shouldn't we call your doctor?"

Summer nodded her head.

Nick anxiously paced the floor as Summer lay in the hospital bed infused with IV fluids and attached to a fetal monitor. The rapid, rhythmic, pulsation of the tiny baby's heart was the only audible sound in the room. It reminded him of one of those relaxation or meditation tapes that played sounds of nature, like waterfalls or birds chirping. Surprisingly the rhythmic sound soon began to have a calming effect on him.

That's my baby in there. I'm gonna be a daddy.

That's what he wanted his son or daughter to call him. Not father like he was forced to call his dad. The title father always felt so cold, so distant. He definitely, under any circumstances, did not want his child to call him father. *Daddy*. The very thought had elicit a lopsided grin. Funny how things change, last year this time the thought of being anyone's daddy was the furthest thing from Nick's mind and heart.

What in the world is he looking at me like that for? And why does he have that goofy grin on his face?

Unconsciously, Summer matched his goofy grin. "What are you grinning for?"

"I was just thinking that I'm gonna be a daddy soon."

Turning serious the grin evaporated from her face "Are you okay with that?"

"I have—"

Nick was about to tell her that he had come to terms with his soon to be status of fatherhood, however, the doctor barging into the room interrupted him.

Summer wanted to scream. Dr. Neil had absolute horrible timing

The doctor walked over to Nick and offered his hand, "Good afternoon, I'm Dr. Neil. You must be the soon to be proud papa."

Nick accepted the proffered hand as Dr. Neil vigorously pumped his hand and smiled with much animation.

Nick eyed the middle-aged balding man who was slightly taller than Summer by an inch or two. He reminded Nick of a cartoon character. "That would be me. I'm Nick Stiles."

Turning his attention to his patient, "Miss Jackson, I thought we were all done with these premature contractions. You were doing so well."

Nick's head snapped back as if he were slapped. *All done with these contractions? I thought this morning was the first time she had them?* Nick felt annoyance creeping into his bones. He cursed under his breath. *Here we go again.*

Summer felt the stare emanating from Nick. Nervously she glanced at him then averted her eyes back to Dr. Neil. Nick's disposition changed as quickly as the Chicago wind. Summer swore she heard him cursing under his breath.

"I was doing fine until this morning."

Even Dr. Neil's walk was animated as he bounced over to the fetal monitor to study the strip of paper that hung from it. "The medication has stopped the contractions for now."

Summer breathed a sigh of relief. "Good, can I go home now?"

The little man pressed his lips together as if in deep thought. "Mmm, I don't know Summer if that's a good idea."

"Why?" She asked with tears filling her eyes. The last thing she wanted was to be in the hospital hooked up to a fetal monitor and IV fluids. Why should she have to when the contractions had stopped?

Reading her thoughts, Dr. Neil expressed his reservations. "Summer, I'm concerned about you being at home alone. If I were to release you home you would need to be on bed rest with very limited activity. That means no going up and down stairs and only getting out of bed to bathe, use the bathroom, and maybe sitting up in a chair for no more than thirty minutes at a time. I know you live alone and you would definitely need someone at home to help you." He paused in giving his speech. He felt terrible because Summer was quietly sobbing. What was he to do? His main concern was that of the health and welfare of the unborn child. Keeping the mother safe and contraction free was the best way to ensure the delivery of a viable infant.

Both men rushed to her side as she expressed being distraught. Nick stood by her side while Dr. Neil sat on the bed and took her hand in his.

"Summer, I'm sorry, but I have to do what's best for the baby. As you know you're thirty-six weeks pregnant, we have to get you to at least thirty-eight weeks so that the baby's lungs are fully mature."

Covering her face with her hands, Summer continued to sob. She felt like she was losing what little control she had. She'd never been sick a day in her life. The worse she ever experienced was having morning sickness during the first trimester of pregnancy.

As a nurse she comprehended everything the doctor was saying, she too wanted a healthy baby. However, there had to be another way to continue her pregnancy without being confined to one room for a month. At least at home, she'd be in her own environment. In between sobs she pleaded with her doctor.

"I know all of that Dr. Neil, but I want to go home. I don't want to stay in the hospital for a month. I promise not to do too much."

Summer's mind ran wild thinking of someone, anyone who could sit with her during the day so she could go home. Starr and Ava couldn't do it they had to work. Maybe she could call her mom to come stay with her. When she learned Summer had begun to have premature contractions she'd been itching to get back to Philly. Summer frowned and nixed that idea. Her mother would drive her nuts!

Nick hated to see her so distraught over not being able to go home. He'd never seen one woman cry so much. Every time he turned around, she was crying for one reason or another. Guilt gnawed at him, he *was* the main source of her recent spells of weeping.

"Dr. Neil, I'm taking Summer home." Before the doctor could object, Nick put his hand up cutting him off. "I'll make certain she has around-the-clock care."

A surge of relief flowed through Summer as she reached for Nick's hand and squeezed it.

"Thanks Nick."

"Don't worry 'bout it."

It was settled, Summer was going home.

Chapter 17

As Nick's vehicle pulled off from in front of the hospital Summer felt a heavy weight lift from her shoulders. Thank goodness she wouldn't be spending four weeks in the hospital. Unless she started to have contractions within the next two weeks Dr. Neil informed her she could stay home. If she went into labor after that, the baby would be fine.

Settling back into the soft leather upholstery of the vehicle, Summer began mentally rehashing the last few hours. Suddenly she felt foolish, downright simple. *I acted like a complete brat! Whining and crying like I was ten years old! And I have the nerve to soon be somebody's momma. Nick and Dr. Neil probably think I'm a basket case carrying on like I ain't got a bit of sense!* Shaking away the thought she gazed lovingly at Nick. He was so sweet, offering to have someone come to her house to watch over her so she wouldn't have to stay in the hospital.

Concentrating on the road, he hadn't paid any attention to Summer intently watching him, her thoughts turning from appreciation of his kindness to appreciation of his good looks. *Oh my goodness brotha is too fine!* Just looking at him had her body tingling all over settling dead smack between her legs causing her to squirm in her seat. It's been months since she experienced such sensations. Only one man was capable of evoking such a reaction.

Summer wasn't sure if he saw her squirming, she camouflaged the movement by maneuvering her body in the seatbelt facing him. She wanted to tell him how much it meant to her that he'd convinced Dr. Neil to let her go home. How she would have been totally depressed if she had to be confined to one room for the next four weeks. Of course if she absolutely had to do it, she would've. However, she would have hated every single minute of it.

The movement of her body drew Nick's attention; he could tell she was thinking about something.

"What's up, Summer?" He asked as he brought the car to a stop at a red light.

"I just want to thank you for taking me home. It's really sweet of you."

Pulling off from the green light he told her, "I'm not taking you home."

"Huh?" *What's he talking about, 'I'm not taking you home?'*

"You're going home with me."

Stunned, Summer stammered, "But... you... said—"

Nick immediately cut her off. "I said I was taking you home, meaning my home."

"What! I can't go home with you!" *This fool done fell and bumped his head.*

Making a U-turn in the middle of the street, Nick started heading in the opposite direction.

"What are you doing? Where are you going, Nick?"

"I'm taking you back to the hospital."

Panic overtook her in waves. *He's not serious. Is he?*

Summer grabbed his forearm. "Please, Nick, I don't want to go back to the hospital.

Nick was gradually losing his patience with her. He had enough of her whining and crying for one day.

"Summer, listen to me, and listen real good. Either you go home with me where I can take care of you, or you can go back to the hospital and let Dr. Neil do it. The choice is yours."

Silence.

"Come on Summer, I don't have all day."

Shifting her body facing forward again, crossing her hands over her chest, she grumbled, "I'll go home with you."

"I thought you'd see things my way."

Glaring at him and rolling her eyes, *he is so smug, get on my nerves.*

"Woman, don't you roll your eyes at me. I'm just looking out for the baby…my baby." Reaching out and lightly rubbing her belly he said, "Okay."

Summer wanted to melt right there where she sat. He really did care about the baby after all. However, the streak of stubbornness she inherited from her mother wouldn't allow her to melt…not now anyway.

Turning back to face him she didn't respond to his tender gesture. Instead she pouted, "I don't have any of my things." She unfolded her arms and rattled off a list as she pointed to each finger on her left hand with the index finger of her right hand. "I need my clothes, my toiletries, my laptop, my overnight bag I packed for the hospital for when I go into true labor, and… and… my stuff. I just need my stuff."

Driving into the garage of the building where he lived an amused grin spread across Nick's face. What he was about to say was going to make her hotter than Mississippi in August.

"Send your pit bulls Ava and Starr to get your *stuff*." He put emphasis on stuff. "They have keys to your place right? They'll sniff your *stuff* out without a problem." Nick stated dryly with a hint of a smirk playing around his lips.

Summer was furious. She wanted to smack that smirk right off his stupid face. How dare he call her best friends dogs! They'd been there for her when he wasn't anywhere to be found! He went too far. One thing you didn't do was talk about her girlfriends. He was about to get it.

Nick totally lost all composure. When Summer turned on him he nearly slammed into a concrete column as he parked. Her face was red and contorted in a furious frown with lips pressed so tight they turned white and eyes squinted so small the whites were barely visible through the slits. Nick couldn't help but to crack up laughing at her. She looked like a cartoon character; the only thing missing was steam coming from her ears. The laugh was cleansing. It had been such a long time since he laughed that hard.

Anger, shock, and then amusement simultaneously coursed through Summer. She must have made some horrendously, ugly face. Summer had never seen Nick so hysterical with laughter. Though she was mad at him for talking about her friends, she too began cracking up. Not because he had totally dissed her friends in the worse way, but because his laughter was so infectious. A few moments later the laughter died down. After catching her breath from laughing so hard she gave him a warning. "You better shut up, calling my friends pit bulls. They'll kick your butt."

Nick rolled his eyes. "Yeah, right. Tell your mutts to bring it on."

Summer's mouth dropped open before she erupted in laughter again. "Ooh, Nick, you are a stinkin'mess. Boy, I'm telling you, you're about to get rolled on for talking all that trash."

Nick's laughter dissolved as he looked at Summer. The sound of her laughter was music not only to his ears, but to his soul as well. He missed this carefree side of her. He'd forgotten how her entire being literally lit up when she laughed. She had gone from upset to playful and giddy within seconds.

She noticed Nick wasn't laughing anymore, but quietly gazing at her.

"What? Did I say something wrong?" *Again.*

"No, not at all."

"Then why did you get so quiet? Why are you looking at me like that?"

"I was just thinking how good it is to hear you laugh again."

"Oh."

"Summer?"

"Hmm?"

"You're really pretty when you laugh."

"I am?"

"Yes, you are."

"Oh."

Chapter 18

Staying with Nick hadn't been at all what Summer expected. Initially she'd thought after he came down off whatever high he was on, he'd be in a funky mood because their trip had been cancelled. "I told you already I just want you and the baby to be safe." Is what his response was when she questioned him about the cancelled trip.

Once she was settled in at Nick's, dread overwhelmed her as she remembered she hadn't called her parents, Starr, or Ava to bring them up to date on the latest events. Biting the bullet she called her parents first. Both her mom and dad wanted to come to Philly right away to be at her side. Summer convinced them to wait until she went into true labor. She assured her folks she would be fine in Nick's care. Although her parents balked at Summer's decision they had to respect it, after all she was an adult.

Much to Summer's surprise Starr and Ava didn't trip at all. They were more than willing when she requested they go to her house and bring her *stuff* to her. When they strutted into Nick's penthouse their eyes nearly bulged out of their heads. "This pad is off the hook!" Starr exclaimed as she went from room to room with Ava on her heels. The penthouse was laid out like it belonged in Architectural Digest. The entire time they were there, Summer prayed that they wouldn't get into a confrontation with Nick. And they would have too, if they knew he'd referred to them as the most vicious dog known to man. Everything ended up cool. Summer's friends and the father of her baby were cordial to one another. It went without saying they were all doing it for Summer's sake.

As the first week faded away, Summer was able to relax in her new environment. When Monday rolled around, she expected to be greeted by a nurse Nick hired to sit with her during the day while he went to the office. To her amazement, he set up shop in his home office. That same morning FedEx delivered files from his downtown office. Everything that was necessary for him to run his business efficiently from his home was at his fingertips. The only time he left was to attend meetings at the office. He detested teleconferences. During those few hours, his housekeeper Joan kept a watchful eye on Summer.

Joan immediately liked Summer. She was nothing like those other snobbish women who would call Nick's home talking down to her just because she was the housekeeper. It was a good thing he didn't flaunt those women in front of her, because the first time one of those heifers said anything out of the way, Joan swore she'd knock them into next week. Humph, she'd tell Nick a thing or two if he had anything to say about it. Summer, however, was a pleasant change from the others.

Joan hid her shock when Nick informed her that the mother of his soon to be born child would be at his place until she delivered. She was shocked mostly because she'd never seen a woman present in his home in all the years she worked for him. Sure, there were times when she occasionally worked a weekend he'd come home on a Saturday or Sunday morning around eight reeking of expensive perfume. As far as she was aware, his mother was the only woman other than herself who was granted entry into his home.

When Joan arrived to work that Monday morning, Summer was curled up on the sofa engrossed in a magazine. When she stepped into the living room she noticed Summer first and immediately stiffened her back. *I know little Miss Thang better not start no stuff with me, 'cause I ain't putting up with her mess! Nick's either. Got me playing nursemaid to this gal. I don't get paid to be no nurse. He should've kept his britches on!* Joan was pulled from her mental fussing when she heard a soft voice.

"Good morning." Summer uncurled her legs, stood and waddled over to Joan. She offered her hand to the older woman along with a bright smile. "You must be Joan."

Taking the offered hand, returning the smile, "And you must be Summer." *She's a pretty little thing. Mmm, got some manners too. I like sweetie already.*

Instantly the older woman and younger woman became fast friends.

❧ ❧ ❧ ❧ ❧

When at home with Summer, Nick was more than accommodating, catering to her every need. "Do you need anything? Can I get this for you? Can I get that for you?" If she so much as reached for the remote while she watched television he would jump to get if for her. All of the attention at times was suffocating. "Nick, I'm fine. I don't need you waiting on me hand and foot."

"Yes, you do. I gave Dr. Neil my word. I don't want my baby born prematurely."

Summer lifted a brow, "Your baby?"

"Okay, our baby," he compromised.

Evenings were no different. Every night he transformed the master bathroom into a luxurious spa. The aroma of lavender candles strategically arranged throughout illuminated the spacious bathroom. While the Jacuzzi bubbled with soothing bath salts awaiting Summer's arrival.

"Oh, Nick, you didn't have to do this. It smells so good in here." *This I can get use to.*

"No Problem. Now stop talking and get undressed."

Summer knitted her eyebrows together. "Huh?"

Nick chuckled. "Come on get undressed."

"I'm not getting undressed in front of you." Summer told him indignantly.

"Woman, stop playing, I've seen it all before."

"Yeah, before I was thirty pounds fatter. I'm not getting undressed in front of you, Nick."

The Mexican standoff began as they both stood facing each other, arms crossed over their chests, neither moving.

"All right…already…you always have to have things your way." Summer ranted as she pulled and yanked at every article of clothing until she was booty butt naked.

"Satisfied?"

Taking a few steps bringing him closer, Nick touched her swollen belly. "Now was that so bad?"

"No, but why–"

"Did I want you to get undressed in front of me?"

"Yeah."

"I just wanted to see for myself."

"What?"

Nick let his eyes seductively scan Summer from head to toe then reverse again. "If you were still…sexy."

Summer blushed with embarrassment as she shyly whispered, "And?"

"Most definitely."

❧ ❧ ❧ ❧ ❧

With Nick lavishing so much attention on her, she found it almost impossible to control her emotions. He was making it difficult for her to keep her guard up. She didn't know how or when things between she and Nick slipped back to where they'd been before he walked out on her. The only element missing was passion.

With Nick's new and improved attitude, she lost focus. Her goal was to get him to understand she was afraid of telling him about the pregnancy for a number of reasons, rejection being the first. She was afraid if she'd told him he would have rejected both her and the baby. She had survived his walking out, had pulled herself together, had managed to get on with her life and had planned to raise her baby on her own. Telling him about the baby wasn't an option. Neither was having herself and her baby rejected like old discarded dishrags.

Summer fell in love the moment she heard the rapid heartbeat at eight weeks of gestation. As she listened to the evidence of life her body would house for nine months, she knew she made the right choice. If she had tracked Nick down back then and told him about the baby, she was early enough in her pregnancy to have aborted it. Hadn't he told her to do so if she'd ever became pregnant with his baby?

As the months passed and she grew, another fear began to take root. Nick would snatch away without regard what was most precious to her. That would be her punishment for keeping their baby a secret.

Summer had to convince him at the time she thought the safest thing to do was to keep the baby a secret. She needed him to understand she'd lost just about everyone that was important to her; everyone that she'd loved. Her parents had moved miles away just before she and Nick started to date. Then just as she believed he'd be a permanent fixture in her life, he moved on too. How did he now expect her to handle being rejected, forced to have an abortion, or have her baby taken away? Hadn't she lost enough?

As good as he made her feel, Summer wasn't one bit disillusioned. She knew the man too well. Sure, he treated her like a princess and pampered her from the time her eyes opened in the morning until they closed at night. She was aware his actions were primarily for that of the baby. Countless times he told her, "I just want the baby to be safe. That's my main concern, so let me take care of you."

Summer believed with all her heart he'd fallen madly in love with their baby. With every opportunity he touched, kissed or talked to her belly. He'd done the one thing he'd sworn to her he would never do, give his love, his heart to another person. Summer was now certain that for this reason he would honor his threat of filing for full custody of their unborn child. She wished a million times she'd told him about the baby. Now in hindsight, it would have been better to be rejected than to lose her baby.

She clung to the hope that when she told him everything he'd believe her intentions were never to deceive or hurt him. All she wanted to do was to keep their baby safe, to keep their baby alive.

Chapter 19

Each evening the pair retired to Nick's king size bed for the night. Summer watched television until she drifted off to sleep, while Nick brought documents from work to bed.

She'd complain, "Do you always have to bring work stuff to bed?"

After *light* reading he'd turn the channel from whatever she'd been watching to the nightly news, usually *Date Line.* If circumstances were different anyone who looked from the outside would have guessed they were a happily married couple.

Shifting in her sleep, Summer rolled from her back onto her side. She threw a slender arm leisurely across Nick's midsection, bringing her swollen belly to rest against his side. A slow smile curved his full lips as his eyes traveled from the television to rest on Summer's soft body cuddled next to him. Having her around all the time was more pleasant than he expected. He was never the type of man who always had to have a woman around him all of the time. Yes, he appreciated the beauty of women, and all they offered to satisfy his carnal cravings. However, it wasn't a necessity to be chained to one.

After that debacle with Veronica, he absolutely refused to bring another woman home to his bed. Other women after her were always taken to luxury hotels. The acts they performed were strictly to alleviate a basic primal need, nothing more, nothing less. The instant a female companion, aka, bed buddy questioned, "Why can't we go to your place or my place?" She was history. Nick didn't play those games.

By the time Summer came along Nick was just plain 'ole tired. Tired of women throwing themselves at him. Tired of women pretending to love him. Tired of women trying to take him home to meet their parents. Tired of women after a month of dating hinting at marriage and a family. What he was most tired of was sleeping and waking up in hotel beds with women he didn't care anything about. *There has to be more to it than this.*

Summer hadn't been anything like the others. She didn't expect him to pamper or spoil her with expensive gifts. Her main interest was in getting to know the *real* Nicholas Stiles, not the wealthy businessman. She wanted to know what he was like as a child. Did he enjoy being an only child? Or did he hate it at times as much as she did? Who taught him to ride a bike? What was his favorite color? What made him happy? What made him sad? Why had he decided on the corporate world and not follow in the footsteps of his father and grandfather and become a lawyer?

Nick detested nosey women who asked too many questions and talked too much. Any other time he would've dismissed the prying questions. Summer's inquiries, however, were a sincere attempt to get to know him. He found himself intrigued with her. Other women assumed his main ambition in life was to gain epic wealth and status. Whereas, Summer's astuteness brought her to the conclusion that he wasn't driven by wealth or status. Though he developed a number of successful businesses from the ground up, his true passion was to recreate. He'd been blessed with the ability of taking a failing company and recreating it into a thriving business. After three to five years of the company performing well, he would sell to the highest bidder for a lucrative profit.

"Wow, Nick, do you know how many jobs you saved? How many people you kept from the unemployment line and possibly becoming homeless statistics?"

The others never appreciated the true man he was beneath the tailored suits, designer shoes, and expensive cars. They didn't care about the long hours he worked to keep a deteriorating company from going under. Nor did they care about how he literally saved people's livelihoods. Their only interest was in how stacked his financial portfolio was.

With Summer, Nick changed little by little. Changes he himself felt were uncharacteristic even for him. Though he made it clear he wasn't interested in a serious relationship he began to exclusively date her. And for the first time in years he had welcomed a female presence into his sanctuary, his home. Initially he'd cursed himself when he offered, "Let me make dinner for you, Beautiful." Later, he learned his reservations were for naught. Summer respected his space. When the time came in their relationship when she'd spend a night or two he never had to tell her, "Don't leave this or that here." Whatever she brought with her to his place went right along with her when she left. There was never any straggling panties, bras, or nightgowns. Not even so much as a forgotten toothbrush to announce she'd been there.

There was one change he would never allow as long as he lived. After Veronica's betrayal he promised himself he'd never let another woman get close to his heart. Breaking up with Summer was the right thing to do. She'd manage to wiggle her way near his heart. If he weren't careful she would be the one reason he would rethink his position on love. And as much as he cared about her, he would never love her.

While away from her he reflected on their relationship. Summer was the only woman he ever dated that never, not once, asked him for anything. No jewelry, furs, shopping sprees, nothing. It wasn't like he couldn't afford it. He wasn't a stingy man. He didn't mind showering beautiful women with gifts.

On Summer's birthday when Nick presented her with a small package wrapped in aqua paper with a white satin ribbon, her hands slightly trembled as she delicately opened the package. She was in awe as diamond earrings sparkled and winked at her. Nick ignored how his heart fluttered when she looked from the exquisite gift then back to him.

"Nick, these are so beautiful. Thank you, no one's ever given me such a gorgeous gift before."

He'd never experienced sincere gratitude from a woman. The others always act as if they had deserved his exquisite gifts.

Who was he fooling? Nick's feelings ran deeper than merely caring for Summer. It had taken months of his being without her to see the light, to see that their relationship was beyond the physical. That night on the plane back to Philly, he confessed to himself that he wanted her back in his life. In the recesses of his mind, thousands of feet in the air he toyed with the idea that one day he could bring himself to love her.

Just as quickly as he toyed with the idea it fled his mind as he stood face to face with a very pregnant Summer. Instantaneously rage rushed through his entire being. He had been played again; in spite of all the defenses he constructed to guard his heart. Here he was making plans to build a solid future, taking a chance on opening his heart, only to be made a fool of again.

What started off as pleasant memories of the petite woman next to him came crashing down like an implosion as anger and doubt overtook him as he hissed a string of expletives.

Nick removed Summer's hand from his midsection as he left the bed.

Chapter 20

Summer, a light sleeper was aware when Nick left the bed in haste. She sensed his irritation as he mumbled angrily to himself. *What in the world is wrong with him?*

Maybe he forgot to do something for work. He had told her he was in the process of taking over another company. Maybe things weren't going as scheduled.

Summer slept off and on, an hour passed and Nick hadn't returned to bed. She was getting worried. Swinging her legs over the side of the bed, waddling down the hall to his office, "He's not in there." Neither was he in the hall bathroom, guest bedroom, den or kitchen. She was relieved when she found him in the living room.

Nick sat in an armchair gazing out the window at nothing in particular. Something wasn't right he appeared troubled. As she eased up to the chair, Summer wasn't sure if she should approach him. His face was unreadable.

"Nick, are you coming back to bed?"

"No, go back to bed." He commanded in a chilly tone. Summer stiffened. He was upset with her, but why?

"Did I do something?"

"I don't know. You tell me Summer, did you?" His voice dripped with sarcasm as the muscles in his left jaw twitched from being clenched so tight.

The atmosphere was thick with tension. Summer quietly eased over to the sofa, sat down, and braced herself for the storm. *This is it. I'm tired. I want this over once and for all.*

With that resolved the next question she asked was the impetus that made all hell break loose. "Is there something you want to know?" Summer said with a hint of an attitude boosting her confidence a little bit.

Nick rose from the chair, took a few long strides then planted his large frame on the coffee table in front of the sofa. Leaning forward on his elbows coming into Summer's space intimidating the hell out of her.

Here we go again, Summer thought to herself.

Seconds ticked by as they stared at each other. Summer was determined to meet his stony stare. *I'm gonna stand up to him this time.*

If she just held her stare, kept her eyes locked with his, she'd be all right. She dropped her gaze the moment Nick's features became distorted. Her resolve to stand up to him crumbled even further when he spoke.

"Yeah, Summer, I want to know why you didn't tell me you were pregnant."

Summer whispered, "I wanted to."

"Speak up! I can't hear you!"

"I said I wanted to tell you, Nick."

"Why didn't you Summer, huh?"

"I didn't tell you because at first I was going to have an abortion."

"Why?"

"Because you didn't want to be with me anymore, and if you didn't want me I figured you wouldn't want a baby either."

"Did I ever tell you I didn't want children?"

"You told me never to find myself pregnant by you. You said if I did you'd tell me to flush it."

The pain was evident in her quivering voice as she replayed his words back to him.

I did tell her that. He remembered the very night he had told her. "What happened, why didn't you get the abortion?"

Tears slowly ran down her cheeks. *He really wanted me to kill our baby.* Wiping tears away with the palm of her hand she silently wished she could wipe the pain away just as easily. "I went to the appointment with every intention of ending the pregnancy but I just couldn't bring myself to do it." Slowly she pulled her gaze up to meet his. Nick's demeanor was unmoved; her eyes drifted from his gaze to the floor.

"Summer, I'm still not getting why you never tried to contact me."

"I thought if I had told you early on that you would have *made* me have an abortion or deny that the baby was yours." Summer took a deep breath then added, "And when I wanted to tell you it never felt like the time was right."

He didn't argue with her on the point about the abortion, she was right. Hell, he would have driven her to the appointment and waited to make sure the deed was done. Honestly, he may have even denied the kid given his history with Veronica.

Nick was never one to hold back, he spoke his mind regardless how blunt or abrasive.

"Yeah, well you're right. I probably would have told you to get an abortion. But never the less I should have had a say so in the decision. Thanks to you, I never had that chance. And what is this lame excuse about the timing not being right? What happened to when you turned three, four… hell, five months pregnant! You could've told me then. Instead I come to your house to find you seven months pregnant, Summer! Seven, damn months!"

Anger was fully consuming him as he bit out every sharp, piercing word. As each word exploded from his mouth his body propelled in Summer's direction, making her extremely uncomfortable.

Summer cringed with every word. Backing up and shifting to the left, attempting to put some distance between them because he was getting angry again and flirting with being out of control. His left eyebrow began twitching involuntarily, signaling he was reaching his boiling point.

Summer's efforts to put space between them only infuriated him. He grabbed her by the shoulders with a firm hold, "Stop moving and answer me damn it!"

The moment he put his hands on Summer the confrontation escalated to a whole new level. Nick had crossed the line. All of his ranting, raving, and yelling was one thing, but this touching stuff while angry was something else. Every fiber she used to maintain her composure shattered, "Nick you promised.....you promised you wouldn't hurt me or the baby."

Quickly he released his hold as she misinterpreted his gesture. "Summer, I'm not going to hurt you or the baby. I just want some answers. Please just tell me why you hid your pregnancy." So far nothing she said made since to him.

He waited as she calmed down and found her voice. Her lips trembled when she spoke.

"I was afraid that you would be angry like you are right now."

Nick nodded in agreement. He was past the point of angry. "Anything else?"

She nodded her head. "Yes." Summer wanted to tell him her greatest fear, but would he hold it against her? Would he truly understand her reasoning? Would he care?

"Well?" Nick said impatiently waiting for an answer that would put him his mind at ease.

"I was afraid of you, afraid of what you would do. I honestly thought I would never see you again. I had no idea you would ever come back to see me. I didn't think you would care about the baby."

When Nick didn't say anything, her heart began to sink. He still didn't believe her. She could tell by the way he looked through her as if she wasn't there.

"Please, Nick, don't..." She whispered as tears fell from her eyes.

Nick wouldn't let himself feel anything for Summer as he disassociated any affection he'd ever held for her. She had kept her secret and now she had to pay the consequences. He would handle this situation like any other opposition. It was cut and dry.

"Don't what Summer? You were willing to keep my child away from me. I'll be the first to admit I didn't want children, but that gave you no right Summer, no right, not to tell me you were having a baby and I was the father."

He walked over to the window and stared out into the darkness. That's just how Summer made him feel, as if he was in complete darkness. He couldn't stand to look at her right now.

Summer sat quietly crying. *He doesn't understand I have to make him understand.*

She rose from her sitting position to stand next to Nick.

"Nick, look at me please."

He ignored her request as he kept his gaze focused ahead.

"Please believe me, I love you and never wanted it to be like this. I was just so scared of you. I knew you'd be angry with me, and that your anger would strike out to hurt me in the worst way. The only way that could destroy me…"

Summer's eyes pleaded with Nick, though he never looked at her. "Nick, can't you understand how I felt? How scared I was?"

"If I had never came back to see you, would you have eventually told me about the baby?" Nick already knew the answer to his question; he just had to hear her say it.

Summer wanted to lie, wanted to tell him that eventually she would have told him.

Silence wrapped around them like a heavy cloak. She couldn't bear to tell him that her intentions were to never let him know that their child existed if that's what it would take to keep her child. Tears continued to fall as no words would come from her mouth to tell him the truth.

Summer's silence confirmed Nick's suspicions. Glaring at her in disgust, he sneered, "Just what I thought. You're no different than Veronica, Summer. You're just as much of a conniving whore as she was."

Stalking off, he left Summer stunned and crying all alone in the living room.

Summer cringed at the words Nick hurled slapping her in the face. He'd said she was like Veronica. Veronica had used him, claimed he was the father of a baby she knew wasn't his. She hadn't loved Nick like Summer had. The only thing she'd been interested in was his money.

Emotions overtook her that were indescribable as she thought about how he'd compared her to a woman he downright loathed. She *was* carrying his baby. And she had never used him the whole time they'd dated. Summer was devastated by Nick's unfair judgment of her. She wanted to hate him for being so cruel, killing her with his words. But hating him would mean hating her child that was just as much a part of him as it was of her.

With lead legs, Summer made her way to Nick's bedroom removing all of her items and taking them to the guest bedroom. Dropping everything on the floor, she crawled beneath the sheet and comforter of the queen size bed. Tears drenched the pillow as she cried until exhaustion and weariness claimed her.

❧ ❧ ❧ ❧ ❧

"Nick, man, what's the hell wrong with you?" Kevin asked as he opened the front door of his townhouse to an enraged Nick.

"Just let me in." He pushed pass Kevin not waiting for an invitation to come in.

Stopping mid-step, he pivot on his heels, "My bad, do you have company?" Nick asked as he looked around Kevin's bachelor pad.

"Naw man, come in and sit down. You want a drink?"

"Yeah, get me the usual."

Kevin excused himself as Nick settled on the leather sofa in the living room. In no time he returned with a beer for himself and a double scotch for Nick. That was his usual drink whenever he was in a mood about something. Handing the scotch to Nick, he frowned as he watched his friend gulp down the drink without coming up for air.

"Dude what gives? What got you all ready to explode?" *This time.*

"Summer." Nick stated with irritation.

Kevin nodded his head as the name rolled of Nick's tongue. Without saying a word, he gave Nick a look that told him to proceed. Kevin sat quiet as he told him about the confrontation he had with Summer.

Letting out a low whistle, Kevin asked in disbelief, "Man, you called the girl a whore to her face?" He didn't even mention the fact that he had compared her to Veronica. Anyone close to Nick knew he detested the woman. Did that mean he felt the same about Summer? *Mmm, poor Summer.*

Nick nodded his head. "I was so pissed off I lost control. I didn't mean to say that to her."

"How much control did you lose?" Kevin gaze was intense as he looked at his friend.

Nick hissed, "Damn, Kev, man I told you once don't make me tell you again. I would never put my hands on Summer to hurt her."

Throwing up his hands signaling he hadn't meant to offend Nick. "A'ight man, my bad. I just know this whole situation has you uptight. I don't want to see you do anything stupid."

"Brotha, uptight ain't the word. I've never let a woman get as close to me as Summer. Not even Veronica. I started feeling things for her I never felt for any woman."

Kevin grinned at his friend. "Don't tell me my man done went and got himself bit by the love bug."

He cracked up when Nick let out a string of expletives. "I wouldn't say love, but I do care about her a lot, especially since she's carrying my baby. Never thought this day would come. Man, that's why I'm all messed up in the head right now. It really hurts to know if I never found out she was pregnant she would have kept my kid from me."

Kevin held his grin. Nick was in denial. He'd never admitted to anyone that a woman had hurt him. Women didn't hurt the invincible Nick Stiles. It was usually the other way around. Not even Veronica had hurt him. He was more outraged, his ego bruised, than hurt. He had never cared for her the way he had for Summer. Nick himself had just acknowledged as much. Kevin didn't understand it; he saw it plain as day. Why couldn't Nick see it? He was in love with Summer. How else could she have hurt him if he didn't love her?

"Man what's up with that goofy grin?"

Shrugging his broad shoulders, Kevin replied, "Oh, nothing man, nothing at all." Kevin didn't dare push. Nick eventually would conclude he was in love with Summer. Kevin just hoped it wasn't too late. A person could only take but so much harshness. As far as he was concerned Nick was tittering on the fine line of being abusive in his behavior towards Summer. He had indirectly told him as much. Whether he meant to treat her that way wasn't the issue, he had. Kevin kept his faith in his friend, his brother. Once Nick simmered down and was thinking with a rational brain in that stubborn head of his, he'd see the error of his ways and make things right with her. After all Nick loved the girl, and to Kevin's surprise embraced the idea of fatherhood.

Kevin made a mental note to restock his condom supply. Rising to his feet, heading to the kitchen, he yelled over his shoulder, "You want a beer, man."

"No, I'm cool."

The two men talked for hours. When Nick stepped outside a new day was dawning. He'd been so angry, needing space from Summer that he'd left her alone all night unattended.

"So much for making sure her and the baby was taken care of."

Chapter 21

Over the next few days, Summer and Nick barely said two words to each other, only speaking when necessary. His stubbornness and inability to forgive were major character flaws she found unbearable to cope with. If it weren't for her present physical condition, she would've packed her bags and left days ago. Instead, she moved into the guest bedroom after that night and avoided Nick at all cost.

Nick had taken to playing the avoiding game as well, spending more hours at the office leaving Summer in the care of Joan. She didn't mind at all. Joan was good company and she liked the older woman a lot. Though Joan was old enough to be her mother they shared some of the same interests. They both loved romance novels, game shows, soap operas and crossword puzzles. When Summer begged her to watch Jerry Springer with her she'd playfully remarked, "Chile you got me watching this silly mess." Within the first five minutes of the show the two would be laughing hysterically at the crazy charades paraded on national television.

Joan was a good listener and a wise woman. With everything weighing so heavy on Summer, she confided in the older woman. Talking to her parents, Ava or Starr wasn't an option. Joan sat next to her on the bed closely listening as she told her every facet of her relationship with Nick. From how they met, to the week they spent at his cabin, to how she was heartbroken when he ended their relationship, and how surprised she was to learn she was pregnant. Joan was the only soul she had told he had threatened to get custody of their baby and how she feared he would go through with doing so.

Joan waited patiently until she was done talking. Taking Summer's small hand in hers, she said, "I've worked for Nick, for ten years now –"

"I thought it was seven years." Summer interjected cutting Joan off with a confused look.

Joan softly chuckled. "Nothing gets by you when it comes to that man."

Summer sheepishly smiled. It was true, she knew just about everything there was to know about the man. "I'm sorry."

"Oh, it's all right sweetie. I worked for him the first three years cleaning his office building at night. He was looking for a housekeeper, when he asked if I wanted the position I jumped at it. Anyway, back to you, sweetie. I know he can be hard, but he's a fair man. I know you heard about that stankin' huzzy Veronica."

Summer wanted to laugh at Joan's description of Veronica, however, her pain wouldn't allow her. Nick had said she was a conniving whore just like her. A hurt expression flashed across Summer's face that wasn't missed by the older woman.

"What's wrong sweetie?" Joan asked as she patted Summer's hand.

"Nothing, I was just thinking about something. Go ahead, I'm sorry."

Joan gently squeezed her hand. *Poor child is hurting so bad. I hope that boy get his act together. Can't he see that this chile loves him? I swear sometimes he's as stubborn as a mule.* "After that gal, Nick never trusted women the same. Never settled down with anyone more than a month if that long, until you came along. Summer you're special to him. Just give him time. He's a good man, he'll come around."

"I don't know Joan; he's hardly said anything to me since the other night."

"Just give him time sweetie." Joan encouraged as she stood up. "Well, I'm gonna leave you to your afternoon nap. I need to get dinner started."

Summer also stood from her seated position and opened her arms to hug the older woman. Joan stepped into the embrace and held Summer closely to her large bosom as she gently rubbed her back. Summer could've stayed there all day.

What Summer said next to the older woman brought tears to her eyes. "Thank you so much for listening to me and not judging me. I know I've messed up big time by getting myself pregnant. But you've been so kind to me, helping me and taking care of me just how my mother would do if she was here."

Breaking the embrace, Joan held Summer away from her, "Oh, ain't you 'bout the sweetest little thing. I'm glad I can be here to help you sweetie. Now come on and get some rest."

Joan waited until Summer comfortably settled herself back onto the bed before she left the room.

After Joan left Summer focused on the ceiling as Joan's words tumbled around in her head. "Give him time." *Time for what?* She was tired of giving Nick time and everything else. Tired of taking a backseat to him. Tired of always putting what he wanted first. Tired of being afraid of him and what he might do to her. Most of all she was tired of loving a man who didn't love her the way she deserved to be loved. Or for that matter, loved her at all. A man who refused to find it within his heart—that is if the scoundrel had one—to understand everything she'd been dealing with for the past several months. He hadn't even considered how all alone she'd felt when she found out she was pregnant knowing he didn't want her or a baby. How miserable she was for the first four months of pregnancy with morning sickness every single day, sometimes three to four times a day. How she had disappointed her parents by getting herself pregnant by a man who simply walked out of her life. Even in this day and age she was embarrassed when her co-workers found out she was pregnant without the father in the picture. Thank goodness for Starr and Ava. When the tongues went a flapping they'd come to her defense putting anyone in check.

If all that wasn't bad enough, he continued to hang the threat of taking her baby away from her over her head. Sometimes she felt her fears were unjustified because the ultimate decision to grant custody of the child to either parent was that of a judge. Summer knew she was a good person, didn't have a criminal record, was educated and had a good job. Anyone who knew her knew she was capable of being an excellent mother.

Pondering all these things, Summer came to a decision to release her love for Nick. Holding onto it was too painful, too destructive. As much as it hurt, she came to the realization that he would never love her. She held onto the hope and even fantasized that in time he would come to love her. No longer disillusioned she accepted he was incapable of loving her. It was evident in his behavior, how he treated her. She still could not believe he had sunk to the level of calling her out of her name.

For the first time in days Summer slept peaceful. Her decision to purge Nick from her heart and her soul was finally freeing her.

❧ ❧ ❧ ❧ ❧

After waking up from her nap Summer called her mother. Four days had gone by since she'd spoken to her. If she had called any sooner, her mother would've sensed something was amiss. Her mother had an internal honing device, which alerted her when the tiniest thing was out of sync with her daughter. The last thing Summer wanted was for her mother to notice her troubled spirit.

"Hi mommy, how are you?"

"Hi baby, I'm doing fine, how 'bout you? Have you had any more contractions?"

"I'm doing well, mommy." Summer lied. "And no, I haven't had anymore contractions."

"You call me the minute you go into labor so your daddy and I can get to you as fast as we can." Her mother wanted to tell her she didn't know why she hadn't let her come take care of her instead of staying with that despicable man. She didn't want to upset her Summer, so she held her peace…this time.

"You know I will mommy." Summer assured her mother.

"Mmm, I hope my first grandbaby wait until next week sometime. The weatherman said we're gonna get a heavy snowstorm in the next day or two like the one y'all had last month.

Talking with her mother lifted Summer's spirits. She'd felt better than she had in days. Lately her mother expressed so much excitement about the prospect of becoming a grandmother. Summer felt horrible in the beginning of her pregnancy. She had let her parents down; she heard it in their voices every time she talked to them.

After four months of being pregnant, she finally got up the courage to tell her parents. They didn't hide the fact she had disappointed them. Her mother flat out told her that nothing good ever came from a younger woman dating an older man. "The only thing the old fool would want with a girl twelve years younger than him is to manipulate and use her." Her father said he had expected better from his daughter. "I raised you to know better than to come home unmarried and in family way. Princess, what were you thinking? If you were gonna mess around you should've been more careful."

She was devastated to say the least by her parents' reaction. It was as if she hadn't done anything right her entire life. The one time she screwed up they hadn't been shy about letting her know it.

However, as the months went by her parents came around and were thrilled they were about to become first time grandparents.

"Oh, really? Well, I hope this little bumpkin holds out too. But I don't know mommy, at my appointment last week the baby had dropped into the birthing position."

"Chile that means you can go anytime. Just try to hold out for mommy, okay?"

Summer laughed. "Mommy, you are a trip. When this baby decides to come I won't be able to do anything to stop it."

"You're right about that baby. My water broke with you while I was in the meat department at the supermarket. You should've seen your daddy fussing at me. Talkin' 'bout, 'I told you Nita to keep your hardheaded behind home. If you have my baby in this supermarket …' Baby your daddy made me so mad. You know I wasn't having him talk to me like that. I said, 'What James? What are you gonna do? Nothing! Now shut up and get me to the hospital!' We argued the whole time on the way to the hospital." Summer's mother laughed as she remembered that afternoon some twenty-six years ago.

Summer laughed at her mother. *They've always fussed, even before I was born. It's a wonder they haven't killed each other yet.* "Well, thank goodness that won't happen to me. I won't be at anybody's supermarket."

Mother and daughter talked several more minutes before the call was ended.

"Mommy, I'm gonna go now. I just wanted to check in with you. Tell daddy I said 'hi' and that I love him. And I love you, too."

"I love you too, baby."

❧ ❧ ❧ ❧ ❧

Knock, Knock, Knock

"Come in."

"Summer, I was just coming to see if you wanted to venture out into the dining room for dinner tonight?" Joan asked with a grin, sure of what Summer's answer would be.

"Yes ma'am! I'm tired of lying in this bed."

"Come on precious let me help you get up." Joan helped her from the bed. Hand in hand, they walked to the dining room.

Joan for a split second envied Summer's mother. This is how she imagined it would've been if she had a daughter. Summer touched her heart earlier in the day when she referred to her as a mother figure. For so many years Joan loathed herself for having that botched abortion when she was barley twenty years old leaving her barren.

Joan admired Summer for keeping her baby in spite of being young, single and alone. She wished many a days she had done the same. That she hadn't listened to that good for nothing Sam Waters. He promised to marry her if she had the abortion telling her, "Joanie, we're too young to have a baby. Let's wait until I finish my pharmacy training then we'll get married and start a family." That was until he found out she was "damaged goods" as he put it. Joan was devastated when Sam ran off with her best friend Alice.

No, she would not judge Summer. She would support and give her guidance as if she were her own daughter. No one was there to do that for her when she was a young woman facing a life altering decision. A decision that brought her years of pain and loneliness because she had listened to a man whom obviously never loved her.

Joan and Summer enjoyed each other's company as they ate their dinner. The food was so delicious Summer ignored the faint twinges in the lower part of her abdomen. The faint twinges felt nowhere as painful as the other contractions that sent her running to the hospital almost two and a half weeks ago. The rest of the evening slight discomfort poked and prodded in intervals every hour or so. Summer ignored them thinking they would pass if she retired early to bed. "I must've been on my feet too long after dinner," she told herself as she gingerly stepped out of the tub toweling off. "I'll go lie down, that should stop them before they get too bad."

❧ ❧ ❧ ❧ ❧

Somewhere around midnight, she heard Nick come into the room.

"Summer, are you awake?"

She pretended to be asleep. She didn't want to deal with him or his mess. He didn't want to hear what she had to say anyway, so why was he bothering her? He believed what he wanted; nothing she said to him would change that.

Not getting a response he left the room. He was sure she was awake; he'd just heard her turn off the television not more than ten minutes before he walked into the room. Since the night of their confrontation Summer kept to herself, mostly in the guestroom reading and watching television or talking on the phone. If she was in the den relaxing when he came home, the second she heard him go into his bedroom to change she'd retreat to the guestroom. Every time he looked into her eyes she'd shift her gaze as if trying to hide something. Her efforts were futile; he saw the pain each and every time. He had hurt her, wounded her. Even in his anger that night he witnessed how her face contorted in pain when he called her a whore. His anger consumed him to the point he had resorted to being down right cruel to her. He wanted so badly to go back in the room and make her acknowledge his presence, to tell her how sorry he was for hurting her.

Yeah, that's what he would do. Heading back to Summer, Nick was stilled by a tiny voice. *She doesn't want to be bothered with you.* His arrogance ignored the voice as he took another step and then stopped. *You went too far this time.*

Summer had never outright ignored him. She had always been accommodating, at his beck and call. Nick had taken it for granted, expected it; not recognizing she had only done those things because she had loved him. All of that was changing. Summer was letting go and he could feel it.

Chapter 22

Between the hours of five and five-thirty the next morning Summer was awaken by a contraction a bit more intense than the previous night. She groaned, "Not now baby," to the tiny life within her as if it would obey.

As anxious as she was to have her baby, she was in no way prepared for its arrival. Mulling over in her mind all the things she had for the baby, she came to the conclusion she wasn't ready yet. *Seven undershirts, three gowns in yellow, pastel green and white, five bibs and a box of newborn pampers.* That was it. Her brain was preoccupied with so much drama she hadn't thought about shopping.

"Trifling, just trifling. Mommy would have a natural born fit." Summer mumbled to herself sucking her teeth. Pushing herself up, swinging her legs over the side of the bed, and standing up slowly to keep the blood from rushing to her head, Summer made her way to the bathroom. "I'll go online and order some more stuff this morning." With overnight express mail she would have just about everything she needed by tomorrow this time.

Within two steps of entering the bathroom, she encountered Nick coming out of his office. He was already dressed in a business suit that was tailored made to fit his very masculine physique. Summer was angry with herself as she admired how good he looked. She had to get out of his environment as soon as possible if she was serious about letting the man go.

When their eyes locked Summer was the first to avert her line of vision. Not ready to face him head on she quickened her pace nearly slamming the bathroom door before locking it. Once on the inside, she leaned against the door and held the lower part of her abdomen as another contraction began to form.

A frown marred Nick's handsome features. *Since when did she lock doors around here?* The small voice taunted, *since you start acting like a maniac.* Nick groaned as he wondered how long she would continue to avoid him.

Looking at his watch he noted it was six-fifteen; he had to leave if he didn't want to get stuck in rush hour traffic. Today he was headed to Harrisburg on business and couldn't afford to be late. Joan wasn't due to arrive until seven-thirty, which meant Summer would be alone for a little over an hour.

Knock, Knock

"Yes?"

"Can you open this door?" Nick hated talking through doors.

Summer's heart began to beat rapidly as she gripped the doorknob.

"Yes?"

Nick's stomach tightened as he looked down into her face. Her eyes still held the hurt and pain from a few nights ago. Hurt and pain he had caused.

"I have to leave out earlier than usual this morning. Will you be okay until Joan comes in?"

"I'll be okay."

"Are you sure?" His gut was telling him something wasn't quite right.

"Yes."

Nick was hesitant as his gut continued to gnaw and nag at him. "All…right… then, I'll be on my way."

"Okay."

Summer's thumping heart returned to normal when she heard Nick leave. After emptying her bladder, she brushed her teeth then turned on the water for her morning shower. Adjusting the temperature of the water just right she stepped under the spray. The hot water streaming down her body was soothing, helping to relax the tightening in her lower abdomen. Grabbing shower gel from the caddy, Summer lathered her body from head to toe with a bath sponge. As she stood under the spray rinsing the suds away, she wished she could rinse Nick away from her life just as easily. Impossible. She was forever connected to the man for life. As long as the tiny life in her womb existed, was healthy and thriving she would have an unbreakable link to him.

❧ ❧ ❧ ❧ ❧

Joan arrived on time as expected her usual chipper self.

"Hi sweetness." She greeted Summer who sat at the kitchen table with her laptop.

"Hi Joan, how's it going?"

"I'm good. How 'bout you?"

Summer dare not tell her about the contractions, she'd be on the phone calling Nick with the quickness.

"I'm doing good, too." Summer lied.

"That's my girl. Have you had breakfast yet?" Joan asked as she moved around the kitchen going from the refrigerator to the cupboards.

"No, I was just sitting here ordering the little bambino some things. You know I hardly have anything for this baby. I don't even have a crib."

Joan chuckled softly. "I'm not surprised, you've had your plate full lately." Joan witnessed the strained atmosphere everyday she came to work.

"Yeah, tell me 'bout it." Summer halfway joked as she put items in the shopping chart. "Hey you want to see want I ordered?"

Joan pulled out a chair and sat next to Summer. "Sure let's see what you got here."

Summer showed Joan all of the adorable baby apparel in the shopping cart. Joan "ooohed and aaahed" over everything. "Summer these things are so cute. That baby of yours is going to be the best dressed baby in town."

"I know that's right, Joan."

Standing Joan said, "Let me get breakfast started. Want anything in particular?"

"Whatever you make will be fine."

"Pancakes, bacon and eggs sound good?"

"Yup, sounds good."

❧ ❧ ❧ ❧ ❧

By ten that morning, Summer had several more contractions lasting forty-five seconds to one full minute. She hadn't said anything to Joan even when Joan mentioned Nick called asking, "Can you stay with Summer a little later than usual? I'll be tied up longer than expected." Throughout the rest of the day, the contractions began to regulate themselves coming every seven to ten minutes apart.

To Summer's disappointment the weather channel reported the snowstorm in the Carolinas was responsible for the delay of all flights from North Carolina to Philadelphia. This meant her parents were grounded until the storm eased up or passed over the region.

Her disappointment slightly dissipated upon hearing Starr's voice on the other end of the phone.

"Starr it's me, Summer. It's time."

"A'ight, girl. You need me to come get you?"

"No, I think it'll be faster if I meet you at the hospital."

"Hey, should I call Ava?"

Summer quickly contemplated calling her. Ava hadn't gone away on vacation in almost two years. She didn't want Starr to call her because she knew Ava would be on the first thing smoking from Arizona. She was living it up being pampered at a five star posh spa. A vacation well deserved. No, she would not call her and disrupt her vacation. Ava would be mad, but Summer didn't care. *She'll get over it.* Besides, she was due back home in two days.

"No, Starr. I don't want to bother her while she's having the time of her life."

"You sure? You know she's going to be mad at you?"

"Yup. I'll call her after the baby's born, then that way if she wants to come home she'll only miss one day of her vacation."

"Okay, but I warned you."

"Starr, get off the phone and get your butt to the hospital before I have this baby at home fooling with you and Ava, and whether she's gonna be mad at me or not!"

"Ooh, my bad, Boo. I'm on my way."

Summer called down the hall, "Joan… Joan… come here for a minute please."

Joan hustled into the room in a hurry. She heard the urgency in Summer's voice, "What's wrong sweetie?"

Summer weakly smiled. "I think I'm in labor for real this time."

"Oh, I better call Nick." Joan said as she hurried to the nearest phone.

"Joan, no, please don't bother him. What if I'm not really in labor and they send me home?"

"Summer, sweetie, I think we should call him anyway." Joan gently insisted.

"Please, Joan, can't we wait until I get situated at the hospital? That way we'll know if this is the real thing or not." She reasoned with the older woman.

Summer winced as another contraction hit her petite body. Joan rushed to her side.

"All right, come on sweetie let's get you dressed and out of here."

The cab ride to the hospital was disastrous. An accident three blocks from the hospital had traffic moving at a snail's pace.

Summer groaned, "Only me. Only something like this would happen to me. I must have a freakin' black cloud over my head."

Joan affectionately patted Summer's arm. "Everything's gonna be okay sweetie. You just hold on." Leaning forward, Joan banged on the plexi-glass partition. "Hurry up unless you want a baby born back here!" *Damn cabdrivers always trying to run the meter. If he'd gone the way I told him we'd be there by now. Gonna have a nerve to want a tip!*

❧ ❧ ❧ ❧ ❧

Checked into the birthing suite on the maternity floor, Summer waited for Starr to show up. Just as promised, she blew in like a whirlwind.

"Girl, are you ready for this?" Starr asked with excitement.

"As ready as I'll ever be."

As promised, Joan waited until Summer was checked in and settled before calling Nick. He wasn't pleased to say the least that Joan had waited to call him.

"What do you mean she's been having contractions all day? Why didn't you say something when I talked to you earlier?"

Joan bristled from the curtness Nick's voice held. "Calm down boy and watch your tone with me. I ain't one of your little gal friends. Summer wanted to be sure the contractions were the real thing before I called you."

Nick rolled his eyes as he listened to Joan rant. Sometimes she thought she was his boss and not the other way around. "I'm on my way. I'll be there as soon as possible."

Summer's and Starr's gaze went to the door when she came back into the room. Neither missed the aggravated expression on her face.

"Joan, what's wrong?" Summer asked.

"Nick isn't pleased at all. Said we should've called him sooner. He's on his way."

"Joan, don't worry. I'll let Nick know it was my fault.

Flagging one hand while the other was on her hip, Joan let it be known, "Chile I ain't stuttin' Nicholas Stiles with his 'ole grumpy tail. And don't you get yourself all worked up worrying 'bout him either. You tryin' to have a baby... *his* baby. I swear he acts like a rotten brat at times. Boy talking all rough to me like he ain't got a bit of sense in his head. Humph!

He don't know me! Get me wrong and I'll put my foot in his behind!"

Summer and Starr both looked at each other wide eyed then back at Joan before they cracked up laughing. Joan was a mess! She didn't take anything off anybody. Not even the benevolent Nick Stiles.

"Oh where are my manners. Joan this is my friend Starr. Starr this is Joan."

The younger woman offered her hand to the older one.

"It is so nice to meet you, Miss Joan. I've heard so many nice things about you."

"It's nice to meet you too, Starr. Summer talks 'bout you and Ava all the time. And chile please don't call me no Miss Joan, makes me feel old. I still got a few miles left in me." Joan teased.

"Okay, Joan it is." Starr agreed, offering the older woman a dimpled smile.

❧ ❧ ❧ ❧ ❧

Time dragged by with each minute seeming like an hour and each hour like a day. Summer walked the halls in an attempt to pass the time and speed up the labor process. Starr and Joan took turns walking back and forth, up and down the hall with her. As she and Starr walked again for what seemed like the hundredth time, a strong shearing force ripped through her uterine wall. Holding onto the wall, she began taking a couple of deep breaths. Starr coached her through the pain.

"That's it Summer, take a deep cleansing breath through your nose and out your mouth." Starr gently instructed as the contraction came in a wave, starting low, rising to a high peak, and then descending down again leveling out.

"Wow that was a rough one. I think I better head back to the room. If I get another one like that you'll be picking my big butt up off the floor."

"Girl, you know I can't lift your big tail. I'll have to drag you by that long ponytail of yours like a caveman or something."

Summer's laugh turned into a soft groan. "Oh no, this is so embarrassing."

"What girl?"

Summer spread her legs and looked at the floor. "Either I just peed on myself or my water just broke."

Starr held Summer's hand as she helped her to step around the clear puddle.

"Come on, let's get you back to bed then I'll go tell the nurse to have someone come clean up your pee-pee."

"Shut up Starr. I didn't pee on myself." Summer said as she playfully nudged her friend.

"You did too. Wait until I tell my godchild how his or her momma peed in the middle of the floor." Starr teased.

"Starr don't make me kick you in the lip."

"As if your fat behind can lift your leg up that high."

"Shut up Starr."

❧ ❧ ❧ ❧ ❧

Nine forty-five rolled around and Nick hadn't showed up. Joan left forty-five minutes earlier to baby-sit her neighbors, the Kennedy's two younger children for them. Joan hated to leave Summer, but she'd committed herself to keep the adorable toddlers last week. Joan gave Starr her home phone number and the Kennedy's number telling her, "Please call me the minute that little precious baby is born."

"Of course I will and thanks for everything." Starr promised the older woman.

Joan wasn't at all surprised when Summer held her arms out to hug her before she left. She gladly returned the hug wishing more than ever she could remain for the birth of the baby.

Every time Summer had a contraction, Starr cringed as she helped her breathe through it. "Summer are you sure you want to go through with this natural childbirth stuff?" Starr questioned her friend; she appeared to be in such agony with every contraction.

"Yeah, girl, I told you I don't want my baby all dopey from those drugs."

Starr sucked her teeth. "Shoot, girl, when my time comes, I'm gonna want the whole dang pharmacy. Demerol, morphine, dilaudid, percocet…give me evvvverything!"

Summer couldn't help from laughing at her friend. "Starr, you are nuts. Just plain crazy."

Moaning replaced Summer's short-lived laughter. "Ooh, ouch, ouch, Starr here comes another one."

For some reason it hadn't taken the few seconds it had earlier for the pain to build and intensify. This particular contraction was intense as soon as it started.

"Come on girlfriend, squeeze my hand and breathe. That's right, breathe. Let the pain go."

Just as the contraction was subsiding, Nick entered the room along with Dr. Neil. The doctor was the first to speak.

"How's my favorite patient?"

"Dr. Neil that last contraction was really bad." Summer moaned.

"Sure you don't want anything for the pain? I can have anesthesiology down here right away. Just give me the word."

Summer shook her head. "No, Dr. Neil, I want to do this without drugs."

"All right then, let me check you. See how far along you are."

After thoroughly washing and drying his hands, grabbing a pair of latex gloves, he asked, "Do you want your visitors to leave before I exam you?"

"They can stay."

Both Nick and Starr focused their attention elsewhere as the doctor prepared to perform the examination.

Properly draping his patient the doctor began his examination. "You're almost ready; your cervix is at nine centimeters. Since this is your first baby it may take another hour or longer." Removing the gloves the doctor asked again, "Are you certain you don't want anything for the pain?" In this day and age he didn't think it was necessary for a woman to suffer needlessly during childbirth.

"I'm sure. If I change my mind, I'll let you know." *Another hour, I'm gonna die. I just might take those stupid drugs if I have to go on like this for more than an hour.*

"Okay, I'll be back in a little while to check on you."

"Thanks, Dr. Neil."

Feeling awkward like she was in the way and needing to give Summer and Nick some privacy, Starr announced, "Summer I'm stepping out to get a bite to eat." It was ten thirty and the last time she had anything to eat was sometime around nine that morning.

"Nick, do you want me to bring you anything back?"

"Naw, Starr, I'm cool. Thanks though."

Summer wanted to beg her to stay and not leave her alone with Nick. But she wouldn't be selfish; Starr had been there with her every step of the way. "Take your time Starr, I know you're just as hungry and tired as I am."

"I'll be back in a few, I promise." Grabbing her coat and purse, Starr blew Summer a kiss as she left out the door.

No sooner than she closed the door, Nick started in on Summer with his inquisition.

"Why didn't you tell me this morning you were having contractions, Summer?"

Summer stared at Nick in disbelief. *Why is he starting with me now?* "I didn't want to....oh no... here comes another one." Summer moaned as she prepared herself for the pain.

Nick hadn't a clue as to what to do as Summer's body stiffened and she moaned and groaned in pain as she held onto the side rail of the hospital bed. When her uterus finally relaxed so did her stiff body. She waited for her breathing to return to normal before answering him.

"I didn't want to bother you.

Now, Nick was the one with a look of disbelief. It had been hours since she'd been laboring. From what Joan told him the laboring started with mild contractions yesterday evening at dinnertime. More than twenty-four hours ago and she hadn't said one word to him. Nick was asking himself why again. Why wouldn't she tell him she was in labor? She had an opportunity earlier that morning. Did she really think he'd rather be conducting business than with her while they await the birth of their baby? No, it couldn't be. Nick was growing weary of Summer keeping him in the dark. Before anger could creep into his bones her words rang clear in his ears. *"Please, Nick don't..." That's why she didn't call me.* Summer had reacted to his threat. The fact she hadn't called him had nothing to do with her bothering him as much as it had to do with her fear of having her baby taken away.

Nick didn't know which was worse, the tight knot in his gut or the fact that he wanted to kick himself. Yes, he'd been angry with her but he didn't want her to have to go through labor without him being at her side. He'd already missed most of her pregnancy; he'd wanted to be with her from the moment her true labor began.

Nick's shoulders slumped as he removed his coat and draped it over the back of a chair. Pulling up a chair to the side of the bed, he sat and watched her saying nothing.

Summer felt his eyes on her, but refused to look at him.

"Hey, look at me for a minute."

As she lifted her eyes to meet his, she noted the gentleness his voice held as he spoke to her.

"I'm not upset. I just wanted to be here with you when the baby is born. I thought I was going to miss it."

"I'm sorry. I know I should have called you." Summer's voice quivered as a tear slid down her cheek. *Damn hormones!*

Nick wiped the tear away. "Don't cry. You don't have anything to be sorry about. Okay?"

"Okay." Summer softly whispered.

Neither knew what to say. This was the longest the two had been in each other's company for days. They sat in silence until Summer needed to speak.

"Nick, please take my hand I'm having another contraction."

Without hesitation he allowed Summer to wrap her tiny hand as best she could around his large hand as she squeezed with all her might as the contraction consumed her.

Before Starr came back Summer had several more contractions. Nick held her hand as she squeezed and breathed her way through each contraction. He couldn't believe how powerful her grip was for such a tiny woman. Every time he watched her suffer through the pain guilt jabbed at him starting with the day he ended their relationship, up until the night a few days ago he had left her standing crying all alone in his living room.

He wished he could take on the pain for her. It didn't seem fair her tiny body had to endure so much discomfort. He was amazed at her strength and determination not to take drugs for the pain. He too had tried to convince her to take "a little something." Nick was relieved when Starr returned from her dinner break. Summer got through the contractions much better with Starr coaching her using the breathing exercises they'd learned at the childbirth classes.

Summer was becoming more and more frustrated with how long it was taking for her cervix to dilate that last centimeter. Nick and Starr were both startled when she burst out into tears. "I can't take this anymore! This hurrrrts too much! I just wanna diiiiie!" Summer screamed as she was hit with searing pain.

"Come on, Boo, you can do this. You made it this far." Starr soothingly coaxed her.

Shaking her head back and forth, "No… no… I can't… I can't… take this anymore."

"Yes, you can baby. Starr's right, you can do this." Nick told her as he rubbed her lower back.

Something suddenly snapped inside of Summer, as if possessed by an evil force. Neither Nick nor Starr saw it coming. Summer's very soft genteel feminine voice dropped a few octaves. Her voice coming out in a deep tenor as she turned on Nick.

"Don't touch me! Get your hands off me! This is your entire fault, Nick! All your fault!"

Nick continued to rub her lower back. He didn't allow her outburst to shake him. "I know baby. You're right, it is all my fault." Nick validated Summer's verbal attack in a soothing voice as he continued to rub her lower back.

This seemed to calm her temporarily as she collapsed against the pillows trapping Nick's hand. Gingerly, he pulled his hand out as he looked at Starr, his eyes questioning, "What now?"

Reading the message in his eyes, "I'll be right back. I'm going to get Dr. Neil to come back in here and check you Summer."

"Thanks Starr." Summer's voice was strained with the weariness of having labored for hours.

Helplessness overwhelmed Nick, as he didn't know what to do to comfort her. He handled multi-million dollar business transactions, yet when it came to comforting the woman giving birth to his child, he was at a loss. He felt like a fish out of water thrashing back and forth.

With all of his resources, there was nothing he possessed that would help to ease her agonizing pain. No amount of materialism he own could console her. Only the delivery of the tiny life in her womb would erase the torturous contractions wrecking havoc on her exhausted body.

Nick tenderly wiped at her damp brow with a cool washcloth. "Summer, is there anything I can do for you? Just tell me and I'll do it."

Summer looked at Nick, tears spilling from her eyes, her voice cracking as she softly spoke. "I only wanted you to love me Nick. To love me how I'm loving you right now."

The wind was knocked out of him as if a three hundred pound linebacker had tackled him to the ground. Immediate revelation floored him, as he finally comprehended the breadth of Summer's love. She had loved him so severely she refused to snuff the life out of what may be the very best of him. She had made a heart decision to nurture, to care for, and to love a baby that was the very essence, the very nucleus of him.

The lump forming in his throat threatened to cut the air supply to his lungs. "Summer, baby –"

His words were cut off by her letting out a blood-curdling scream similar to that of a wounded animal. The scream brought Dr. Neil, Starr and two nurses running into the room. Quickly washing his hands, Dr. Neil snatched a pair of latex gloves from a box, donning them and examined her again.

"The cervix is measuring at ten centimeters and a hundred percent effaced. Okay, Miss Summer, you're ready to start pushing."

"Thank you Jesus." Those were the sweetest words Summer ever heard in her life.

Removing the gloves, Dr. Neil left the room to scrub and dress for the delivery. As the doctor was preparing himself, the two nurses efficiently and quickly transformed the ordinary hospital bed into a birthing bed. Just as the nurses were placing Summer into the birthing position with her feet in the stirrups, the doctor backed through the door careful not to touch anything as he took his place at the end of the bed on a stool between Summer's open legs.

"Summer, I'm going to massage a little mineral oil onto your perineum to help stretch it, hopefully preventing you from tearing as you push the baby out."

Summer nodded her head in compliance as the doctor worked at further preparing her body for delivery.

Placing a hand on her belly, Dr. Neil instructed, "Summer, with the next contraction you can push."

No sooner than the doctor gave the command, a contraction reared its ugly head prompting Summer to grab Nick's hand as he stood at her side.

Taking a deep breath, squeezing her eyes shut, Summer pushed, "Ahhhhhhhh."

"Come on that's it, push, push, push." Starr coached until the contraction ended. "Okay Summer, relax and breathe."

This cycle went on for thirty minutes until Dr. Neil told her to stop pushing.

"Summer, the baby's head is beginning to crown. I'm going to inject a little lidocaine into your perineum just in case you do tear you won't feel a thing."

Summer winced as she felt the prick of the needle and burning lidocaine. Relief washed over her as the burning quickly faded into a numbing sensation. If she did tear she wouldn't feel a thing.

"With the next contraction, I want you to give a *big* push, okay?"

Summer gave a weak, "Okay." *Never again, never again,* is what she chanted in her head as she waited for the next contraction to come. Upon the decent of the contraction, Summer squeezed her eyes shut and pushed with all her might. "Ahhhhhhhh! Come on bayybee!"

The excitement and exhilaration of delivering a baby came in waves over Dr. Neil. Every time he assisted in bringing a new life into the world it was just as thrilling as his first delivery twenty-five years ago as a young intern. He excitedly cheered her on. "Come on, Summer… Push! …Push! …That's it! …That's it! … Push! …Push! This baby has wide shoulders. Push!... Push!"

Summer was obedient as she pushed with all her might the life inside of her body out. Relief came with the last push as the warm solid mass slipped from her body.

"It's a boy! You have a baby boy! Congratulations!" Dr. Neil sang as he guided the tiny, squirming, loudly exercising its lungs baby out of its mother's birth canal.

Summer eagerly reached for her baby before the doctor could fully wrap, let alone wipe off the birthing residue and clamp the umbilical cord. Once the baby was within her embrace she collapsed back against the pillows as she hugged him close, feeling the warmth from his tiny body.

Summer didn't want to let him go when the nurse announced, "I have to take the baby now." Although he was only a few feet away from her as the pediatrician made sure he was healthy, it felt like miles to her. She patiently waited for her son as Dr. Neil delivered the placenta and sutured her lacerations.

Nick glimpsed at the clock on the wall in the birthing suite. It was 1:45 am, February 14. The entire experience for Nick had been surreal from the moment he stepped into the birthing suite. Though he and Summer had issues to resolve, he gained a newfound respect and admiration for her. She was determined to take this journey alone if necessary. The desire to work things out between Summer and himself became a burning obsession as he watched mother and son.

After the pediatrician examined the baby, the nurse thoroughly cleaned, weighed and dressed him. Starr used this time to say her goodbyes so that mother, father and baby could have their privacy. As is, the hospital staff was constantly in and out of the room intruding on their intimacy.

Wrapping the baby in a receiving blanket the nurse placed the tiny bundle in Summer's arms. "If you want you can nurse him now."

"Okay, I will. I just want to look at him real good first."

A mixture of excitement and exhaustion plagued Summer when the baby was placed on her abdomen directly after delivery. His features barely noticeable as he was covered in birthing residue and slightly purple from making the exchange from maternal oxygenation to breathing on his own.

Laying the infant on her lap she slowly loosened the snug blanket from his tiny body. Summer studied his tiny face. He must have known his mommy was looking at him as he stretched with tiny fist balled up, yawned, then gradually opened a pair of tiny eyes that immediately locked with hers. Summer's breath caught, the tiny pair of eyes were identical to his father's. A faint smile curved her lips as she further inspected his little face. He had the cutest nose and lips. Lifting her hand she caressed the locks of silky dark curls. With care, rubbing the silky strains between her fingers she noted the texture was like hers. Delicately as if he was a porcelain doll she touched his hands and his feet making sure there were ten fingers and ten toes.

In slow motion she brought her head down as she lifted a tiny foot kissing the sole of it. The baby was light in complexion. However, closer inspection revealed ears that were the same rich chestnut coloring as Nick's complexion.

Perfect. Her baby was perfect. Wrapping the infant up she was so happy she hadn't succumbed to the aid of pain medication. The infant was alert and wide-awake. Summer was so caught up in her bundle of joy she'd almost forgot Nick was in the room. Really looking at him for the first time in days their eyes locked and held. She hadn't expected to see the tenderness in his gaze.

"Do you want to hold your son before I feed him?"

As much as he ached to hold his son in his arms, he declined the offer.

"No, go ahead and feed him first. I'll hold him afterwards."

Summer exposed her right breast positioning the baby for feeding. Instinctively the infant opened its mouth, latched on and began nursing. Mother and son affectionately gazed into each other's eyes, bonding as she gave him life-sustaining nourishment from her body.

Sauntering over to the head of the bed, Nick watched the baby looking into Summer's face with interest as he suckled her breast. *He adores her already.* Bending down he feathered a kiss on Summer's forehead, then leaned in further to kiss the baby's forehead. Pulling up a chair, he sat as close as possible to them.

"Summer, look at how he's looking at you. He knows you're his mother."

"You think so?"

"Of course he does. He's so beautiful."

"Yes, he is. He looks just like you Nick, he has your eyes."

Peering into the baby's little face, Nick couldn't help but to grin.

"Yeah, he does have my eyes."

"Don't you think he looks like you?" She quietly asked, praying he would see what she saw, that their son was a complete replica of him.

Nick commented on the fact they had the same eyes, but said nothing when Summer mentioned the baby looked like him. Did he still have doubts about the baby being his she wondered?

"Most definitely. He does look like his old man." Nick responded in a quiet thoughtful voice.

A nurse came barging into the room without a clue she'd interrupted a poignant exchange, "Summer, we're going to be moving you upstairs to your room as soon as you finish feeding that handsome little guy." The nurse's voice was too animated to be so early in the wee hours of the morning.

"Okay, I think he's almost done anyway. By the way how much did my baby weigh and how long is he?"

Beaming at Summer, the nurse told her, "Seven pounds- nine ounces and he's twenty –one inches long. He's a nice size for a first baby."

"Thanks." *Good grief, no wonder I feel like I've been dragged behind a herd of elephants.*

Removing the baby from her breast, Summer kissed him on the nose before handing him over to the hyperactive nurse. *Oh Lord, please don't let this hyperactive woman drop my baby.*

The nurse secured the baby in her arms as she checked the identification band on Summer's wrist and then on the baby's ankle making sure they matched. "I'll be back to take you up to your room as soon as I take baby boy Jackson to the nursery."

Nick frowned as the nurse swiftly walked passed him with the infant. *Baby boy Jackson?*

The instant Summer was settled in her room she requested the baby be brought to her though she was bone tired. It was as if she couldn't get enough of holding the precious tiny gift. As soon as the nurse placed the baby into her eagerly waiting arms, Summer was filled with an awareness she couldn't find the words to describe. She found it extremely hard to keep her eyes off the now sleeping newborn. *This must be what true love feels like.* Though she loved him while he grew day by day in the protectiveness of her womb, seeing him, touching him, nurturing him from her body took on a whole new meaning. It was a love that was pure, unselfish, protective, trusting, giving and never expecting anything in return. It was a mother's love.

The picture before Nick was breathtaking. Summer and his son were a beautiful pair. Just as she couldn't keep her eyes off their son, he was having difficulty doing the same. Nick's heart trembled as she looked from the sleeping infant to meet his gaze. She wore the prettiest smile, that of an angel's.

Summer was aware he was staring at her and the baby. His reaction was what she'd hoped and prayed for. Smiling she asked, "Do you want to hold your son now?"

Summer stiffened her body sore from just giving birth as she shifted on the bed to make room for him to sit. With great ease he sat his large frame down next to her, so close, their bodies touched sending an electrical current through the both of them. Summer's face blushed with embarrassment letting him know she too, felt it.

A minute or so past before either said anything, neither of them wanted to spoil the warmth of the closeness. Summer was the first to speak, breaking the silence.

"Have you ever held a baby before?"

Nick chuckled. "No, never had a reason to before."

"Well, you better get used to it. I don't want you letting this little cutie pie slipping out your hands." Summer teased as she instructed Nick on how to support the newborn's tiny head in the crease of his elbow.

"Don't you worry your pretty little head about that Miss Summer, I plan on getting plenty of practice." He countered with jest as he received the sleeping bundle in his arms.

"Good for you, Mr. Nick."

Enjoying the easy flowing bantering between them, Nick started to say something else witty but was silenced after she placed the baby in his arms. His heart began to accelerate as the tiny bundled squirmed. The emotion of fear seized him.

"Summer, you better take him back."

Summer furrowed her perfectly arched brows. "Why?"

"Because he's moving, I don't want to drop him." Anxiety laced the new father's voice.

Summer giggled, "Nick, you won't drop him. He's probably just trying to wake up again, that's all."

"Okay, if you say so."

Nick relaxed as he peered into the slumbering face identical to his. *A son. I have a son.* Nick's chest swelled with pride. This was the most incredible feeling in the world. Suddenly the hollow space in his heart no longer felt empty. A smile tugged at his mouth as he took his attention away from his son to Summer. She had quietly drifted off to sleep. She never looked more beautiful. Nick figured she had to be exhausted. Giving birth had been excruciatingly painful for her as she repeatedly refused medication so their baby wouldn't be exposed to any unnecessary risks.

A sickening feeling washed over him at the realization that if Summer had tracked him down, telling him she was pregnant, he would not be holding the seven pound nine ounce gift in his arms so close to his heart, loving him with everything inside of him. If it were up to him, nine months ago she would have had that abortion. He would have seen to it, even if it meant him dragging her kicking and screaming to the nearest clinic.

Nick hadn't been to church since his mother's funeral. He refused to go every time Summer offered the invitation to go with her. He wasn't much of a praying man either. But everything in him hoped and prayed that she would find it in her heart to forgive him for the hell he'd put her through, starting with the day he turned his back on her.

Chapter 23

Later that morning, Nick arrived at the hospital with two dozen long stem white roses trimmed in baby blue. Knocking on the door he heard Summer say, "Come in."

Immediately, he sensed the strain in her voice.

Opening the door, he found her lying on her side staring at the baby as he slept in the clear bassinet.

"How you feeling?" He asked as he laid the roses and his coat on a bedside table before washing his hands at the sink.

Summer's tone was flat when she responded. "Fine."

Lifting the sleeping baby from the bassinet, Nick further inquired. "You all right, Summer?"

"The lab technician from BioMed just left." Enough had been said; he needed no further explanation for her reserved mood.

"I see." Nick was tested last week, all the lab needed were Summer's and the baby's buccal samples. Knowing this was the reason for her mood, he mumbled a curse under his breath. He wasn't thinking when he innocently told his attorney, Mr. Steinberg he was on his way to the hospital because Summer had gone into labor. The business he'd been discussing with the attorney had nothing to do with her or the baby. Nick had no idea the lawyer would contact the independent lab before he had a chance to tell him he'd changed his mind about the paternity test and filing for custody.

"Summer, we need to talk."

He wanted to tell her he didn't need a test to prove the baby he held in his arms was indeed, unquestionably his. He wanted her to know she didn't have to worry about the threats he slung her way in anger.

Nick wasn't prepared for Summer's response.

"Nick, I'm tired. I don't feel like talking."

Not now or ever, she wanted to say. Summer was devastated when the lab tech showed up eight that morning. *Well, dag-gone it! Couldn't he at least wait until I could see straight*? It had been barely six hours since she had given birth.

Sitting down in a chair, Nick carefully adjusted the sleeping infant in his arms.

"Then when?" He asked as he struggled to keep the tightness from his voice.

"Not now. I can't handle anymore conversations with you right now." She wanted him to leave but didn't dare tell him to do so. He was there to see his son and not her as far as she was concerned.

Agitation crept in his voice, as he demanded, "What is that supposed to mean?"

"Nick, I'm tired of you treating me like I'm the enemy… your enemy. I'm exhausted; I don't have the energy to sit here and have you yelling at me."

Placing the infant back in the bassinet, Nick turned to Summer. "When you feel like you have the energy, we *will* have this conversation."

Snatching his coat off the table taking long strides to the door, Nick stopped without turning to look back at her. "Trust me, if you were my enemy you would've known it by now."

Summer shuddered at his words as he stalked out the room slamming the door.

❧ ❧ ❧ ❧ ❧

Nick was disgusted with himself. He hadn't handled Summer well at all. What was it with him? Why did he always seem to hurt or upset her? She was only reacting to how he had been treating her. Was it too late? Had he pushed her to the point of no return? He had every intention on apologizing to her for being a jackass and treating her so badly. He was planning to tell her he would do whatever it took to make things right between them, to put the past where it belonged and move forward. Somehow, things had taken a tragic detour. Summer ended up crying and he ended up storming out the room slamming the door.

Needing to burn off frustration, he decided to walk instead of taking a cab back to his office in the blustery February air. The biting cold didn't seem to bother him as he walked against the gusting wind. Several blocks into the walk his frustration still present as the cold air began to chill him. Fastening the top button of his wool overcoat, the rectangle box in the breast pocket shifted. The elderly woman he passed gasped, "oh dear" as an expletive exploded from his lips.

"Pardon me ma'am for my rudeness."

The rectangle box made him think of the sweet, sleeping Summer he'd left at the hospital earlier that morning. Not wanting to wake her he left her a note on the bedside table.

Summer,

I didn't want to wake you. You looked so peaceful.

I'll be back later this morning to see you and the baby.

Sweet dreams,

Nick

Before coming to the hospital, he stopped at Tiffany's on Walnut Street. The platinum three-carat diamond tennis bracelet in the display case caught his eye. Beautiful and sparkling, reminding him of Summer. Nick let out a deep sigh. *Enemy. She thinks I treat her like an enemy.* For her to make such a statement meant her feelings for him were changing, if they already hadn't. Summer was slipping threw his fingers; he felt it in his gut.

❧ ❧ ❧ ❧ ❧

How they did it, Summer didn't care. She thanked the Lord in heaven her parents made it to Philly. It was only by His grace that they had. Their surprised arrival was just the pick me up she needed. She hadn't expected them until later that night or the next day. Summer was sitting in a chair nursing the baby when her mother barged through the door with dramatic flair startling her.

"Baby, I tried to get here as fast as I could."

Rushing over to her daughter, Nita awkwardly hugged her tight, making sure not to squeeze the baby.

Summer leaned into her mother's embrace. "Mommy you made it. Where's daddy?"

Waving her hand, "He's out there. Saw the sign 'Mother is Nursing' on the door. Said he wait until you're done."

Removing the baby from her breast, Summer laid the infant against her chest gently patting his back. Her mother smiled as tears shone in her eyes. "My baby is a mother. I remember the day you were born, seems like yesterday."

"Yeah?"

"Of course baby. That's something you'll never forget." Holding her smile, "You'll see."

Summer nodded her head in agreement. After all the pain and suffering she'd gone through, she was sure she would never forget it either.

"You want to hold your first grandbaby?"

"Yes, but let me go get your daddy first. You know how impatient he is. Probably complaining 'bout what's taking you so long."

Summer's mom left the room quickly returning with her husband.

"There's my princess." Summer's dad announced loudly with a smile in his voice as he went to his daughter with outstretched arms.

"Hey daddy."

Summer held the baby in her mother's direction, prompting her to take him. She wanted, no, needed her father to hold her. It had been so long since she had been in his arms.

As soon as her mom took the baby her dad held her in his strong arms making her feel safe. The moment her head hit her father's shoulder she started to weep.

"What's the matter with daddy's princess?" Her father's deep vibrating voice soothingly caressed Summer, making her almost forget about Nick, his funky attitude and the fight they had earlier.

"I'm just glad to see you and mommy." Summer said as she clung to her father.

"Princess you know the minute they cleared that runway we'd be here. We would have been a lot longer getting here if that Nick fella hadn't chartered us a jet."

Summer's father smoothed her hair, stroking the long strains as he talked. Summer felt like a ten year old again as her father called her by her childhood name and stroked her hair. Usually she cringed every time her dad called her by her childhood name; after all, she was a twenty-six years old woman. However, for the moment she allowed herself to go back to that safe place when she was a child and her daddy could make anything all right.

Something her father said made Summer break the embrace. She must have heard him wrong.

"Nick chartered a jet for you and mommy?"

"Humph, at least he was good for something." Her mother stated turning up her nose with an attitude.

"Now Nita behave yourself." Her father chided.

Ignoring her husband's chiding, Nita waved him over to her. "James, come look at your grandson."

Going over to stand by his wife who was sitting on the bed, a bright smile lifted to his eyes. "Princess, he is a handsome little guy."

"Thanks daddy. I think so, too."

"Mmm, he sure is." Her mother agreed, then quickly added in the next breath with distaste, "Must look like the daddy."

Summer's smile faded as she shot her mother an exasperated look.

"Mommy." Summer loved her mother dearly, but she was wearing on her nerves already.

"What? I only said he must look like his daddy. He looks nothing like you, Summer."

"Nick, mommy. His name is Nick. And yes, my son looks just like his daddy."

"I know his name and watch your attitude missy. I'm still your mother." *Thinks she's grown just 'cause she done went and had a baby. She ain't too big for me to take a switch to her yella behind.*

Summer rolled her eyes at her mother the second her mother shifted her gaze back to the sleeping infant in her arms.

Defending Nick came so naturally to Summer, it scared her. Even after their run in earlier that morning, she felt devotion for him. *Lord, why can't I shake this man?*

The tension in the air was obvious. As always, James acted as the buffer between mother and daughter as he smoothly changed the subject.

"So princess, what are you going to name this little guy?"

"I haven't decided yet daddy. What do you –"

Just as Summer was speaking Nick knocked on the door and without waiting for an response he strolled into the room as if he had a right to.

He grimaced when three pairs of eyes landed on him. Twice in one day his impulsive behavior made him appear rude. Rudeness wasn't his intention, he was anxious to see and hold his son again. Anxious to see Summer again.

As Nita roamed Nick over from head to toe she thought, *hmmm, he definitely is handsome, I see how my baby feel for the 'ole scoundrel.* Nita struggled to keep from smacking the man who turned her daughter's life upside down. *I just want to hit 'em one good time.*

James initial thoughts as he appraised Nick were completely opposite from that of his wife's. James understood what it was like to be a man unsure of commitment. *He ain't all that bad of a man. Just need to stop running, settle down and do right by my princess and her boy.*

Nick offered his hand to James, Summer's father first. He could tell her mother wasn't too pleased with his presence. "Nick Stiles, glad to meet you, Sir."

"James Jackson, same here. I've heard a lot about you, Mr. Stiles." James facial expression was unreadable as to whether what he had heard was favorable or not.

"Please, call me, Nick."

As he was speaking, he released James' hand then proceeded to offer his hand to Nita. The resemblance between Summer and her mother was striking. Both women were petite, shared identical facial features and had long, thick beautiful hair. The only contrasting feature was their complexion. Summer's caramel coloring was like that of her father's, whereas Nita was a rich medium brown.

Nita glared at the large hand as if it were a rattlesnake. Reluctantly she accepted the proffered hand that refused to withdraw. Nita's indifference didn't faze Nick one-way or the other.

"Nice to meet you, Mrs. Jackson. I see where Summer gets her beauty from."

Nick couldn't resist displaying his charming trademark smile followed by a playful wink.

Nita rolled her eyes refusing to smile at Nick's flirtatious behavior and devastatingly handsome smile.

Lawd a mercy, would you look at this fresh boy trying to flirt with somebody. "Mmm hmm."

Summer shot daggers at her mother. Nita returned a look that said, "What?"

James also shot her a warning look that said, "Don't start woman."

Nita rolled her eyes at her husband. Not wanting to upset Summer further, she decide to make an attempt to be civil.

Clearing her throat, she said, "Thanks, Mr. Stiles for getting James and I here to see Summer and our grandbaby."

Though she didn't like Nick, she was grateful she and James were able to get to their daughter as soon as they had. If it hadn't been for him, more than likely they'd still be at the airport in North Carolina waiting for a flight.

"Please, call me Nick. It was no problem. I know Summer wanted you here with her and the baby as soon as possible."

As much as Nita wanted to dislike him, Nick's smooth velvety voice held sincerity as he spoke of Summer and what she'd wanted. Maybe there was more to this story than she knew. She made a mental note to talk to her daughter when they were alone.

The next hour passed with Nita and James acquainting themselves with Nick. Summer sat on pins and needles as her parents practically interviewed him as if he was applying for a position with the FBI. She watched as Nick answered every question without flinching.

The interviewing was going well until Nita went for the jugular. Summer nearly choked on the water she was drinking when her mother stared Nick dead in the eyes and asked, "Are you married and do you have any other children?"

"Mommy!"

"Nita." James firmly warned his wife through clinched teeth.

Nick chortled. *This woman is off the chain.*

Nita lifted a perfectly arched brow. *What's so darn funny?*

"I assure you Nita, I've never been married and no I don't have any children. Except for the *one* you're holding."

Smiling at her grandbaby, she brought her gaze back to Nick. "Are you sure 'bout that, Mr. Stiles?"

"Absolutely."

"Good."

James and Nita Jackson were like night and day. Their temperaments were complete opposites. James was easy going and laid back.

Nick expected him to be overbearing and threatening considering he'd impregnated his daughter without the benefit of marriage. Summer had told him how her parents reacted to her pregnancy. Therefore, he was surprised her father was so pleasant.

Nita, however, was out spoken and opinionated. Nick was acutely aware she wasn't fond of him though she never came right out and said it. The only time she expressed any semblance of kindness was when he'd mentioned the untimely death of his mother.

Nick smiled on the inside; grateful Summer had inherited her father's temperament. If she'd been anything like her mother, they would've never made it past the first date.

As the conversation flowed, Nick concluded he and Summer were opposites as well. She was soft, gentle, easy going, patient, kind and understanding. And he tended for the most part to be harsh, abrasive, uncompromising, unforgiving and explosive when angry. The only time he allowed himself to be different was when they were together. Kevin often teased him about how Summer had transformed him into a *nice* guy. At the time he viewed this as a weakness, rather than an evolution of becoming a better person.

No one in the room noticed as he felt the internal turmoil eating away at him. For so many years he had allowed his egotistical ways rule him and every aspect of his life. Whether it was his personal or business life, it didn't matter. Always needing to be in control he never cared how he captured or maintained it. For once in his life his need to control may very well have destroyed the one special relationship with a woman, other than his mother, that would have given him true fulfillment.

Breaking into his thoughts, he heard James announce, "We better get going. I think we've stayed long enough."

Summer didn't let her apprehension show about being alone with Nick. She didn't want a repeat of their exchange earlier that morning. She could tell he wouldn't be leaving anytime soon. *I hope he doesn't bring up that "we need to talk Summer" speech.*

After her parents left, Summer took small painful baby steps in the direction of the bathroom. Nick watched as she all but dragged her feet as she walked into the bathroom and closed the door.

When she came out she slowly made her way over to the bassinet to look at the baby. Soon as the infant started to squirm, she immediately picked him up. So what if she was spoiling him, he was hers.

Summergaspedwhenshefeltherselfbeinglifted.Automatically, she leaned her head against his chest and inhaled his scent as he carried her and the baby the short distance to the bed. With their faces mere inches apart, lips almost touching, eyes locked on each other, Nick told her, "You look like you're in a lot pain."

He was close, too close. He was making her dizzy. Making her head spin as his words came out in a deep husky whisper. She had to say something, but what? Out of nervous habit

she bit her bottom lip before she spoke. "I am. He has broad shoulders like his father." She whispered keeping her eyes locked with his.

Leaning further in, he whispered against slightly parted lips, "Sorry."

When he covered her mouth with his, Summer further parted her lips allowing him entry.

Breaking the kiss, he eased her down onto the bed. For the first time in weeks, she hadn't looked terrified or uneasy, but rather content as she gazed into the tiny face of the infant. There was no way he or anyone else would ever take their son from her. Nick wanted desperately to tell her that, but couldn't. His threats had been so severe; even if he told her he would never follow through with them, she wouldn't believe him. He would have to show her he would never destroy her in such a way, or any other way for that matter.

"He makes you happy doesn't he?"

Summer lifted her gaze to meet his. The sweetest smile played at the corners of her mouth. "Yes, he does."

She wanted to tell him that they could be happy together, too. That they could start over again with their son. But before the words could come out she reminded herself that she was letting go of her love for him. So instead, she asked in a small voice, "How about you Nick? Does he make you happy, too?"

Nick chuckled. Summer frowned. She didn't understand what was so amusing.

"Yes, Summer, he makes me happy."

"Then what's so funny?"

"Nothing, other than the fact we keep referring to our son as he or him."

"Oh."

"Have you come up with any names yet?"

"No, have you?"

Summer wasn't even about to tell him the day he threatened to take their son she'd stopped thinking about names. Her main concern was how she was going to keep her baby.

"Naw, not any names for a boy anyway. I was hoping you had a girl."

Tilting her head to the side to get a better look at him, she asked, "Why did you want a girl?"

Should he tell her the truth? That he didn't want a son that possibly one day may grow up to be hard and callous like him. As much as Nick hated to admit it, so many of his unbending ways were just like those of his father's. That's why they never got along; they were too much alike. Three generations of male stubbornness was a bit too much. No way was he about to admit that truth to the mother of his child. Admit that she had nurtured for nine months in her body a potential stubborn jackass with the likes of his father and grandfather. He was determined to teach and show his son a different way. He purposed in his heart he would teach his son that hardness and cruelty did not make you a better man, only a lesser one. Even if it killed him, he would change the error of his ways to become an example to his son. He would teach him that being slow to anger, having patience, love, and understanding are characters that build a man.

Nick had gotten so caught up in his thoughts that he hadn't heard Summer calling him.

"Nick?" Rolling her eyes to the ceiling, "Earth to Nick."

Snapping out of his reverie, he pulled his attention back to Summer.

"Yeah babe?"

He chuckled at her annoyance with him. Feeling particularly mischievous, he decided to rattle her further.

"I heard you. I was hoping you had a girl so we could name her Beautiful Stiles." He grinned from ear to ear as if he were a poor man who had just won the lottery.

Turing up her nose as if something smelled horribly rotten Summer snapped, "Nick that is the most ridiculous name I've ever heard of. You've got to be kidding, right?"

"Serious as a heart attack."

It took everything in him not to laugh at the astonished look on her face.

"Well, thank goodness for small miracles," she muttered.

"Small miracles like what, Miss Jackson?"

"That he is a boy and not a girl. There is no way a daughter of mine would be named no ridiculous Beautiful."

"But that's what I call you. Beautiful."

Summer's sucked in her breath and held it. The squirming baby in her arms reminded her brain that she needed to breathe. *How in the world does he do that?*

His voice had dropped seductively low as his gaze caressed every inch of her face. He had the ability to transition right before her eyes like a chameleon. Changing from mischievously teasing, to seductively teasing in the bat of an eye. Shifting her gaze from his, back to the squirming baby, "That's different."

"How so?"

"Because, that's not a real name, it's a nickname."

Before he responded, he remembered a time when his hands roamed and touched every soft, sensual, sexy curve of her petite body as he would moan "Beautiful" over and over again from the pleasure he would get from exploring her body.

"You're absolutely right."

Quick to change the subject, Summer brought the issue back to the forefront of what to name their son. After tossing several names around, they hadn't decided on one they could agree on. All the names she was fond of, Nick detested. She had the same response to his choice of names, especially Fredrick. Nick said it was a proud, powerful name of African-American heritage. Strong and powerful or not, Summer refused to name their son such an old-fashioned name, uggggh!

An hour later, they still hadn't picked a name. Nick helped her from the bed to the chair as she prepared to nurse. As the baby fed, the one name they never discussed all but rolled off her tongue. Staring down into the tiny dark eyes intently watching her, Summer felt in her heart that the name she decided on was perfect.

Stretched out on the hospital bed, Nick flipped through channels as she nursed. He needed to focus elsewhere as she fed the baby. Summer's exposed breast was making his mind go places it had no business going. It didn't seem right to lust after her as she tended to the infants needs.

"Nick."

"What's up?"

"I have a name."

Sitting up, he swung his long legs over the side of the bed disregarding the rampant lustful thoughts running amuck in his head. He wanted to give her his undivided attention.

"You do?"

He figured it would be another day or two before deciding on a name. So far they hadn't agreed on a suitable one.

Summer nodded her head. "I want to name him, Nicholas Christopher Stiles, Jr."

Stunned he asked, "Are you sure?

Even after everything he had put her through she wanted to give their son his name.

Summer nodded.

"No, Summer. I want to hear you say it. Tell me that you're sure." This woman, *his* woman was talking about giving their son his name. That's right, Summer was *his* woman. If he hadn't been sure before he was sure now…she still loved him.

"Yes, I'm sure. He looks so much like you. I think the name perfectly suits him. We'll call him NJ, short for Nick Jr."

Rising up from the bed he went to her, kneeling down so that they were at eye level, he brushed his lips against hers, "Thank you."

Summer raised her hand to Nick's face gently stroking his jaw. "You don't have to thank me."

For the second time that day Summer had to remind herself of her resolve to let Nick go.   Would she be able to do it? For the rest of the night she considered that very questioning in her heart over and over again.

Chapter 24

The next six weeks rushed by in a fuzzy haze as Summer returned home from the hospital with parents and baby in tow. She enjoyed having her parents with her, but by the fourth week she was ready to pull out every strand of her hair from frustration. As much as she loved them they were driving her crazy, especially her mother. Her father continued to act as a buffer between the two.

The first argument was over Nita wanting to go to NJ's first doctor's appointment. It was a no brainer that Nick would accompany them. When Summer suggested her mother stay home, Nita nearly had a bird.

Summer didn't really care. She wanted her baby's first appointment to the pediatrician to be a pleasant memory. That wasn't likely to happen since every now and then her mother slipped a snide remark past her lips aimed at Nick. On this special day she did not want it marred by unpleasant memories of any smart comments, courtesy of her mother.

Though Nita was outright rude to Nick, he remained on his best behavior. He would patiently hold his composure, ignoring the remarks of the older woman.

Like always, James stepped in sternly informing his wife she would wait at home until Summer and Nick took *their* child to his first doctor's appointment. After hearing the sternness in her husband's voice, Nita resentfully complied with her husband.

During those six weeks, Nick and James became at ease with one another. On many occasions they would leave Summer and Nita at home while they went to the sports bar with Kevin to watch whatever basketball team was playing. It didn't bother either woman one bit since the men act like teenagers hooting and hollering when their favorite team scored a point. Or let out a string of foul language when a basket wasn't made. Not to mention all the beer cans that littered Summer's living room while they watched the game. Summer had to put her foot down when Kevin came over and pulled out a cigar to smoke which was absolutely ridiculous since he didn't even smoke cigarettes.

Coming out of the kitchen with a bowl of chips she spied Kevin about to light up. With chips in one hand and the other on her hip, "Kevin, you know I love you like the brother I never had and everything, but if you think you're gonna smoke that stinking cigar in my house, around my baby, you've got another thing coming."

Flashing his trademark boyish grin, "Come on Sis, NJ's upstairs sleeping, this smoke isn't gonna bother him."

"Kevin, if you light that cigar up in here you'll be eating it instead of smoking it." Summer warned as she glared at him.

"Oooooh!" Was the response from the other two men in the room.

Kevin chuckled. "Girl, you are mean since you've became a momma."

"That's right. Now put that nasty cigar down. It stinks and you haven't even lit it." Summer said tersely as she placed the bowl of chips on the coffee table before retreating back to the kitchen with her mother.

So as far as the women were concerned, having the men at the sports bar was definitely okay by them.

Things between Summer and Nick hadn't progressed any further. Although he came over everyday to see and bond with the baby the two never had a chance to discuss how they would plan on raising their son. It hadn't yet been determined who would be the primary caregiver of NJ. Summer still had no idea Nick no longer had plans on filing for custody.

She maintained her distance whenever he was around. If he were in the nursery with the baby, she would go in her bedroom to watch television or downstairs in the living room to talk with Ava or Starr on the phone. In her mind putting distance between them was crucial to her emotional and mental wellbeing. She felt she had to do this especially after receiving a call from BioMed three days after coming home from the hospital. During the call she was informed the paternity test confirmed ninety-nine point nine percent Nick was NJ's father. Summer was so pissed she told the technician, "Tell me something I don't know," before slamming the phone down in his ear.

Summer hadn't meant to be rude, but if she received a phone call giving her the results, she was certain Nick received the results as well. Now she would wait until he approached her. She was in no hurry to have her world come falling down around her like a house of cards. Six weeks had gone by and Nick hadn't mentioned one word about the results. If he ignored the pink elephant in the room… so would she.

Later that evening after the Jacksons departed, Nick showed up as usual. Summer heard his footsteps walking in the direction of the downstairs closet off of the living room as she stood in the mirror wrapping her hair in a bun. She had given him a key the night before for the sake of convenience since her parents wouldn't be around to answer the door.

The house was extremely quiet now that her parents were gone. Nick smiled to himself. Now he would be able to put his plan into action to win Summer back. He had been a patient man as he waited the six weeks out. During those weeks he had been methodical in his plan. Whatever it had taken to get along with her parents, he did it. James hadn't been a problem; he truly liked the older man and enjoyed the times they hung out. Nita however was a different story. Whenever she let a snide remark slip, Nick didn't let it faze him, he couldn't. He had bigger fish to fry, like winning her daughter's heart back. In time he was confident that things between him and Nita would be just fine.

Taking two steps at a time, he made his way to the nursery. Peeking in he saw that NJ was squirming in his sleep, about to wake up at any moment. Deciding not to wake the baby, he sauntered down the hall to Summer's bedroom. Leaning against the doorjamb he crossed his arms across his chest, *When I get you back I'm never going to let you go,* he thought to himself as he watched her fussing with her hair.

"I'm gonna cut all this mess off." Summer grumbled to herself as she put the last pin in securing her tresses.

"Please don't. I love your hair."

The fine hairs on the back of her neck stood up from the low baritone voice she was so familiar with. Glancing over her shoulder, "I thought you were in the nursery."

"I peeked in on him, but he's still asleep."

"Oh. He's due to wake up soon."

As Summer crossed the room to the dresser pulling out a pair of silk pajamas, his gaze followed her. She looked good, real good. The knit blouse she wore clung snuggly to her full breasts, while she nicely filled out a pair of jeans something fierce. Nick tilted his head to the side as he watched her hips sway naturally from side to side.

"What?" Summer asked when she caught him staring at her with that look. She felt herself being drawn in by it. *Uh huh, nope, I'm not going there with you Nick,* she told herself as she broke eye contact.

Nick pushed himself away from the doorjamb uncrossing his arms and rubbed his hand over his goatee. "I was just checking you out in that blouse and those jeans. Girl you look tight, can't even tell you had a baby six weeks ago."

"Thanks." Summer mumbled. She wasn't about to tell him it was the breastfeeding that helped her body to bounce back to its pre-pregnancy state. He was having hard enough time keeping his eyes off her breasts as it was.

"Nick?"

"Summer?"

"When NJ wakes up change him and feed him for me."

He lifted a dark brow as his face knotted into a perplexed expression.

Summer laughed. "I pumped a few ounces earlier. It's in the fridge; just put the bottle in a cup of hot water to take the chill off."

"A'ight, that makes sense. I was beginning to think you had postpartum madness or something," he chuckled.

"No, Mr. Smarty Pants, just a desire to take a nice long hot shower."

Easing pass him in the doorway Summer's breast accidentally brushed against his arm. Instantaneously their bodies reacted to the intimate touch. When they briefly locked eyes the passion they saw was undeniable.

Unconsciously, Summer crossed her arms concealing her breasts. "Excuse me."

"Not a problem." Nick mumbled as she closed the bathroom door in his face.

Stripping out of her clothes down to her bra and panties, Summer looked at her form in the full-length mirror on the back of the bathroom door. Nick was right her body had retained all its former curves after giving birth. A frown flashed across her face as she stared at her full breasts remembering how her body betrayed her, awakening a strong need for him.

"I need to be taking a cold shower instead of a hot one." Summer mumbled to herself hating the very fact that she still craved the man.

The hot water was soothing and just what she needed to ease the sudden tension her body felt as muscles in her neck began to tighten. With her back facing the stream of water, she forced her thoughts away from Nick and to her baby. Tonight would be the first night they would be together all alone. A part of Summer was glad about it. Yet another part of her was anxious, giving her thoughts up and over to paranoia. *What if someone tries to break in? Or the house catches on fire. Maybe I should ask Nick to spend the night. He could sleep in my room and I'll sleep on the daybed in the nursery. Oh goodness... why am I tripping like this? Nothing's going to happen...right?*

The last thing she needed was for that man to spend the night under her roof. Although she had determined in her mind a thousand and one times she was letting him go, her heart and body had a hard time cooperating with her head. The very sight of the man made her weak in the knees. Why did he have to stand in her bedroom doorway looking all sexy and everything? Talking in that deep voice that had the hairs on the back of her neck standing up. Telling her he loved her hair and that her body looked tight. What kind of game was he playing anyway? He barely said "boo" to her in the last six weeks while her parents were there. Besides, by now he should have known that there was no going back for them. Too much damage had been done. The only thing they had in common was the tiny gift lying down the hall sleeping. NJ would be the only thing that kept them involved as parents and nothing else.

After showering, Summer stepped out of the tub turning off the cold water and leaving the hot water running giving the bathroom a sauna effect. Before she could reach for a thick terrycloth towel to dry off her wet nude body she jumped turning towards the door as it flew open. The barging in of her intruder startled her something terrible as she stared wide-eyed at him.

"Summer...." Nick's words trailed off mid-sentence. He was not prepared for what he'd barged in on. Unconsciously he licked his lips as he drank in the vision before him. There she was completely nude as the day she was born. Body glistening as drops of water lazily glided down breasts, abdomen, thighs and legs. Immediately his body responded. In his head he screamed, *"Daaayum! Double Daaayum!"* as his eyes roamed her petite body from head to toe and then in reverse again.

"Nick! What are you doing?!" Summer yelled crossing her arms shielding her breasts from his roaming eyes.

"I just ...wanted... to know ...how long to let ...the bottle sit ...in the hot water. And is... hot tap water okay... or should I ...boil it?" He asked distracted, hardly able to get the words out as his eyes were still a roaming.

"About three to four minutes. And yes, hot tap water if fine. You should have knocked before barging in here." She snapped, irritated with him.

"I thought you were still in the shower. I heard the water running." Getting over his initial shock of what he'd stumbled onto, Nick could no longer suppress the sly grin widening across his face.

Stomping her foot, crossing her arms tighter, Summer yelled, "Stop looking at me like that!" *A dirty dog !*

"Like what?" His grin remained fox like.

"Like you've never seen a naked woman before," she snapped.

Shutting the bathroom door he advanced a step closer, Summer withdrew a step. "I haven't."

Summer snatched at a towel on the rack. Nervous jitters replaced irritation as she fumbled, dropping the towel to the floor. "You haven't what?" She asked breathless.

Too self-conscious to bend down to retrieve the towel she stood as if rooted to the floor.

Nick moved with the grace of a large cat as he stooped down in front of her picking up the towel with his left hand as his right hand caressed her from ankle to hip as he rose to his full height. Summer took the towel backing away from his touch as she covered her nakedness.

Continuing his advancement until her back was against the wall, he had his prey trapped. Placing his hands against the wall on either side of Summer's body boxing her in, he said, "Seen a naked woman in a very, very long time."

What in the name of...? Summer's heart began to pound in her chest as Nick lowered his mouth to her neck. Just as he was about to zero in on the area of her neck he wanted to taste, she said, "You hear that?" Craning her neck further to the side straining her ear to hear beyond the closed bathroom door gave him exactly what he wanted. It wasn't her intention, but unwittingly she'd given him absolute access to his target. Like a vampire he descended upon her, biting into, then sucking the soft, succulent exposed flesh. Nick's eyes rolled in the back of his head as he ravished her flesh. Never before had anything tasted so sweet, so tender.

Summer let out a yelp from the pain of having her tender flesh bitten, soon to be followed by eyelids heavily drifting shut as she gave into the pleasure. Right at that moment, she never wanted him to stop. One second she was whimpering and the next moaning as he sensuously alternated between biting, sucking and licking. It was as if her body was craving the attention he was giving it. Soft moans escaped her lips as he kept up his assault, giving her the perfect balance between pleasure and pain. Her body again betrayed her as her stomach quivered and the sensitive spot between her legs throbbed and ached for only him.

Oh this feels so good, too good. I need to stop this before I do something stupid. Like…

The noise she heard earlier was like a bucket of cold water being doused on her as her eyes popped open.

"Nick, you hear that?"

"Hear what?"

Summer pushed against his chest with the palms of her hands.

"Stop, Nick, listen."

He lifted his head tilting it to the side, shrugging a muscular shoulder, "I don't hear anything." He was too engrossed in breaking down her defenses he hadn't heard a thing.

Summer turned her head as Nick tried to capture her mouth with his. As much as she wanted to lose herself in his kiss, she pleaded with him again. "Come on, Nick, please stop. I think I hear the baby crying."

Backing up Nick heard the frantic cries of a hungry infant before he even opened the door. The urgent cries of his son immediately brought him under control.

"Duty calls," he said as he left to tend to the needs of his son.

Good timing little man, Summer said to herself, holding the towel close to her traitorous body as she watched Nick's retreating back.

Turning off the water, stepping in front of the mirror and wiping it off with her hand, "I knew it." On her neck was a hickey the size of Texas. "What was I thinking? A second longer we'd be knocking boots. I wish he'd leave me alone and go find somebody else. I ain't never gonna get him out of my system if he keeps sniffing after me like some dirty old hound dog," Summer hissed aloud.

Summer was flat out lying to herself. She didn't want Nick to find anyone else. She wanted him to find *her* with his heart. But the only thing he had managed to do once they were alone was to get her all hot and bothered. And that upset Summer. Wasn't she supposed to flee temptation like the pastor said on Sunday? But how in the world could anyone flee a drop dead gorgeous, six-three, two hundred twenty pound temptation?

❧ ❧ ❧ ❧ ❧

Going down stairs, Nick stopped in the living room long enough to put a pacifier in NJ's mouth to quiet him as he lay in his bassinet crying so hard his little face was as red as a tomato. "I'll be right back buddy." He crooned soothingly to the baby.

Once in the kitchen he prepared the bottle as Summer instructed him. Shaking the bottle on his wrist like the model in the baby magazine, he tested the milk. Satisfied the milk wouldn't scorch the baby he made his way to the living room and picked his son up before settling down on the sofa.

Becoming inpatient, NJ spit the pacifier out, squirmed and squealed, demanding to be fed. He greedily accepted the bottle as Nick placed the nipple in his mouth. The baby sucked and grunted at the same time as his hunger was being satisfied.

"Buddy, you were hungry."

Every time Nick held his son, he tripped. It was a good trip though. For years, he told himself he didn't want children. That he didn't have time for them or that he would never find the right woman to have any with. In spite of all he believed, here he was with a child on the heels of turning forty in two short years.

Raising a child was a serious commitment. He never committed himself to anything in his life other than his business. It amazed him how such a tiny baby had impacted his life and filled his heart with so much love. Love he never knew he had, nor knew he was capable of giving. No longer was he that self-proclaimed bachelor. He was now accountable and responsible for someone other than himself, and it scared the hell out of him.

He'd been wrong about everything. Having a child was a wonderful gift. Each and every time his son gazed at him with eyes identical to his own, Nick feel in love with him all over again. He refused to have the same strained relationship with NJ that he had with his father. The strained relationship was partly because his father never had time for him. He was too absorbed in his career to be involved with Nick as a child. His father's main objective was becoming a federal judge. His primary love was for the law and not his family.

Every game, boys scout outing, field trip, or any other activity he was involved in as a child his mother was the one to attend every event as if she was a single parent. As a small child around the age of five or six he remembered an argument between his parents. "You never spend time with your son. All you do is take on case after case, leaving me to raise Nicholas on my own. He needs you to be a father to him," his mother tearfully complained. Nick never forgot his father's harsh rebuttal to his mother's complaint. "You wanted a baby. Now deal with it, and leave me the hell alone!"

Nick until this day resented his father for placing that burden on his mother. He promised himself that he would never treat his son as nothing more than a mere interruption to his life.

For years, he couldn't figure out why his mother put up with his father. That wasn't the first, nor the last time he had witnessed his father's gruffness towards his mother where he was concerned. The first thing Nick did when he made his first million was offer to take his mother from his father's house. She refused telling him, "Son my place is with your father. I made a vow before God to love him until the end." And that's exactly what she had done up until the last breath left her body.

The night of his mother's death, he and his father nearly came to blows as Nick released years of pent up frustrations. The sight of his father weeping over his mother's dead body made him sick. After years of neglecting his wife, he decided to be a husband. However, it had come a little too late for Nick's mother. After thirty-five long years of marriage, she had been diagnosed with an aggressive form of pancreatic cancer. That night he accused his father of never loving his mother. "You never loved my mother. You practically ignored her for as long as I can remember. She should've left you years ago. Maybe she would've had some happiness in her life." When his father angrily defended himself, Nick brought up every overheard argument beginning with the one he'd heard as a very small boy.

He would never place that heavy burden on Summer. Never would she be made to feel like a single parent. He was involved with their son from the moment of his birth. Summer was very accommodating and sensitive to Nick's needs of being a new father. Before he could even tell her he planned on going to NJ's first doctor's appointment, she had called him at the office suggesting he go with her so he would be familiar with the baby's pediatrician. When she first brought NJ home he would call to make sure it was okay to come over to see his son. "Nick, you don't have to ask permission to see your son. Just come over whenever you want to see him."

She was making the best out of a situation that had the potential to be downright ugly. And Nick appreciated her for doing so.

After feeding NJ, Nick placed him on his shoulder and gently patted his back the way Summer showed him. When the baby gave up a big burp, Nick cradled him with his head in his hands and his little body resting on his forearms.

"Buddy, what am I going to do about your momma? Your old man messed up real bad. It may be too late for me. I treated her like s—" Nick abruptly stopped, not letting the foul word escape his lips as he remembered he was talking to an infant. Lately he was making a conscious effort to curb his inappropriate language around the baby. He didn't want NJ picking up his nasty habit when he got old enough to talk.

The entire time he talked the baby intently held his gaze as if he understood. When NJ's little lips curved in a toothless smile and cooed as if to say, "You better hurry up and figure it out daddy." A deep rumbling laugh rose from the pit of Nick's stomach. "I'm straight up tripping."

Tripping or not, Nick was on a mission to get his woman back.

Chapter 25

Floating down the stairs in a pair of lavender silk pajamas, Nick got a whiff of Bath and Body Work's newest scent, Brown Sugar and Fig as Summer rested a hip against the edge of the sofa closest to him.

Flicking through cable channels with the remote in one hand while holding the baby in the opposite arm he tried to ignore the tantalizing scent dancing beneath his nostrils.

"Do you want something to drink or to eat? She asked as she leaned across Nick and touched NJ lightly on the tip of his nose with her finger.

"Sure, what you got in there?"

"My mom made some baked chicken, greens, candied yams and macaroni and cheese before she left."

"Cool, I'll have that."

Summer's mom was mean as all get out, but the woman sure could burn. Nick was the recipient of many a tasty meals while she stayed with Summer and the baby over the past six weeks. And he had enjoyed every single meal.

Pushing off the edge of the sofa, "Okay, coming right up."

While she was in the kitchen preparing his food, Nick sat holding the infant struggling to get himself together. Summer's scent was too provoking. She had him feeling like a starved man who desperately needed to be fed in the worst way.

Minutes later she placed a tray with a plate of hot steaming food and a glass of her famous strawberry lemonade on the coffee table.

"Here let me take him so you can eat."

"Thanks." Was all he said as he concentrated on the piping hot plate in front of him as an effort to clear his head.

Tenderly the sleeping infant was transferred from father to mother. Once the baby was settled in her arms, Summer gently kissed his forehead.

"You're going to spoil him rotten Nick if you keep holding him like this while he's sleeping."

"Come on now, I don't get to see him as often as you. I can't help it if after a long day at work all I want to do is hold my son."

He loves his son so much. Is this the same man who almost lost his mind when he found out I was pregnant with his baby? Now look at him, can't keep his hands off my baby. "Yeah, my little man kinda have that effect, doesn't?"

"Yup, he does." He agreed as he turned to the movie, *Training Day*. Picking up his plate he patted a space on the sofa next to him. Having them close always made him feel complete. Made him feel whole.

Sitting down she asked, "Did NJ take the bottle okay?"

"Yeah… he did good…Why?" He asked in between bites.

Evading Nick's question she wanted to know, "Did you burp him good?"

Raising a brow, "Yeah, why you ask?"

"Because I don't want him to get a tummy ache from all the air in his little belly." She said in baby talk as she held the sleeping baby kissing his tiny lips.

"Not why to that. Why did you ask about how he did with the bottle?" He noticed how she squirmed at his clarification of the question.

"Because he didn't like the bottle at first, he kept crying and spitting out the nipple."

"Why?" Nick was now even more curious as she squirmed even further with her explanation.

"He likes the breast better than the bottle." She all but mumbled under her breath.

"That's my boy." Nick commented with a cheesy savory grin.

Rolling her eyes and scooting away from him feigning disgust, "You so nasty. Just nasty."

Nick chuckled, shrugging a broad shoulder. "I'm only telling the truth."

Sucking her teeth, "Whatever, Nick."

Summer swatted Nick's hand as he leaned over and poked her in the side. "Come on, you know you want to laugh."

"Leave me alone nasty boy. Watch your movie." She said swallowing her giggles as she stood holding her son close to her chest.

"Where are you going?" He asked almost in panic fearing he had gone too far in his jesting.

"I'll be right back. I want to put my little prince to bed."

"A'ight, hurry up back so you can watch the movie with me." *Hurry up back? What is up with that?* Nick mindlessly scratched the side of his head, wondering when had he become so desperate. *Since you feel in love with her you stubborn fool,* the tiny voice in his headn taunted.

Returning from putting the baby down, Summer found Nick in a more relaxed position. He had removed his tie, unbuttoned the first few buttons of his shirt and rolled up his sleeves. His long legs were stretched out and crossed at the ankles.

"Are you comfortable?' She asked as she plopped down next to him.

"Uh huh, why you asking?"

Shrugging a slim shoulder, "Because, you look awkward to me that's all."

Nick frowned. "I do?" He certainly didn't feel uncomfortable.

"Mmm hmm. Here, give me your leg." She removed a shoe, "now your other leg," and then the other. Placing the size thirteen Kenneth Coles under the table, she asked, "Is that better?" as she sat back next to him.

Wrapping an arm around her slender shoulder, he pulled her head to his chest. "Yes, thank you, baby."

"You're welcome."

When Summer pushed away from the embrace, he tightened his hold and kissed her forehead. "Stay and watch the movie with me."

Obediently, yet with some reluctance, she submitted to his request. Lying in his arms feeling the steady rhythm of his chest rising and falling was hypnotizing. Her resistance to be near him was effortlessly dissolving the longer she stayed in his embrace.

The movie came to a scene Summer enjoyed though it was a bit on the violent side. She didn't care though. Shoot Denzel was fine!

"You look like him?"

"Who?" Nick asked confused. "The white dude?"

"No simpleton, Denzel." She replied rolling her eyes towards the ceiling.

Nick looked at the television screen then back at Summer. "I do?"

"Mmmm... hmmm... yup...yup." Summer purred as she watched Denzel swagger across the screen.

"That's the only reason why you dated me?" Nick asked pretending to be offended by Summer practically drooling at the television screen.

"But why of course. How else do you think you hooked me?" Summer teased saucily.

"Woman, please. I look ten times better than that chump."

Summer pushed away planting her hands on slender hips. "Negro, pullease! As if! And don't be calling my man a chump! Chump!"

Within a flash he had flipped her on her back and straddled her midsection.

"Nick! What the heck are you doing?!"

Grinning with mischief in his eyes, "Take it back."

With a stubborn glint in her eyes she shook her head from side to side.

"I said take it back."

"No! Now get off me!"

"Okay, have it your way, Miss Summer."

Summer screamed and squirmed as Nick mercilessly tickled her. Being extremely ticklish, she tried with all her might to get him off her petite body. It was useless he was too large.

Covering her mouth with a large hand, "Sssh, woman, you're gonna wake up the baby."

Nick snatched his hand away when she nipped his palm with her teeth.

"Hey, what you bite me for?"

Laughing at his mock anger, "Because… now… get your… big… butt… off of me!"

Summer's screams bounced off the walls as he unrelentingly tickled her not showing any sign of mercy whatsoever. Again he silenced her with a tighter grip. Summer's small hands didn't have strength as she attempted to pry his hand from her mouth.

"Want me to let you go?"

Summer nodded her head.

"When I let you go are you going to tell me what I want to hear?"

Again she nodded.

"Good."

Slowly he released a hand from her mouth.

Summer said nothing as she gave him the evil eye.

"Well, Miss Jackson."

"Let me up first. My back hurts," she pouted.

Nick was agile as he stood pulling her to her feet with him. Backing away towards the steps, Summer taunted him. "You wish you looked as good as Denzel on your best day buster."

Making a mad dash for the stairs was futile. With one powerful swoop of his arm, Nick had Summer around the waist carrying her.

"Whoooa!" She yelled as he dumped her on the sofa straddling and pinning her arms to her side.

Laughing she said, "Nick, this isn't fair!"

Nick loved that Summer was laughing, and that he was the cause of her laughter. As he laughed with her he asked as if confused, "What isn't fair, Beautiful?"

"You out weigh me by more than a hundred pounds."

His laugh dwindled to a grin. "So."

"Boy, what are you about to do to me?" Summer could tell he was about to be up to no good.

"You should've told me what I wanted to hear."

"Okay, I'll tell you."

Shaking his head, "Nope, too late."

Summer went completely still as he slid a hand in the waistband of her pajama bottoms. This was one time she wished she'd wore panties underneath her pajamas.

"What are you doing?"

"I just want to make you feel good." He nibbled at her earlobe as his voice seductively dropped to barely a whisper while his hand expertly glided further inside in search of her hidden treasure.

Oh…oh…o-o-o-oh!

Summer moaned and writhed as his long strong fingers worked their magic, stroking and caressing, finding her hidden pearl.

She felt herself being pulled back into Nick's vortex as he took her to a place she hadn't gone to in over a year. Struggling with her emotions as she slipped into a haze of ecstasy she told herself she couldn't get caught up again in Nick's world again at any cost.

But it was easier said than done to refuse him, to resist being pulled into his web when he was giving her body such pleasure. *This one time. Just this once.* She told herself as her body went tumbling out of control.

Summer lay on the sofa, her thighs quivering after having a longing she hadn't realized was so deep satisfied. Nick captured her mouth in a penetrating kiss that sucked the oxygen right out of her lungs. When he felt her struggling to break the kiss, he was sure it was to replenish the precious air he'd just depleted her of.

Breaking the kiss, his mouth mere inches away from hers, he wanted to know, "Now you were saying, Miss Summer."

Not hesitating to conceal the lazy satisfied grin she let out a soft sigh and purred, "Honey, you're ten times finer than Denzel."

"I thought you'd see things my way." Of course, his response was one of an arrogant, self-assured lover.

Oh, honey you have no idea how much I love seeing things your way, she thought to herself, not giving him the satisfaction of knowing he'd given her body what it had been screaming for. Though she was sure by his cocky statement, he knew exactly what he had done to her

Summer lifted her hips as Nick pulled her pajama bottoms up. Changing positions on the sofa he pulled her against his solid body. She felt his heat pressed against her as she lay nestled between muscular thighs. Immediately she reacted by jumping up and away from the intimate contact. Her actions had been so instantaneous she nearly tripped over her own feet.

What in the world was I thinking?! No! No! No! History will not be repeating itself again! I am not ending up pregnant…again! Oh hell to the NO!

Gazing at her, bemused by her reaction, he asked, "Hey, what's wrong?"

Before she could answer, he reached for Summer, grabbed her firmly, yet gently by the wrist and pulled her onto his lap.

"We went too far, Nick." Summer whispered softly.

She had felt how his body responded to her and was still responding as she sat in his lap. He was ready to make love to her, and that scared her. If she went all the way with him, she would never be able to free herself of him. Not to mention possibly end up in trouble again.

"Summer, look at me."

He needed to look into her eyes to see what she was feeling. Nick was very much aware of her state of vulnerability. All evening he had sensed her need to pull away from him and not to give into her desires. A battle, which they both knew she was losing the longer she remained in his presence.

Slowly Summer lifted her gaze to meet his. Her eyes said it all. She wanted to love him, and to be loved by him, but was too afraid to do so.

"Are you afraid I want to make love to you?"

"Yes..." Summer paused trying to get her thoughts together. "But I can't, Nick. I'm sorry about earlier. I should have resisted you more than what I did. I didn't mean to lead you on."

"Baby, you didn't lead me on. I would be lying if I said I didn't want you. But I would never force myself on you."

She believed every word he had said. Not once had he ever taken advantage of her in that way. "I know you wouldn't do that to me."

"Good. Now can I hold you before I leave?"

Though she momentarily hesitated, thinking, *I got it bad for this man.* Letting out a soft sigh, trustingly she allowed him to pull her back into the warmth of his embrace.

As Nick held Summer, he dreamed of the day not if, but when Summer would completely be his again.

Chapter 26

After that night with Nick, Summer was extra cautious when around him. He was a constant figure in her life and in her space. She had seen more of him in the last three months than she did the entire time they dated. His level of attentiveness without a doubt increased as well. Whenever he paid special attention to her she would brush it off as, *he's only doing this because of NJ.*

As strange as it was she couldn't deny the fact she looked forward to Nick's daily evening and all day weekend visits. No longer being in the hustle and bustle of going to work every day was getting to Summer. Certainly, she loved her son more than life itself; however, she was itching to get outdoors, to be a part of the outside world. So when he showed up at her home she was more than grateful for his company. When she wasn't living vicariously through Starr's and Ava's lives, she was doing so through his. Nick would crack up when she'd meet him at the door and drag him in by one hand as she chattered away. "So tell me about your day. I want to hear all the nitty, gritty. Don't leave out any dirty details. Tell me who got on your nerves today. Because I know somebody did something to piss you off, you're so dag-gone picky about everything. It's a wonder—"

He'd cut her off with, "Woman slow down. Your mouth is moving too fast. You're giving me a migraine."

Bringing some excitement to her day, he would answer every question as she hung onto his every word.

Summer decided to join one of those Baby and Mommy exercise classes to get her out of the house. She'd get to meet other new mommies, women she'd have something in common with. She had been so excited about the classes only to find out NJ was too young. He had to be at least six months old for them to join any of the classes that were offered.

Nick listened attentively over dinner at how thrilled she'd been about the classes only to be disappointed. "I love NJ, but sitting in the house all day is driving me bananas. You know I'm used to getting out and about."

When he responded, "Uh huh," Summer felt foolish. She felt like she was complaining about nothing.

❧ ❧ ❧ ❧ ❧

Brrrrrg. Brrrrrg. Brrrrrg.

Placing the baby in his crib, Summer ran to her bedroom shoving her left breast back into her bra.

"Hello?" She breathed heavily into the phone. *I really need those exercise classes.*

"Hey, baby, why you so out of breath?"

Summer smiled. She loved it when he called her baby. "I was running from the nursery and shoving my boob back in my bra to get the phone." *He's gonna say something smart.*

Nick chuckled. "That was a lot of shoving, huh?" He loved how nursing had further filled her out. Not that there was anything to complain about before.

Summer sucked her teeth. She hadn't underestimated him. "Do you think you can ever keep your mind out the gutter nasty boy?"

"You make me that way." He teased.

"Yeah right. You were that way looong before I met you.

Nick chuckled again. "Girl, I was a perfect gentleman with you." He could feel Summer's smile as she softly said, "Yes you were."

During the silence that followed, both Summer and Nick remembered a time so sweet.

Clearing his throat he asked, "Are you busy this afternoon, Miss Summer?"

"Other than taking care of your son, no. Why do you ask?"

"It's a surprise. Just be ready by one."

"Okay. I'll have me and the baby ready by one."

"Umm, Summer?"

"Yeah?"

"The baby won't be coming with you."

What is he talking about? She wondered. The baby went everywhere she went. They hadn't been separated since his birth.

"Nick, what do —"

He cut Summer off before she could finish her sentence. He could tell she was going to have a problem with being separated from NJ.

"Baby, don't you trust me?"

"Yes." Summer answered softly.

"Do you think I would do anything to harm our son?"

"Of course not, Nick."

"Then trust me. I've taken care of everything. Okay?"

"Okay."

At twelve forty-five, Summer stood looking at herself in the full-length mirror in her bedroom. Peeping over her shoulder at the baby lying on his back in the center of her bed brought a smile to her lips.

"Your momma doesn't look so bad, huh, little man."

The burgundy long sleeve jersey knit dress clung to every curve on Summer's petite body. The v-neck neckline plunged just enough to show a modest amount of cleavage. The hemline stopped just above the knees showing off shapely legs. Matching burgundy pumps added three inches to her height.

Further inspecting her reflection, Summer's attention was drawn to her hair that was pulled back in a bun.

"This won't due." Pulling out hairpins, she mumbled, "I look like a librarian." After the last pin was removed, Summer went over to her dresser, picked up a wide-tooth comb and began to comb through the black silky strains that now fell slightly below her shoulder blades.

Everyone was shocked when she talked her longtime hairdresser Julie into coming to her house and cutting several inches of her hair off. She would rationalize, "It's easier to take care of my hair this length now that I have the baby, "to all those, especially Nick who'd asked horrified," Why you cut your hair?" Each time she'd roll her eyes thinking, *my goodness one would think I shaved my head clean bald. It's only hair it'll grow back.*

"Why am I so intent on trying to look so good for that man?" *Because you still love and want him,* the tiny voice in her head jeered at her. "Oh shut up," Summer mumbled to herself.

Picking up a sheer burgundy lip-gloss coating her lips just enough to give them a little color, she said to her reflection, "I guess I'm ready now."

Going over to the bed, she picked up NJ and held him close to her. She wasn't so sure about leaving her baby. She wanted to call Nick and tell him that she couldn't go, that something had come up. "Mommy's going to miss you. Yes I am." Summer whispered as she kissed the soft curls on the top of her son's head.

The doorbell rang interrupting her tender moment with NJ. Summer glanced over at the clock on the nightstand, *one o'clock on the dot.*

Laying the baby in the playpen she went to answer the door. A megawatt smile lit up her face.

"Joan! What are you doing here?! It's so good to see you. How have you been?" Summer rushed all this out as she affectionately hugged the older woman.

Joan laughed as she hugged the young woman back.

"I've been good sweetie. How 'bout you and that precious little baby boy?"

"We're good. Come on in," pointing to a corner in the living room, "he's over there in the playpen." Taking Joan by the hand she led her over to the infant.

"Oh, sweetie, he's getting so big and just as handsome as ever. Looking just like Nicholas Stiles."

"Thanks, Joan." Summer stood there smiling at her son, adoring everything about him. Agreeing with Joan that NJ was the exact replica of his father.

"Well, you better get going, Missy. You know how Nick hates to be kept waiting."

Summer's smile radiated with relief. "I'm so happy you're keeping my little man."

"Yup, now grab your coat and purse and go! I know how to take care of a baby!" Joan playfully admonished Summer. "Hurry up chile! There's a car waiting outside for you."

"Okay, Okay, I'm getting my stuff."

As Summer grab her things she informed Joan there was milk in the fridge for the baby's two o'clock feeding as she ran out the door, down the steps into the black Lincoln Town Car waiting at the curb.

❧ ❧ ❧ ❧ ❧

Nick watched as the maitre d led Summer to the table. A hint of jealousy coursed through him as he observed a few drifting eyes. He held his composure, refusing to reveal an emotion that was foreign to him. Standing, he took a few steps closing the gap between Summer and himself.

Reaching out he possessively splayed his hands on her waist pulling her closer giving her a quick peck on the lips.

"Baby, you look sexy, too sexy. You see all eyes are on you, don't you?"

Summer looked around the posh restaurant as Nick helped her out of off her coat and into her chair. Just as she sat a middle-aged man smiled at her. Politely she returned the smile.

"Is that what that little kiss was all about?" She asked as she lifted an arched brow.

"Damn straight."

"Come on Nick half these men are old enough to be my father."

"And?"

"Possessive, aren't we?" she asked teasing.

The expression faded as Nick stared at her through dark eyes before responding. "Beautiful, I don't know any other way to be with you. Especially when you look the way you do right now."

"Oh."

Over lunch, the couple enjoyed each other's company immensely. For the first time in months, Nick was able to free an entire afternoon to do whatever he wanted that didn't pertain to work. Spending time with Summer was where he wanted to be, where he needed to be. With every passing day the gravitational pull to be near her grew stronger and stronger.

As they talked, he noticed every little nuance about her. From the way she tilted her head when she was interested in something he said. To the way she bit down on her bottom lip when she was in deep thought. To how she threw her head back and laughed when he said something amusing. His also picked up that she was missing their little boy every time she glanced at the gold Bulova watch on her slim wrist. He was even aware of how she attempted to camouflage the gesture by twirling the stem of her water glass.

He covered her hand to still the twirling. "You miss him don't you?"

Giving up a weak smile she responded, "It's that noticeable?"

Nick nodded. "Yes."

"I love him so much. I can't imagine being without him."

"What are you going to do when it's time for you to go back to work?" Nick was curious to know as he held both her hands in his.

Summer shrugged a slim shoulder. "I don't know." She answered truthfully with sadness in her voice.

The six-week maternity leave was officially over three weeks ago. Summer was living off of her savings because the Family Leave Act she'd taken didn't provide any sort of income. The only thing the Act did was secure her job for the next twelve weeks.

Summer was a saver; she would be able to stay home with NJ until he was at least two years old without having to dip into her 401B plan. It certainly didn't hurt that she had inherited a trust fund from her paternal grandfather when she was twelve years old. It wasn't enough to make her rich, however, it would allow her to pay the bills for a few years without having to work. Besides, if things got really bad she could always go to her parents for help without a problem.

For several seconds, Nick held Summer's hand. It was apparent she was in deep thought. If he had to guess, it was because she would have to ultimately deal with having to return back to work. He treaded cautiously as he approached her with an offer she was going to accept, whether she wanted to or not.

"Do you want to go back to work?" Nick asked breaking the silence.

Summer hesitated before answering. She did not want to admit the words she was about to speak. "Eventually, I have to go back to work."

"That's not what I asked you. I asked if you want to go back to work."

"No, Nick, I don't *want* to go back to work leaving NJ at some daycare all day. I'm his mother. I should be the one taking care of him."

Bringing her hands to his lips, he kissed her palms. "Then that's what you'll do."

Summer's heart thumped not just from the tenderness of his touch, but also from what he was offering.

"Nick, I can't. I have bills—"

He cut her off with, "Don't worry, I got you."

"Nick, I can't allow you to do that."

"Why?"

"Because, it's not right. I don't want to take money from you."

Nick softly chuckled.

"What's so funny?"

Summer's feelings were hurt. How could he make light of what he was offering? What would she have to give in return for such generosity?

"You are. I know inside that pretty little head of yours you're wondering what I want in return."

A frown marred her pretty features. As Summer opened her mouth to refute him, Nick held up his hand.

"If it makes you feel better I can have my lawyer draw up a contract stating that my offer is free of any conditions."

"No, I don't want to complicate things. You already buy everything the baby needs as is."

"Summer, I bring my son a bag of pampers every week. Your mother is constantly sending him clothes. You breastfeed him, so that for now eliminates buying formula. Look baby, all I want to do is take care of you and my son. I don't want you worrying about how your bills are going to be paid. And to be honest with you I'm not at all down with a stranger keeping my son." *I'd have to kill somebody if they hurt my boy.*

Summer nodded her head in agreement. She wasn't thrilled with the idea either of leaving her helpless baby alone with a stranger. She'd heard horror stories about babies having diaper rashes so severe they'd gotten skin infections from laying in soiled pampers all day. The thought of it sent chills through her. She didn't want to think about the other poor innocent babies that were sexually abused by some sick psycho freaks.

"So, Beautiful, are going to let me take care of you and my son or what?"

What he was offering would allow her to continue to nurture her son during the most critical time of his young life. An offer of this magnitude could not be turned down. "All right, but how long should this arrangement last?"

She was hoping at least until NJ started pre-school. He'd be four years old and then she could definitely return to work. If someone did something to her baby, he could at least tell her about it.

"I was thinking until little buddy is... uh...at least eighteen."

Summer nearly spite out the last bite of cheesecake she'd resumed eating. "You've got to be kidding?" She asked in total disbelief.

Nick never answered her as he signaled for the waiter to bring the check. That's what he wanted, for her to stay home with his son, like his mother had done with him. But knowing Summer she would return to work as soon as NJ was somewhat independent. He would just have to change her mind about that. Tilting his head to the side, he thought, *Maybe another baby might do it.*

Summer frowned as Nick slyly grinned at her. He was up to no good, and she knew it.

Chapter 27

Nick turned the key and stepped through the door. The aroma of a mouth-watering roast greeted him. The frustrated mask he wore easily faded. Every evening Summer had a hot delicious meal waiting for him. On the nights he ran late, she would have already bathed and fed the baby and patiently waited for him so they could have dinner together.

Setting his briefcase down on the coffee table, he shrugged off his suit jacket throwing it over an armchair. Strolling into the kitchen, he loosened his tie and rolled up his sleeves. He wished he could as easily roll the day away he'd had.

Earlier that day Nick discovered one of his executives, Thomas Jones had a serious drug problem, which became evident by a major screw up. Nick was livid when he learned important documents weren't prepared and forwarded to the legal department because of Thomas' cocaine addiction. Apparently, Thomas was going through a wicked withdrawal and ended up leaving work in search of his dealer. Everything came crashing down when the DEA surrounded the dealer's headquarters while the two were settling their drug transaction.

Nick flipped his lid when Thomas called the office literally crying like a baby as he unloaded all the ugly details of his descent into the underworld of drugs. Nick inhaled deeply as anger threatened to consume him again for the umpteenth time.

Entering the kitchen, he encountered Summer's back as she stood at the sink rinsing off a head of lettuce. The motion of her hands circling the lettuce as she washed it was a soothing movement. The anger that threatened to tip him over all day dissipated as he imagined it was his neck, shoulders and back her hands were massaging.

Summer's mind was miles away thinking about the day she and NJ had when she sensed his presence. She lifted her head tilting it to the side as Nick wrapped his arms around her waist.

"Hey, Beautiful." He whispered against her ear.

"Hey, yourself."

Their lips met in what he thought would be a decent kiss. Instead, he was greeted with a quick peck.

Summer never noticed the frown that marred his handsome features. Turning back to the salad, "Dinner'll be ready in about ten."

Letting go of his hold of her, he leaned against the counter. "All right."

The longer he looked at her the more aggravated he became. Her indifference caused him to recall how he had tried reaching her earlier at home, then on her cell. Needing someone to talk to he decided to give her a call. When he couldn't locate her ugly visions played with him as he slammed down the phone refusing to leave a message. Nick told himself it was all the mad drama going on at the office taking his mind to a place he thought he had overcome. Pushing the thoughts as far away as possible he pressed on to deal with the present circumstances at hand.

"Where were you today?"

Summer noticed the coolness in his voice. *I knew it! Sooner or later he'd pull rank because he's paying my bills. What's he doing? Keeping me on lock down or something? Next he'll start with his custody crap again.*

"What?" She asked with a bewildered look on her face.

"Where were you today?" He repeated in a tight voice.

Setting the lettuce on the chopping block, Summer faced Nick as she began to explained her whereabouts to him.

"NJ and I went to what I thought was going to be lunch with Ava and Starr at the Spaghetti Warehouse."

She felt she didn't need to give him any further explanation. After all, she wasn't a child and he wasn't her father.

"What do you mean by 'what you *though*t was going to be lunch'?"

Summer stared at Nick in disbelief. Mostly from his tone that held a hint of nastiness to it as he spoke to her. Before answering him she did a mental check of what she had done to make him act the way he was acting. *Nothing*. She hadn't done a thing.

"Ava and Starr along with several other co-workers gave me the baby shower I never had." Summer never took her eyes off him as she spoke. *He's a fool. A complete stupid fool. I can't believe I'm standing here explaining myself to this nut like I'm twelve years old!*

"Is that right?" Nick asked tersely.

What does he mean by that? "Nick, don't you believe me?" She wanted to know. Still not believing how he was tripping.

When he didn't answer she went on to say in an irritated voice, "All the gifts are in the NJ's room *if* you don't believe me." *And I even brought your evil butt a piece of cake home. I should put some ex-lax in it.*

Nick didn't bother to answer her as he continued to push. "Why didn't you answer your cell phone?"

"I forgot to recharge it."

Pushing away from the counter he looked down at Summer. Hurt and anger was clearly etched across her face. However, his stubborn pride wouldn't let him back down on his assault.

"Try to remember to charge your cell phone the next time you go out." Nick made it half way out of the kitchen before turning to say, "I needed to talk to you."

❧ ❧ ❧ ❧ ❧

NJ was lying on his back sucking his tiny fist when Nick somberly walked in the nursery.

"Hey little buddy you're just the medicine I need."

Recognizing his father's voice, the infant's tiny dark eyes twinkled with excitement. All tension was assuaged the moment Nick lifted his son from the crib into his arms. Sitting in the rocking chair he gently rocked the baby and felt at ease for the first time all day.

The relaxing motion of the rocker was calming. This felt so right. Coming home to Summer and his son every night. *Summer. I screwed up again.*

Most of his frustration had come from knowing Summer had no obligation of being committed to him at all. The reality of it all hit him when he couldn't reach her earlier in the day. He had no right to expect her to be there for him when he needed someone to be there. At any time she would be well within her rights of telling him to get lost and come see NJ on court appointed visits. Just the thought of it made him draw NJ closer to his chest, to his heart.

After Nick left the room, angry tears fell one after the other. Summer wiped at them as she set the table. A million things ran through her head so fast she felt a headache coming on. For the life of her, she didn't understand what he was so irate about. All she had done was taken *her* baby out to have lunch with some friends. Did he expect her to stay held up in the house all day, every day? Knowing Nick, he probably thought she was out doing only God knows what. Was he going to use this as an excuse to finally file for custody? More tears spilled at the thought. *He wouldn't be that cruel? Would he?*

⁂

Dinner was unusually quiet. Summer wouldn't even look at Nick. She focused all of her attention on NJ as she nursed him. After she fed and burped the baby, she settled him in the infant swing that sat next to the table. Having been recently changed by his daddy and fed by his mommy, NJ was just as content as he sat gurgling and gumming his fist.

Pushing the food around on her plate with her fork, Summer had lost her appetite because she was so rattled by Nick's funky attitude.

Nick sensed her troubled state. He knew he was the reason for it. "Summer, I'm sorry about earlier."

Summer heard the sincerity, but could she believe it? He was sorry this time. Would he be sorry the next time he blew up at her for no reason at all?

"Okay." Was all she said as she stood taking her plate into the kitchen.

Nick watched her walk away. Again he managed to hurt and upset the only woman other than his mother who had ever truly loved him unconditionally.

❧ ❧ ❧ ❧ ❧

"Come in." Summer called out just above a whisper to the soft knocking on her bedroom door.

"Do you mind if I sit?"

Summer gestured with the nod of her head it was okay for him to sit. When he sat she unconsciously reached behind grapping a throw pillow bringing it to her chest and tightly hugging it.

"I'm really sorry for how I talked to you. I had a hell of a day and took it out on you. I know I was wrong for doing that to you."

"Okay." *What more does he want me to say?*

Dragging a large hand down his face, Nick let out a deep sigh. This was going to be harder than he thought. He felt there was more to it than her being upset about his blowing up at her.

"Summer, baby, what's wrong? Each time I apologized all you have to say is 'okay'."

It's now or never, she thought to herself. She had to tell him what she feared most. She couldn't take walking on eggshells anymore every time he was pissed about something.

"I'm afraid."

"Of what? What are you afraid of Summer?"

"That you're going to take …." The words so painful they were lodged deep in her throat refusing to leave.

Nick was profoundly confused. *What is she talking about?* "Take what Summer?"

Summer choked the words out. "Take NJ from me."

Still confused he questioned, "Why would I do that?"

"You said if the paternity test proved you were NJ's father you would file for custody and I'll never see him again."

Nick clenched his jaw, hissing a string of expletives. "Summer, I was pissed because you didn't tell me you were pregnant." His tone had suddenly become cool.

"I tried to tell you, but every time…" Her voice trailed off in a soft whisper.

"Every time what?"

Taking a deep breath she continued. "Every time I tried to tell you why I hadn't, you wouldn't let me explain my side of things. Explain what I was feeling, what I was going through."

Nick dropped his head, closed his eyes and pinched the bridge of his nose. He counted to ten as he wondered why she was bringing this all up. *Must be PMS.* For the most part he had put the fact Summer deceived him behind him and out of his mind. She didn't know how close he was to losing his cool. He would hear her out he decided for once and for all. But after tonight he told himself this issue was dead. They were putting it to sleep forever.

Slowly, Nick lifted his head and gazed into her eyes. His intense stare softened as he took in how fragile she appeared. His voice was low and soft when he spoke. "I'm listening, explain yourself."

Summer's voice quivered as she spoke softly expressing what she had wanted to tell him months ago. It wouldn't be long before the river flowed.

"When you told me you didn't want to see me anymore I was devastated. I kept trying to figure out what I had done wrong to make you want to leave me. I thought that I..." Summer paused, trying to maintain her composure, "Made you happy. But I was wrong." She wiped at the tears that started to fall with the palm of her right hand. "I was so hurt. It hadn't been that long since we'd spent that week in your cabin. I believed that we had something special. But I was wrong."

Nick shifted, uncomfortable from the pain that was so evident in her voice. He'd been selfish; never thinking of the impact his decision to end their relationship would have on her.

"I was in denial. I didn't want to believe it was over between us. I called you at home the next day. When you didn't return my call, I called your office the day after that."

Summer's voice dropped an octave lower as she lowered her head and began to fidget with her hands in her lap. No longer could she hold his gaze. It was too painful reliving that difficult time in her life.

"Your secretary told me you weren't taking any calls. I knew that meant my calls."

Nick remembered. He disregarded the messages telling himself he didn't have time for Summer's hysterics. He figured she would get over it, get over him, all the others had.

"I realized then that you *really* didn't want to be bothered with me... that I hadn't meant anything to you." Summer let out a painful sigh. "So I tried to forget about you, to get on with my life. But two weeks after you left the states is when I found out I was pregnant."

Summer looked up at Nick through red swollen eyes. "I told you that, remember?"

Nick nodded.

"I also told you about my plans to get an abortion."

Again he nodded.

"Nick, I really wanted to tell you I was pregnant with your baby." Her voice pleaded with him to believe her.

Nick had been quiet letting her emote up until that point. He wouldn't be silent either, he finally wanted answers to his questions.

"Why didn't you, Summer?"

"Because I thought if I told you about the baby that you would have thought I was trying to trap you into being with me… marrying me. And, I knew you didn't want a child … or me. I thought that you would have probably forced me to go through with having an abortion whether I wanted to or not."

Lord, help him. Nick cringed at the words she spoke. He knew within his heart all those months ago that that's exactly what he would have insisted on her doing.

"I guess I was a little selfish. I still loved you, so in my mind and heart carrying your baby was a way of holding on to a part of you."

Nick gently lifted her chin with his forefinger to meet his gaze. "Do you still love me?"

Summer nodded. "Yes, I still love you, Nick," she whispered as she wiped away tears.

"Go on, I'm still listening." He prodded gently.

"As the weeks and months passed I accepted the fact that I would never see you again. Then one day I read in the paper you were coming back to Philly to take on another business venture. I knew I had to avoid ever seeing you or letting you know about the baby."

"Why?" He could feel the heat creeping up his neck.

"Because I knew what you did to people when you felt that they had used or crossed you. Like how you did Veronica."

A flash of disgust waved over his features at the mention of *her* name.

"What did you think I'd do?"

"Exactly what you did, threaten to sue for full custody. To take my baby from me."

"Summer, what did you expect me to do? I felt like I had been kicked in the gut?" Nick let out a frustrated sigh as he felt his composure slipping. "I came to see you that night with the intention of telling you that I had made a mistake… that I wanted you back." He dragged his hand down his face. His voice was eerily quiet. "You threw me for a damn curve Summer. You were seven months pregnant. You knew at the time that I didn't want children. Yet you still allowed yourself to get pregnant."

Summer winced at his admission of not only wanting children, but the fact that he had blamed her for getting pregnant infuriated her. He acted as if she had gotten pregnant on her own! All by herself!

"Nick, you are being so unfair!" An indignant anger dried up her well of tears.

"How am I being unfair Summer?! You should have told me! I had a right to know!"

Jumping up from her position on the bed, Summer paced the floor from the shot of adrenaline her anger set off.

"Why are you blaming me for everything?!" Summer shouted, her face contorted in emotional anguish. "You told me to trust you that night in the cabin. I trusted you. I gave into what you wanted, regardless of the consequences because I loved you! I loved you so much I was willing to raise our son all alone so you wouldn't have to be bothered with a baby I knew you didn't want!"

She couldn't stop, wouldn't stop. She was determined to let free every pent up emotion she had held bondage in her broken heart.

"You're always crying about why I never told you I was pregnant! How do you think I felt?! Huh! Crying myself to sleep every night over you! Knowing you didn't want me anymore! Carrying a baby that I knew you didn't want!" She shouted as she pointed to her heaving chest.

"And how do you think I felt when people who I grew up with all my life at church pointed their fingers and talked about me when I showed up big bellied at church! Trying to find just a little bit of peace and comfort in my miserable life! You weren't the one being ridiculed or judged! I had to go to another church because of you!"

Summer was so overcome with raw emotions she wasn't aware that she was now stomping her feet in a tantrum like fashion.

Nor was she aware Nick had become completely paralyzed. The breadth of her hurt and how he had hurt her was breaking his heart as she emotionally crumbled before his eyes.

"I gave you everything I had to give! I never asked you for anything, Nick! Whenever you gave me something it was because you wanted to… not because I asked or begged you for it! Whatever you wanted to do… we did! Wherever you wanted to go… we went! I never complained when you showed up hours late for a date without so much of an 'I'm sorry for making you sit around like a stupid fool waiting on me'!

"Noooo, that was too much like right! Instead you always acted like a freakin' god or something and treated me like I was your stupid little follower worshipping the ground you walked on." Stopping momentarily, catching her breath, "You even called me out of my name, Nick! You said I was a conniving whore like Veronica! How could you compare me to her! I never lied to you or try to use you like she did!"

If there were a hole in the floor or a crack in the wall, he could have crawled in he would have. The viciousness of his words had come back to haunt him as Summer painfully reminded him of his cruelty.

Summer's tone lowered and she trembled as she went on to remind him of their past together. "Nick, you were my first… the *only* man I ever gave my body to. I gave it to you freely…whenever…wherever… and however you wanted it. I compromised my values for you. I gave you my most precious gift."

Emotionally spent, Summer slumped to her knees on the floor. By now her voice was hoarse and barely above a whisper as she looked up at Nick. "I knew you never loved me. I just hoped… even prayed that you had at least cared about me."

Immediately, Nick found himself on the floor pulling Summer onto his lap, hugging her in a tight embrace.

"Oh, baby, I'm so sorry. I wish I could take it all back. I wish I could make it up to you."

"Let me go, Nick! You're not sorry! All you want is to take my baby from me!" She cried, attempting to push herself away from him.

He was holding her so tight she gave up her fight to free herself. "No, sweetheart, that's not what I want."

"Then what Nick? What is it that you want?

Kissing her forehead, "I want you and I want our son. At first, I didn't understand, but after NJ was born and I watched you holding him, loving him, I knew then I would never see the two of you separated. I won't lie to you, Summer. I was still pissed about not knowing about your pregnancy. But I had to man up. It was my fault you didn't tell me. You were thinking about me, and what I wanted. You are so right. I was so wrapped up in living my life as a carefree bachelor, not being, nor wanting to be committed to anyone at the time."

Releasing Summer from the tight embrace, he lifted her chin and gazed into her eyes. "I truly am sorry for everything. I've been a complete bastard. Nothing I can say or do will change that. That's something I'll have to live with. I also know I've hurt you repeatedly. I'll have to live with that, too. I just pray that I haven't destroyed everything between us." What he was about to request of her, he had no right to. " Do you think you could ever forgive me?"

Nick patiently waited for her to answer. If she had told him to go to the nearest bridge and jump he only had himself to blame.

"I forgive you. But do you really mean what you just said about NJ." She asked, wanting to believe that what he said was the truth.

He put a finger to her lips. "Ssssh. Sweetheart our son is staying right here, where he is with the both of us."

Summer's tiny frame collapsed against Nick's. For the first time in months, she finally felt free. Free from the miserable dark cloud that constantly threatened to storm over her. Free to not have to worry about Nick thinking the worst of her. Most important, free to know in her heart that her precious baby would always be with her in her care where she could love and nurture him forever.

"Thank you." Summer whispered as she kissed his lips.

Standing, he gently placed Summer on her feet. "Come with me."

Hand in hand they walked to the nursery. Summer stepped in front of the crib. Her hands were itching to pick up her baby, but she didn't want to disturb his sleep. Nick eased up behind her and wrapped his arms around her waist. On cue, she leaned back into his strong, solid body as they silently watched the sleeping infant.

Summer whispered, "He's so beautiful."

Nick kissed the side of her face. "He's his mother's child."

"What are you talking about? He looks just like you."

"Are you calling me beautiful?"

"Yes."

Slowly, he turned her to face him. Silently they stared into each other's eyes communicating without words just like that night of their first date. In the sweet stillness of the room, they both understood that they would always be an integral part of one another.

Nick was the first to break the silence.

"Um, I think I better get going, it's late."

Summer didn't want him to leave her and NJ tonight or any other night.

"Stay the night with us." Summer had spoken so softly Nick thought he was hearing things.

"What did you say?"

"I said, I want you to stay the night with me and your son."

He pulled Summer close. "Are you sure?

"Positive."

❧ ❧ ❧ ❧ ❧

Sleep eluded Nick as his mind filled with thoughts of his life and what had become of it. With all of his accomplishments, they did not compare remotely to the newfound joy he felt from the petite woman snuggled against him and the sleeping infant down the hall.

Holding Summer so close he was even more determined never to let her go. She had not lied; she had given him everything, and then some. In return, he had uncaringly taken everything she offered and more. He had blamed her and labeled her as a deceitful and a conniving whore. When in all actuality he was to blame. After all, it was his primal lustful desire that changed the course of their lives a year ago. Now they both were living according to the consequences of their actions. During that time in their lives neither one of them had a desire to be a parent. But none of that matters now, because here they are in the present with another precious life added to the equation. Their infant son, Nicholas Christopher Stiles Jr.

Every time he looked at or touched his seed, an indescribable feeling washed over him. Within a span of a few seconds, NJ's life would flash before Nick. He would envision NJ taking his first step, his first day of school, pitching at his first little league game, starting high school, and going off to college.

Nick gently squeezed Summer. He thanked God she had the strength and willpower not to cave into the pressures of terminating her pregnancy. Killing their child. In the past, he believed the lie that, 'it's not a baby, only a mass of cells' during those first few weeks after conception. The truth revealed its self the instant NJ emerged from his mother's body full of life. He had always existed and was born with a purpose regardless of the circumstances of his birth. For whatever reason, he and Summer were the vehicles responsible for their son's existence. And he thanked God for that blessing.

Overwhelming shame and guilt tied a knot around Nick, suffocating him as he replayed Summer's tearful admission of what she had gone through. Abandonment, humiliation, chastisement and rejection, all by people she had loved and cared about. And he was the main culprit who gave her the greatest degree of heartache and pain.

Without even thinking, he quietly questioned himself. "How could I hurt love? Hurt Summer?"

Nick accepted what he'd tried so hard to resist. Love. He was in love with Summer and knew he needed her like the oxygen he needed to breathe. She was his oxygen. This time when he squeezed her it was with all of the love he had for her. All of the love he denied her. Love he should have freely given to her from day one when he realized she was special and different from the others.

Summer squirmed and shifted in her sleep as a shapely leg slid between Nick's muscular thighs. The feel of her soft flesh so intimately close made him close his eyes tight as his body responded to her sensuous touch.

"Summer?" He whispered in hesitation not sure if she was asleep or not.

"Hmmm."

"Uh, do you think you could move your leg?"

He was close to losing it. To flipping her over on her back and doing… well you know. It had been so long since he had touched or held another woman. It was almost impossible for him to restrain himself.

Soon as she came into contact with Nick's hard flesh she became aware of his desire for her. He wasn't alone, she wanted him too. But she was also conscious of the fact that he was holding back. He wouldn't take things any further than she allowed.

Keeping her hot scorching flesh in place, she made a request. Speaking softly she, said, "Nick … make love to me."

There was nothing in the world Nick wanted more. He wanted to love Summer, but wasn't sure where her heart and her head was. True, she had admitted to loving him. However, he wasn't certain if Summer was still *in* love with him. Finally after all this time he knew where his heart belonged and who it belonged to. What he didn't know was if Summer's heart still belonged to him?

She sensed his hesitation. "What's wrong Nick?"

"Get up for a minute please."

Reaching over, he turned on the lamp on the nightstand before sitting up and resting against the headboard. Nick rubbed his eyes with the heels of his hands then looked down at Summer lying on her stomach with her elbows supporting her as she held her chin in her palms.

She was watching him anticipating what he would say. Would he make love to her or not?

"Nothing's wrong, baby. I want nothing more than to make love to you. But are you sure this is what you really want? We don't have to do this. I don't want you to have any regrets."

Regrets would be what they both would be left with in the morning if she were no longer in love with him.

Straddling his lap, Summer held his face between her hands and gave him a quick kiss on his full lips.

"I won't have any regrets. I just want you to love me."

Threading his fingers through her hair, palming the back of her head he pulled her to meet his lips. Neither one of them wanted to let the other go as their tongues danced to a rhythm of their own.

Looking into her brown eyes, he exposed all his vulnerabilities as he opened his heart and his soul to her. "Baby, I'm going to love you for the rest of my life."

A single tear slid down her cheek. "Oh, Nick."

Not bothering to turn the lamp off, Nick slid down on his back pulling Summer to his chest lightly kissing the salty trail on her cheek. He didn't bother to hush or quiet the other tears that followed. His admission of loving her was the beginning of her healing. Of his healing.

Summer felt her heart completely opening up to him places she thought were closed off forever. Summer exhaled the breath she'd been holding for months as she gazed into Nick's dark eyes that held a longing for her that was so deep, so sweet, so tender. It was a longing not of lust, but one of genuine love. A soft smile danced at her lips as she blinked the tears away. Yes. He loved her. He had pledged to love her for the rest of his life.

"Nick, I really do want you… I need you.

"Are you sure?"

Summer nodded.

"It's been a long time, Beautiful. There hasn't been another since you."

Summer was stunned. She had thought for sure he'd found another lover. Just the thought of him doing all those intimate things he had done with her to another woman used to send her into fits of crying spells.

"For real?"

"Yes, Beautiful. I never could get you out of my system. And now I know why."

Chapter 28

For the longest time Nick and Summer laid facing one another staring into each other's eyes. The love, which shined through their souls, was undeniable. Neither wanted to rush the inevitable. They had all night. They had forever.

Slowly Nick began to caress every curve, every inch. The entire time he explored her body Summer writhed under his glorious touch as he again familiarized himself with her body. When he worshipped her most delicate feminine zone she nearly shattered into a million pieces when her release over took her.

Positioning himself over her, Nick wavered. *Is this what she really wants?*

He got his answer when her hands lightly tugged on his shoulders. "Nick?"

With her consent he slowly entered her and began moving in and out. Falling into sync, Summer wrapped her legs around his waist taking him in deeper as they moved as one being. Working themselves into an erotic haze, simultaneously they crashed into wave after wave, drowning in an abyss as their bodies trembled in ecstasy.

As the last aftershock left Nick's body he squeezed Summer in a tight embrace, vowing again never to let her go. Though many had come before her, he knew in his heart that she would be the last.

"Summer Jackson, I love you. I've always loved you. I was just too damn stubborn to admit it."

"I love you too, Nick." *And I never stopped loving you.*

Chapter 29

The next morning sounds of a gurgling and cooing baby over the intercom aroused a very exhausted Nick and Summer. They had just drifted off to sleep not much more than an hour ago. Their lovemaking lasted until early dawn. It was as if they couldn't get enough of each other as they made up for lost time. She wasn't sure if she'd be able to walk. Nick had definitely given her a workout, proving to her she was his last. Summer smiled to herself, biting down on her bottom lip as she remembered all the naughty things and positions he did to her. Her body was sore from all the twisting, turning, bending, and stretching she'd done.

"Someone's awake." Nick whispered in Summer's ear as he held her in a spooning position.

"I'll go get him." Summer said as she went to remove Nick's hand from her hip. Nick held her firmly; he wasn't ready to let her go.

"Stay, don't go. He's not crying yet."

It felt so good lying so close to Nick. Summer snuggled back into his embrace. "Okay, just a little longer, then I need to get the baby."

"He'll be okay for a few more minutes."

"Nick?"

"Yeah, baby?" A smile tugged at his lips. He remembered how she talked incessantly the next morning after a vigorous night of sensual activity. As if she was getting rid of residual energy.

"This is the first time you spent the night here with me." Summer wanted to ask him "why?" because in the past he would always leave before the break of day. She would joke with Ava and Starr that she was dating Blackula. More than once she had pleaded with him, "Don't go." That was then, and this is now. As far as she was concerned all that mattered now was that her man, her baby's daddy was in her bed and had been there all night.

"Yeah, it is. You've always stayed at my place."

Getting frisky wanting to do away with the small talk, Nick slid his hand down her hip and between her thighs. He loved how she felt, soft and silky.

Rolling over facing him, his hand dislodged from its intended target as Summer continued to chatter. "I always liked staying at your place. It's so big and roomy. I bet you can fit my whole little two bedroom townhouse in it."

Nick chuckled as he smoothed his hand over her round firm behind. That last move told him she'd had enough. He couldn't blame her. She had allowed him access to any and everything he wanted. And still he wanted more.

"You and the baby can stay with me sometimes."

That sounded real good to Summer. She wanted nothing more than for her and their son to be as close to Nick as possible. Waking up next to him was what she had dreamed of for months.

"That would be nice, but where will the baby sleep?" Summer frowned as she finished her sentence.

"What's that?"

Nick grinned mischievously. "What?"

Lifting the covers over their heads she pointed to his groin area. "That?"

"Come here and let me show you."

With one smooth move, Nick had flipped Summer onto her back and mounted her.

Summer giggled. "Boy, you better stop it. Are you crazy?" *I'm sore enough as it is.*

NJ's gurgling and cooing turned into a frantic, almost panicking cry, halting Nick's seductive persuasion. The poor little guy was probably wondering what was taking his mommy so long. As soon as he would start his early morning gurgling and cooing, she would be right there picking him up and showering him with kisses.

Nick leaned down and kissed Summer on the lips before rolling off her.

"I'll go get my boy. Just let me freshen up real quick." He said pulling up his boxers as he jetted to the adjoining bathroom.

Rising up on her right elbow, Summer laughed at him. "Yeah, you do that. And while you're in there brush your teeth, too. There's an extra toothbrush in the top vanity draw."

Nick shook his head grinning as he looked in the draw retrieving the toothbrush. When he brought his head up to look at his reflection. He almost didn't recognize himself because of the glimmer in his eyes. He was happy, content. Something he had not been in a very longtime.

The moment NJ saw his daddy's face his cries became soft whimpers. Picking up the baby, Nick kissed him as he carried him to the changing table to change his pamper. Finishing up, he lifted the baby back in his arms. "Come on little buddy, let's go see your beautiful momma."

Summer was coming out of the bathroom from freshening up as she tied the belt on her satin robe as Nick was entering her room. Taking the baby from his arms she cooed, "Come on let mommy feed you."

Settling down in a wingback chair Summer prepared herself to nurse. NJ kicked and squirmed as she exposed a breast. Once he had latched on his kicking and squirming quieted as he hungrily grunted and fed at the same time.

Perched on the foot of the bed, Nick gazed at Summer and NJ. His heart swelled with love as he watched his woman nourish their child. This is where he needed to be…always. Nick slightly tilted his head to the side as he envisioned NJ as a toddler sitting at his mother's feet as she nursed another baby. This time things would be different. He would be there for Summer from the very beginning. Yes, Nick wanted it all. He wanted Summer as his best friend, lover, confidant, wife and mother of his babies.

Moving from his spot on the bed, he knelt on one knee beside Summer as she continued to nurse the baby. Nick's heart melted when Summer lifted her gaze from NJ's to rest on him with a smile.

"Did I tell you I love you?" He whispered in a husky tone.

"Every time you made love to me last night and early this morning." She answered softly.

"Well, I'm telling you again. Summer, I love you and I want you."

Summer lifted a brow. "You want me?" *Okay you sex maniac you're getting carried away.*

"Yes, I want you… forever." He told her as he traced a finger down her jaw and over her bottom lip.

"Forever?" He possibly couldn't be saying what she was thinking and feeling in her heart.

"Yes, forever." He slowly brought himself closer until their lips barely touched. "I want you to be my wife and give me more babies. Will you do that for me, Beautiful?"

Summer blinked as she looked into Nick's dark eyes. *Ohmygowd, ohmygowd, he's serious!* She was completely stunned. Staring at him wide-eyed she couldn't get her thoughts together. This couldn't be. He couldn't be asking her such a thing.

"Beautiful, please answer me. You're making me nervous."

"Yes, Nick. I'll be your wife and give you all the babies you want."

Kissing her he said, "Did I tell you I love you?"

"Uh huh, at least a hundred times."

Epilogue

Summer stared out the kitchen window mesmerized by the heavy falling snow. Country snow was so much prettier than city snow. The glistening flakes sparkled as they fell to the ground, growing deeper and deeper. By morning, there would be at least three to four feet of the white fluffy stuff. The last time she had seen that much snow was four years ago when she was pregnant and held up for three days with Nick.

Things had come full circle for Summer and Nick since then. They had worked through their issues by going to premarital counseling with their pastor. Now they were happily married. Sure, they had their moments like any other married couple. He got on her nerves, and she got on his nerves. Nevertheless, they loved each other with a passion that was mad crazy. Everyone teased them saying, "It's about time the two of you got your act together!"

No longer was there strife between Nick and her parents and friends. He and his dad were even on speaking terms, thanks to Summer. When she insisted he tell his dad about her and the baby, Nick had initially refused. "Baby, I told you it's not that kind of party with me and my father." Summer in her subtle way convinced him that until he resolved things with his dad a part of him would always hold resentment and bitterness in his heart. "Nick, you need to give your father another chance and forgive him. Hating him not only hurts you but your son as well." She knew that would get him to thinking and reconsider his position. There wasn't anything he wouldn't do for his son NJ.

To Nick's surprise when he showed up unannounced one evening on his father's doorstep his father was ecstatic to see his only son, his only child. The older man was beside himself with joy when Nick told him about Summer and NJ. Tearfully he begged Nick not to make the same mistakes in his life that he had made.

"Son, please show your family that they are the most important thing in your life. Don't be the kind of husband and father I was. I know I wasn't there for you and your mother. In spite of it, you've turned out to be one hell of a man. No doubt because of your mother. I can't take credit for the man you've become. Son, I am proud of you."

Nick was touched by his father's humility. He thought he never see the day when his father would apologize for his past deeds. Although they couldn't replace the years of hurt and disappointment, Nick graciously accepted his father's apology.

Having failed at being a decent father, the elder Stiles was determined to be the perfect grandfather to NJ. Like clockwork every Saturday morning he would visit his son, grandson and new daughter. Even on occasion the elder Stiles accompanied his newly expanded family to church on Sunday mornings.

Going to church was another area of Nick's life Summer enriched for the better. Every Sunday he'd have NJ bathed, dressed, fed, and ready to go as Summer scurried around getting herself together. "Come on, Beautiful, you're gonna make us late. I don't want to miss the choir."

Hoping on one foot while putting a pump on the other, "All right, I'm hurrying, stop rushing me already!" Though she pretended to be annoyed by his rushing, Summer always sent up a silent prayer of thanksgiving for her husband's newfound interest in going to church.

"Isn't the snow beautiful?" Summer said as Nick eased up behind her circling her tiny waist drawing her away from her reverie.

"Not as beautiful as you are," he told his wife as he nibbled on her earlobe.

"You better load the dishwasher before you get yourself into trouble, Mr. Stiles."

Summer knew exactly where he was trying to go as she untangled herself from his embrace and moseying over to the kitchen table taking a seat.

Glancing around the huge country kitchen, which she, her mother, and Joan decorated, Summer was still as elated as the first time Nick surprised her bringing her to the cabin for a quiet weekend.

Unbeknownst to her he had built their family a six bedroom, four bathroom home. And of course the master bathroom had a gigantic Jacuzzi in it with enough room for at least four adult bodies. The house was just as enormous with a spacious living room, formal dining area, family room, office, library, and exercise room. The outdoor grounds rivaled one of those fancy resorts with an in-ground pool, hot tub, tennis court and basketball court. A playground with swings, sliding board, sand box and jungle gym was also on the grounds. This new luxurious home was built a half a mile down the road from the old cabin.

Rising from the chair, Summer stretched and yawned. It had been a long day. They had celebrated their second Christmas in the new house with Henry, Nick's father, Summer's parents, Starr, Ava, Joan, and Kevin. Summer softly chuckled to herself as she thought about the obvious attraction between Kevin and Starr that they both tried to down play. It was useless on their part. Summer had seen the attraction clear as day. She was certain that if the others were paying attention they saw it too. Shaking her head she also thought about how Henry, Nick's dad shamelessly flirted with Joan. All the women cracked up when Joan teasingly told him, "Go on now and leave me alone. I ain't stuttin' you, you old fool."

"What's so funny?"

"Nothing. Are you almost done honey?"

She'd tell him later about Starr and Kevin. Now was not the time when all she wanted to do was to snuggle up next to her husband and watch the snowfall as she drifted off to sleep.

"Yeah, just let me put this last dish in."

❧ ❧ ❧ ❧ ❧

Slipping under the covers and quilt, Summer nestled against Nick's large frame.

"You sleep?" She whispered softly.

He answered by rolling over gathering her petite body in his arms.

"No, I'm not sleep. What took you so long woman?" He asked as he kissed her on the forehead.

Summer smiled as she wiggled trying to get even closer to her husband. "I was just checking on everyone. Making sure everybody was comfortable."

Summer's parents had left earlier to stay at the cabin down the road while everyone else filled up the other five bedrooms.

"Doing your nightly rounds, Nurse Stiles?"

Summer threw a shapely leg suggestively over a muscled thigh. "Mmmm hmmm. Now it's time for your back rub, Mr. Stiles."

Neither one of them heard the sounds of tiny feet padding down the hallway as Summer pulled her gown up to her waist straddling Nick's hips.

"I think you'll enjoy this better than a back rub." Summer rotated her pelvis as her hands caressed Nick's bare chest.

Nick slid his hands up her gown massaging her nipples with the pads of his thumbs. "Girl, I thought you were tired."

Summer smiled seductively, "I was until—"

Neither one of them heard the turning doorknob.

"Mommy, what are you doing to daddy?" The tiny boy asked as he grounded his eyes with his small fists.

Summer nearly hit the ceiling as she shrieked and jumped off Nick pulling down her gown and landing on her bottom next to him. Thank goodness she thought to herself that Nick hadn't taken off her gown and she his pajama bottoms.

Nick snickered as he deflated. There was nothing like a wondering toddler to douse you like a bucket of ice-cold water. "Yeah, mommy, what are you doing to daddy?"

Cutting her eyes at Nick, she held her hands out to her son. Climbing onto the king size bed the toddler sat in his mother's lap. Summer ran her finger through the soft curls on his head then kissed him. "I was only playing with your daddy, that's all." She nudged Nick with her elbow. "Right daddy."

Nick snickered again. "Yeah, mommy whatever you say."

"Oh," the little boy said with large expressive dark eyes.

"Momma, daddy?" A tiny voice called as another toddler entered the room rubbing sleepy, tired eyes.

Throwing back the covers, sliding out of the bed, Nick's face lit up as he held his arms open.

"Come here sweet pea."

The little girl's long braids bounced as she ran and leaped into her daddy's arms. Nick sat down on the bed with his daughter in his lap.

"Daddy, I couldn't sleep. Autumn kept moving around in her bed," NJ complained.

Nick's voice was soothing when he spoke. "Sweet pea, you're having a hard time sleeping?"

Snuggling against her daddy as she sucked her thumb, Autumn nodded her head rubbing her eye with a tiny fist.

"My poor baby is probably scared." Summer pouted.

Last year Autumn had been only a year and a few months old, still sleeping in a crib in the room with her parents.

"I can't sleep either, mommy," NJ told his mother feeling left out.

Summer gently pulled her son's head to rest against her chest kissing his forehead.

"Baby, I know you can't sleep, too," Summer told her little boy making him feel better.

Within five minutes, the sleepy toddlers had fallen asleep in their parents lap. Smiling at Nick Summer whispered, "I guess we'll finish playing later, maybe tomorrow?"

"You can bet your sweet little a—"

"Nick! The babies. I thought you said you were working on not cussing like a drunken sailor." Summer hissed between clenched teeth.

Nick hushed the laughter that wanted to rumble through his chest at Summer's reaction. "Baby I am. Their sleeping, they can't hear me."

"The first time one of them says a bad word I'm washing *your* mouth out with soap."

Nick chuckled. "Come on baby let's go to sleep, it's been a long day."

Placing the sleeping toddlers in the center of the bed, Summer laid on her side next to her baby girl, while Nick lay on his side next to his son. Gazing lovingly at each other over the tops of the heads of their sleeping children, Summer was the first to speak.

"Nick?" She said softly as not to wake the children.

"What's up, Beautiful?" He whispered.

"We almost made a baby tonight."

Summer had stop taking her birth control pills three weeks ago when Nick mentioned one night after making love that their children could use another sibling as a playmate. He even went on to confess how he loved having her pregnant. He loved the way her body transformed to accommodate the growing life in her womb. He loved feeling the baby's movement beneath his hands. Then later when it came time for the baby to be born, he expressed how he felt as if he was being reborn again. Tears came to her eyes when he told her, "Beautiful, I know God created you for me and me for you. He created you to be the mother of my children and me to be their daddy."

"We still can."

Summer frowned. "Man, what are you talking about?" *I know my freaky husband don't think we're doing it with my babies in the same bed.*

Nick leaned up on his elbow and tilted his head towards the bathroom with a sly grin. The light came on for Summer as understanding dawned on her.

Summer returned the grin. "All right, but you better be good. Don't be in there making a bunch of noise."

"Yeah right. You're the noisy one. 'Oh Nick, Oh Nick, Ohhhhh Niiiiick,'" he teased.

Sucking her teeth, she popped Nick on the forehead with the palm of her hand. "Shut up, boy. You know you like it."

"Never said I didn't. Now stop playin' and get your sexy self out this bed."

Tip toeing out of bed the lovers met at the bathroom door. "Come here woman." With one swift movement, Nick had Summer in his arms going through the bathroom door and gently closing it with his foot.

COMING SOON!

Starr's Story

When Love Comes Around

by Victoria Wells

Prologue

"You know what Kevin? You make me sick! You're a low life bastard!" Starr screeched, trembling with anger.

Kevin stepped into her space, inches from towering over her. Through clenched teeth, he warned, "You better watch your mouth."

"Don't tell me what to do! You're not my father!" Starr yelled even louder than before. He had some nerve telling her to watch her mouth. What did he expect after being caught in his own web of lies?

"Maybe if you had one, you'd know how to act!" Kevin shot back in frustration. From the moment she barreled into his home, all she had done was sling accusation after accusation. Whenever he attempted to defend himself, she'd cut him off, calling him everything but a child of God.

The defiant scowl that masked her features moments ago transformed into one of hurt, then disappointment as she swayed from the harsh, yet truth of his words. He was right. If she had a father who cared anything about her, she would know how to act. He would have been there to protect her from the leeches that just took and took. He would have taught her never to lower her standards just to have a man. He would have schooled her on slick, silver tongues that slithered their way into her bed. Instead, all he had taught her was to fall for men just like him.

Seconds ticked by as the couple stood staring at each other. Neither saying a word, both wondering how they had come to this place.

Immediately after the words slipped from his lips, Kevin regretted them. The stricken look on her face was more than he could bear. He had cut her deep. Wanting to soothe the ache he caused, he pulled her to his chest in a tight hug. "Baby, I'm sorry. I didn't mean to say that."

Too many harsh words had been exchanged in the heat of the moment.

Starr was drained, downright defeated. She had expected too much, had too many high expectations of her herself, and of Kevin. What was she thinking? Men like Kevin never changed.

Pushing out of his embrace, her voice was low, barely a whisper. “I’ll be back tomorrow to get my things.”

Kevin stood motionless as he watched his future walk out of his life.

Printed in the United States
109204LV00003B/46-75/P

9 780979 975776